NOT
A BRAVE NEW WORLD

GILLIAN

FOR ADAM

MORE ABOUT *NOT A BRAVE NEW WORLD* CAN BE FOUND AT
WWW.KIPFENN.CO.UK

NOT
A BRAVE NEW WORLD

PAUL K LYONS

A TRILOGY IN THREE WIVES

BOOK ONE

GILLIAN

PIKLE
PUBLISHING

NOT
A BRAVE NEW WORLD

GILLIAN

PROLOGUE

I was born, at our home in St Albans, two days before the end of the century, on 29 December 1999. My dad, Tom, tried, or so he boasted, to bribe the doctor into filling out a false date on the health authority paperwork so that Julie would be able to register my birth on 1 January 2000, but he refused. I am glad about this since, if I survive as planned until next January, I will know that I have lived a life spanning three centuries – not many can say that.

My mother, Julie, never told me why she decided on a home birth, nor was it ever explained why a doctor rather than a midwife was in attendance. But I remember meeting him, the doctor, at an afternoon drinks party hosted by a solicitor friend. It was the day before my tenth birthday. I had never seen a house so full of Christmas cards. I was nibbling my way through a bowl of sweet nuts when a tall man, smelling of alcohol, edged up to me.

'I delivered you, boy,' he said without so much as a hello, and confident I would understand what he was talking about. I didn't. I looked down shyly.

'I'm Dr Jessop. I delivered you, boy,' he repeated with such urgency I had to raise my head and respond.

'Thank you,' I said. This seemed to satisfy him and he lurched off to impose on someone else.

I lie here, all these years later, reflecting carefully back over my life, editing and dictating, editing and dictating to the wallscreen in front of me. I have a wealth of personal and more general material to help the process, not least a lifetime of email communications which, from my 20s, I collated and stored. One day they may be net-published along with this, the bare bones of a biography – or what might better be called 'Reflections', all three volumes of them – which I am preparing in these last months of my life.

You may have heard of me, Neil or Kip Fenn, thanks to my career within the United Nation's International Fund for Sustainable Development, better known by its acronym – the

IFSD — or my modest efforts within an organisation called REACH in the aftermath of the Grey Years. You may also have heard of me in connection with my daughter Crystal, who fell victim to the suicide epidemic of the 2040s, or my son, Bronze, whose idiotic caper in the 2060s disrupted both our lives, his tragically more so than mine.

Or, possibly, you may recall my name in connection with a sexual weakness, but which was, essentially, a private matter and should never have been exposed in public. I will not ignore the personally painful and embarrassing, but I hope other areas of my private life, for which I am thankful, will take precedence: my co-op children, Guido and Jay, for example, or my role in launching The Josephine Collection archive of 19th century photographs.

I should explain this thing Tom had about dates. He was born on 12 April 1961, the day Yuri Gagarin went into space. It was eight years later, on 21 July 1969, when he sat with his father, Barry, watching (on 'a dinky black and white') the live coverage of Neil Armstrong's walk on the moon that he realised the significance of his birth date, although he was shocked to learn that Gagarin had already died. By the age of 15, Tom knew more about the moon, the planets and rocket technology than most boys did about football or popidols. Unfortunately, his knowledge was generally undermined by a failure to be accurate with details, other than dates. He dreamed of studying aeronautics at university, but only managed to scrape through into a second-rate college course on business studies. In consequence of his enthusiasm, perhaps, and some talent for spiel, Marconi admitted him to their graduate training course on marketing, but he never made the grade. By 23, he had settled for a well-paid job selling oil field equipment.

It was a wonder Tom asked Julie to marry him, given that she was born on 3 September 1973, a nondescript day if ever there was one. The best he could do in later years was to talk about his wife as having been born in the year of Skylab, or to suggest she should have delayed emerging into the world by a few days so as to coincide with Jackie Stewart's retirement – motor racing being another of his interests. I like to think that love overcame that early obstacle to their relationship, although there was scant evidence of it left by the time I was old enough to notice.

Julie, née Hapgood, came from an average mid-20th century family, one with traditional values, and traditional hopes. She had one older brother, Alan, my uncle. The father, Oswald, was a manager with the Central Electricity Generating Board, and the mother, Eileen, was a housewife and a teacher. After difficult years at school and college, not least because of Oswald's untimely death, Julie followed her mother into teaching, and took a place at a large comprehensive school in Harpenden.

Tom found her one Saturday night in a tenpin bowling alley, slightly drunk, and playing on a fruit machine. The next weekend he took her to the British Grand Prix at Silverstone. Although Tom had a predisposition for exaggeration while Julie usually had an umbilical relationship with the truth, I am inclined to believe Tom's version of events that weekend. I do not suggest my mother lied to me, rather that her memory became distorted in order to accommodate her subsequent resentment to the man. She remembered how hot and bothered she was in the traffic jams during the drive, and how she hated the noise and the crowds during the race itself. Tom told me, though, that Julie had sparkled all day, like a shop girl taken to a palace, and that she had accepted his chancer invitation for them to spend the night together with undisguised enthusiasm.

Despite all that happened, my mother could never completely extinguish her love for him. There had been boyfriends before, but none had lasted. I do not think she fell for him as such, but rather that she made a decision to love him, as if he were a last chance, a last credit in that fruit machine, and once the decision was made, she allowed herself to fall. I can see her now, after his funeral, standing outside the crematorium in the sunshine. She is slim and frail, dressed in a dark grey suit, her hair clasped up in a silvery bun, and she is crying.

'I've met with him three times in 20 years, why these tears?' she asks me apparently puzzled. Behind her I can see my first wife, Gillian, with our children, Crystal and Bronze, all anxious to depart.

'Perhaps you are thankful for what was, and regretful for what wasn't,' I say.

'My little wise man, you, my little wise man,' she says for the first time since I was a child. I smile despite myself. 'No. It is that I am sorry for what was, but grateful for what wasn't.' This is so unlike my mother, never one for complicated or psychological analysis of behaviour, that I avert my gaze from Gillian who is now marching towards me, and look directly at Julie as if to ask for further explanation. Her tears have evaporated.

Writing in the Reflections mode means I am less con-strained by time – although I wish to keep to a rough chronol-ogy – and I can embellish the facts more generously than in a formal biography with feelings and impressions. More impor-tantly, I need not worry where failures of memory, especially in middle and later years, or records would otherwise leave me struggling to fill in certain obvious gaps. I am struck, for example, that I recall nothing about my own emotions at that funeral. This leads me to the more unsettling thought that my writing might be unduly biased in favour of my mother, or even, perhaps, in favour of Tom. But then it occurs to me that another advantage of the Reflections format is that I need not worry too strenuously about being fair.

I keep trying to find a beginning, but there isn't one. Did my life begin with birth, or with conception? Will it end with death? In a physical sense, the answers may be yes, but surely the least interesting part of my life is its medical record. Or should my beginning be confined to what I can remember all of a hundred or so years ago? Yet these are only memories of memories, photographically fixed and collaged, not dissimilar to a Henry Peach Robinson print, and re-photographed in my head, or digitally recorded and re-remembered in soft focus, or in the wrong colours, or ...

I could call up the transcribed video recordings taken by Alan of me as a baby, or as a primary school child, but, to be honest, I can't be bothered. Meanwhile, I could introduce Neil, my personal digital memory store for more than 60 years. I was named after the astronaut, but the memory store was named after me, in a backhand gesture towards my father. I swapped my given Neil for Kip not long after he left my mother and me. It began as a school nickname. A teacher had caught me napping in religious studies, and Horace, that's Horace Merriweather, called me Kip as a taunt. Later, he decided Kip was a more suitable name for a friend of his than the dull Neil. Although he never took to the name Hip that we gave him, as I did to Kip, we became known for a while as Hip and Kip, he in the foreground, and I in the background. He died a while back, in the mid-2080s. I remember thinking at the time how, in general, civil servants like me often age with more dignity than politicians like Horace who never quite become accustomed to living beyond the limelight.

I see I have not yet mentioned Arturo, the second greatest surprise of my life, second only to Tom's drunken revelation on New Year's Eve 2019. Nor have I mentioned Diana or Lizette, with whom I came to know something of the love that people talk and sing and write about; but they each deserve a separate volume of Reflections, and so they shall have them.

PART ONE
Tom, Julie and School

'When every snowflake and every thumbprint is different, and we have no idea how to predict or control the formulation of their patterns, why do we still have the conceit to believe that we can fix and formulate the minds and characters of our children? Let us teach them with wisdom and humility, not try and change who they are.'

The Snowball Effect or Parenting made Difficult
by Julia Derwent (2006)

CHAPTER 1
IN WHICH IT IS NEW YEAR'S EVE IN 2019

It is New Year's Eve 2019, I am remembering, a memorable night. I should have been at a college ball in London, and my father, Tom, should have been in Dorking at a marquee fest with his latest companion. Only my mother, Julie, was in the right place, in Edinburgh, after being pestered for many years by an old school-friend to visit her there. I was staying at the house in Godalming, my past home, over the holidays to recuperate, having badly sprained an ankle during a volleyball league match against the Richmond Reelers. Julie had wanted to cancel the trip north, but I insisted she go. Coincidentally, Tom phoned, not knowing where I was, to tell me he had been dumped by his girlfriend, and was on the M25. I told him I was alone at Julie's house in Godalming and suggested he come and keep me company. He arrived half an hour later.

I used the crutches lent me by St George's Hospital to hobble to the front door and back. Tom was as dapper as ever, even in his late 50s, wearing a dark blue overcoat and light blue scarf round his neck tied like a cravat and tucked into the lapels. He tried to hand me two bottles at the door, but when I declined for obvious reasons he put them down on the side table, next to an oversized picture of me aged 11 in school uniform.

'Do you know what the bitch did to me?' he said; and continued without waiting for an answer, 'she set me up, she bloody well set me up.'

'And you didn't see it coming?'

'Did I hell. Let's have a drink son and I'll tell you more.' But then he remembered he had left something in the car, and dashed out to return a few moments later with two large plastic boxes.

'Dad! One for my birthday and one for Christmas.'

'If you want.' He beamed, but it wasn't a smile that had flourished for seeing me, rather it was the one he wore as easily as his suit when he had some new toy or product to show off, or some new joke to tell. I worked my way back to the sofa, while Tom deposited the boxes, removed his over-coat, and disappeared to the kitchen to open one of the bottles and bring us both a glass of champagne.

'You'll have to sort out food for us too, there's some decent ready-mades in the fridge.'

'Later, later. So, how did you bugger up your ankle? Mmm this is good.' I told him as briefly as I could, knowing he would not be very interested.

'After jumping to block a smash, I landed on the foot of one of the Reeler's hitters, it shouldn't have been there on my side of the net – the goon. My foot and ankle and leg crumpled beneath me, and I was reduced to a shrieking mass of pain. The coach ice-packed the ankle for me, and then, after the game, took me to the hospital.'

'Did you win?'

'Yes.'

'And was that African chappy there.'

'No, Dad, Alfred's studying and playing in Manchester.' Once, and once only, my father came to see me play. I was about 15, and my school team had reached the final of the inter-school southeastern cup. We won, but this was of no interest to Tom. After the match, he wanted to know why I was always slapping hands with the black chap, and to remind me – for he had told me a few times – that Africans were a dodgy lot. There was a grin on his face, but I walked off in silent fury.

'Mea culpa. I'm a bit distracted, you understand. How's your mother?' Tom asked.

'OK. You could call her yourself.'

'I could. Neat place she's got, but then it ought to be, seeing as it cost me an arm and a leg.'

Within minutes Tom had emptied his glass and refilled it. He told me about Kerry, or was it Cherry – I forget, there were so many after Julie. This girl's brother was hosting a large marquee party to celebrate the birth of a child and New Year's Eve. Unfortunately for Tom, it was also a splendid occasion for Kerry to show off her new man – not my father. He was staggered at the depth of her hostility. Poor Tom. I watched his false smile transform into a grimace as he explained how she had taken exception to all the times he had talked about past girlfriends.

'What a bitch. She must have been a great actress.' He emptied his glass. 'All the way here, I've been trying to work out when exactly, in our three month relationship, she turned, and I've no idea, no idea at all.'

'Put it down to experience, Dad,' I said. This was one of his stock phrases, yet, already at 20, I felt wiser than him.

'Fuck experience.' I laughed, he didn't.

'What's that there, then?' I asked pointing to the boxes. I saw the weight lift from his brow, and a glint appear in his eye.

'Guess.'

'A new dinner service for Julie.' This was a joke, but elicited no more than a grunt. 'An Earthmate with Zeta gaming facilities?' I was never a huge fan of computer games, but I did know this had been an object of desire that Christmas.

'You wish. Better than that.'

'A model space station? I give up.'

'Scalextric. It was for Kerry's boy. I liked him. He liked me, but I'm buggered if I was going to give him 800 euros worth of two tier racing track and RC cars with programmable features and a computer console, after what she did.'

'No, I don't suppose you were. So what are you going to do with it?'

'Play with it. Now. With you.' He looked around the room. 'Could be bigger, but it'll do. I'll get us a refill, and then get us going. But first there's something else.' He opened the smaller of the two boxes and produced a battered but serviceable video cassette player, which he deftly plugged into an adaptor and then into Julie's very old freestanding television. From his overcoat, he retrieved a cassette (the size of a book) and set it going.

'A bit of nostalgia son. You won't mind if we keep it playing. You were two days old, I was 20 years younger, the world was in a happy mood. This is a non-stop recording of BBC 1 on 31 December 1999, from early evening through to the early morning. You, son, only saw about half an hour of this, when your Mum brought you in to breast feed.'

'Where did you get it from, and, more to the point, why?'

'Bought it. A week ago, in a Jester shop. A whim.'

'It's a good idea,' I said.

The first programme which came on, while Tom was setting up the track, was a famous episode of *Eastenders*, but one I'd never seen. I was a faithful addict during my early teens, before the BBC sold the show for a fortune to William Caxton who used it to help launch the People's Channel in 2021. And, during that time I probably took in a few historical episodes on the repeat channels or in anniversary slots. Although Caxton slowly drained its quality, the most famous UK soap lasted into the 2030s.

Only after its demise, of course, did *Eastenders* become the classic it is today, beloved and analysed endlessly in English drama departments around the world. Gregory (one of my favourite pop-historians, brilliant but also often flawed) claims that, during the golden era of oil and chips, *Eastenders* became more culturally important in Britain than Shake-speare.

'It's coming back to me now,' Tom said as he crawled around the floor, 'I don't believe it – they haven't changed the connecting mechanism after all these years. You have to place one at an angle to the other and then wiggle it in. What do you think?' I could see he had made good use of the furniture, for tunnels and bridges, and several pots crafted by my grand-mother, for underpinning bends or for raised sections.

'I'm not covering for you, if one of those ceramics break.'

'They won't. Let's give it a go.' He reached into the box and pulled out some model cars. 'Do you want the silver Rhyme, the red Jaguar, the cream Princess – bloody hell, I remember those – or the turquoise Rigatoni Mini?' I may have mixed up the colours, but my memory of those model cars is surpris-ingly fresh.

'Which do you recommend?'

'Do you want speed or traction?' And so we played for an hour or more, stopping occasionally whenever he wanted to adjust the circuit, or to fill our glasses. He won every race, whichever car, whichever track, and I blamed my losses on having to keep one eye on *Eastenders*.

While eating microwaved lasagne and drinking a bottle of wine stored in the pantry for cooking purposes (the champagne having long since disappeared, largely down Tom's gullet), Julie rang. She didn't want to wait until midnight in case I'd gone to sleep. We wished each other all the best for the new year. I saw no reason to mention Tom's presence. It would only have upset her.

CHAPTER 2
IN WHICH MY PATERNITY IS BROUGHT INTO QUESTION

Perhaps Tom, fuelled by drink, had already lost his playful facade before the phone rang, but, as I manoeuvred round on the sofa to speak to him, he suddenly appeared all washed out, lost, empty, vanquished. Sitting there sloppily in the old armchair he had always used, his legs wide apart, I watched while his head fell forward as if asleep, leaving the loosened bulky knot in his bright red tie sticking out below his chin, and his arms, clothed in the well-ironed sleeves of his expensive shirt, sprawled out along the arm-rests.

'Dad.' It was only a word, to get his attention. But it was the wrong word, or the right one depending on which way you look at it.

'I'm not your Dad.' He said it without raising his bowed head. I thought I didn't hear what he said, and was about to say 'pardon', but stopped myself. The words and their meaning, nevertheless, filtered through into my consciousness; and then he repeated them anyway.

'I'm not your father. I can't be.' I said nothing. Everything had gone blank, but vividly blank, if that's possible. I kept on looking at him, and eventually he raised his head.

'Well, fucking say something,' he said. 'Well, fucking say something.' I'm very fond of that phrase. It might have come from *Eastenders*, except that the recording was showing crowds of celebrants in Moscow, and, in any case, by then, *Eastenders* had not gone downhill under Caxton's ownership.

I could make up the next bit, but the truth is I don't remember emerging from the blankness. I might have asked the primary questions, or he might have asked them for me, 'How do you know?' and 'Who is?'. Secondary questions, such as 'Why haven't you told me before?', came later.

This is what I learned that night. Tom was first alerted to his infertility during a serious affair in his early 20s with a 'busty social worker'. She was very keen to have children, but when she didn't become pregnant, she demanded they both get tested. When he came back with news of a very low sperm count, the relationship broke down. He told himself it was only a low sperm count, not a zero sperm count, and put it out of his mind. He went with a succession of weak women after that to restore his confidence, and eventually decided to marry Julie, who had youth, if not beauty, and was fool enough to have him. But he never told her. When she fell pregnant, after more than a year without contraception, he quashed any idea than she might have been unfaithful, and believed his own internal propaganda. My paternity was never discussed. As I grew up, however, without any physical characteristics similar to Tom (he was fairish, slightly built and of medium height, while I was dark, full-boned and tall), he allowed his suspicions to grow. Who knows whether he did this to justify his own infidelities, or whether his unfaithfulness escalated as a consequence of his suspicions. It was only on the brink of their separation that Julie hinted, in one violent argument, that Tom wasn't my father. Given Tom's insecurities in this area, which he had never revealed, this sparked further arguments. Julie, though, stubbornly refused to discuss the subject further. Long after the separation and divorce, Tom found himself unable to forget the matter. Furtively, he arranged a paternity test by post (using some of my hair, apparently). This was after the Bangkok trip and during my first year at university.

As for the who, Tom had no idea, no clue.

My memory re-engages about the time he is shaking his head and saying 'sorry' several times in a row. 'For what?' I asked mechanically.

'I'm sorry I'm not your real father, sorry for you, but much sorrier for me too. You're a fine son, the best.' This must rank as the nicest thing he ever said to me, and I was about to become emotional when he reeled out a rescue line. 'But hey, it's just as well you don't have my genes or you'd never have made it into the volleyball team.' I lay there uncomfortable but immobile on the sofa, while Tom eased himself out of the chair and left the room. The recording was showing crowds along the Thames, and firework celebrations from places further east around the globe.

I tried to think if I could recall any tall men from my childhood. There was only my uncle Alan, Julie's brother, but such a liaison was too horrible to contemplate. Moreover, although my mother was not religious she was morally upright. I may, youthfully, have wished Alan to be my father on occasions, especially when Tom was away so much or appeared disinterested in me, but Alan's relationship with Julie was too honest, too straightforward for them to have hidden a secret. I could barely believe my mother capable of such a deception, one so deep and dark. Nevertheless, at that moment, I had no doubt I would find out my father's identity as soon as she returned from Edinburgh.

Tom re-entered the room some minutes later, more sober, more in control of himself, and proposed another game of Scalextric. I declined, pleading enough was enough. I too needed the toilet so hobbled my way there. On the way back, coming through the breakfast room, I passed a photo of Tom, Julie and me taken when I was about six. I have it on the wallscreen now. I am in school uniform again (what would one expect with a teacher for a mother) and standing between my parents, but looking up at Tom, with something akin to love in my eyes. Julie is glancing down at me, and Tom, as usual, is staring forthrightly at the camera. How strange that I should be able to touch the very same emotion now, looking at this photo, that I felt then. Love for my father, love of my father, warts, Bangkok and all. It made no difference, I realised, standing there, held up by crutches, only 20 years old, that he was not my genetic parent, he was still my Dad, always had been, and always would be. I told him as much then, and it felt good.

At about 11pm, we switched off the video, and flicked through various broadcast programmes looking for one hosted by someone both of us could put up with, which was not so easy. I vetoed any game shows, and Tom blocked any political or current affairs-type discussions. We finally compromised on a truly old comedy, *Some Like it Hot* with Marilyn Monroe, to lift our spirits. Since it was a film we both knew, we could let it fill the silences, or switch easily into the laughter when our talk faded. I wanted to know why Tom had not acted earlier to confront Julie or tell me. I did not get a straight answer, but I did come to understand, more or less. With Julie, he felt no responsibility: whatever his own mistakes, her deception had been the greater. As for me, I believe he was afraid of what it might do to our relationship, especially since it had gone downhill after the horrible trip to Bangkok three years earlier (about which I will have more to say later). As it happens, Tom's revelation that New Year's Eve served to re-establish our friendship, albeit an intermittent one, which lasted through to his death in 2038.

We fell asleep in situ, only to wake groggy and cold in the early hours. I told Tom he should take my bed, but he wanted to leave. He packed up the Scalextric and old video player, when I said I didn't want them, and ferried the boxes to his sleek car, I think it was a Ford Presumption, but it could have been one of a dozen, he was forever switching models. Rain clouds had gathered overnight. We said goodbye on the doorstep under the porch, embracing awkwardly, and one of my crutches fell to the ground.

CHAPTER 3
IN WHICH I FIND A TEAR-STAINED LETTER

I spent most of New Year's Day 2020 searching through all Julie's private belongings for a clue about her infidelity and my paternity. Fortunately, she was a tidy, ordered person – a characteristic she pressed into me from an early age – and I was able to find her personal papers without much trouble. An old pine dresser in the kitchen held various items such as bills, home accounts, tradesmen's flyers, job quotes and jumble sale notices. There was nothing of interest there. Nor was there much to find in the small oak desk, dominated by a dark green personal computer console, or in the three drawer old-fashioned wooden filing cabinet, both of which were tucked into the darkest corner of the lounge. Everything here was connected with her teaching work. I decided against checking the computer hard disk, despite the potential treasure of email correspondence, in case she had a security mechanism which might give me away, and require explanation.

I saved the white-painted desk in her bedroom until last. Here, where I spent several hours, I was extremely careful to ensure that every bundle of letters and email printouts (organised by correspondent, and with neatly printed copies of her own missives), every packet of photographs (labelled), and every diary (largely blank with only intermittent entries) were replaced exactly as I found them. I should note that I never saw any of the letters again (with one exception), nor any of her email correspondence except for some extended email dialogues between her and Alan, which I acquired after my uncle's death. Since I did not find any correspondence among the personal possessions I inherited from my mother, I assume she destroyed or lost them during her later years.

I discovered much about my mother that day, although, from this distance, it is difficult to untangle all of what I learned then from what I had already known, especially from Tom during the Bangkok trip, or from what I may have found out later. Also, whereas some of the information was pertinent to my search, some may have been stored and lain dormant, to be appreciated in conjunction with other events. I recollect, in particular how the letters to Alan, who lived abroad mostly, and the occasional diary entries, mostly in the period up to when I was 11 or so, revealed the depth of Julie's misery.

While the journal entries were unrestrained, the letters told the same story in more coded language, a consistent tale of Tom's frequent trips away, his disinterest in Julie or in me or in any domestic matters at all, and his ugly belligerence. Where he was brutish, she was sensitive, the subtext read, where he was cold, she was warm, where he was hard, she was soft. Oddly none of this was a surprise. I had lived with an atmosphere between them until I was 13, and my mother's written expression of the difference between the male and female character appeared rather normal. It was more shocking to realise that my mother saw herself as a martyr, and that she considered the self-sacrifice of staying with Tom as necessary for my well-being. She must have camouflaged this side of her character well, at least from me. Or, maybe, children have so many other daily petty grievances against their parents they never see the bigger faults. A year or two later, when I no longer felt the need to be so loyal to Julie, I recall Tom, in a pub, choking with laughter when I suggested she had a secret martyr complex. Not secret, he spat, but 'plain, plain as a bloody pike-staff'.

It was easier to forgive another fault that eked out of Julie's writing, especially in letters to an old friend who had given birth at a similar time to her but had then emigrated to Canada: an overly zealous anxiety about me. I had had glimpses of this when overhearing her talk about me to friends on the phone, but the letters and journal entries were stronger stuff. How strange it is to read about oneself in the third person. She wrote in great detail about my physical development, my behaviour, my progress at school, for example, as well as about my faults – disobedience, stubborn silences, insufficient effort. There was nothing unusual there, even at age 20 I could tell that, and yet she wrote with the intensity of an obsessive. I imagine this came from a deep sense of responsibility towards me, which I had never properly appreciated, and one she had never come to terms with – perhaps because she had chosen the wrong husband, or because her husband was not my father.

The first time the house phone rang that day I was already installed in my mother's bedroom, on her bed in fact, which was the most comfortable place for me, even though I had to hop backwards and forwards to the desk for each new bundle. But, as I had forgotten to bring the receiver upstairs, I was obliged to try and hop-rush down the stairs to answer it. On the way, I fell quite badly and bruised my thigh. It was Julie. She kept asking if I was well because I sounded so funny, so tense. And she asked, with that slight accusatory tone of hers, if I had a girl with me. I improvised well-ness, allowing her one more holiday day.

Of all the letters/emails to my mother, the most absorbing were those written by Alan. (Indeed, if anyone were to investigate the extensive files of my own correspondence stored on Neil, they would find the Alan Hapgood file one of the longest, the most easy to read, and the most stimulating. Not that emails have ever replaced the warm satisfaction of receiving a real letter sent by postal courier.) This was not only because, of all her correspondents, his life, spent working for the environmental organisation WWF, was the most interesting, but also because of his warmth and humanity, and the relaxed style with which he wrote to his sister. At this time, he must have been posted in Brussels or Geneva or another of WWF's offices, otherwise I would surely have seen him during the Christmas period. As I have said, he was a great, as in excellent, uncle, and he became a great friend, but since it was clear from the letters that Julie had never confided in him, there was no need to quiz him on this particular matter.

And what of my paternity? There was little to help me, except for this one sad handwritten (in green ink) letter, which alone was housed in its original envelope.

'Dearest Julie, How abysmal, how awful, how lonely these days. I can hardly bear to see you in school. You are so cold, so unfriendly. I'm not sorry for what I did, what we did, nor for who I am. Are you ashamed of me? Did you fall out of love with me in the space of one weekend? Did I do something wrong? Say something terrible? I know you feel something for me, you told me so. And I know you loved me in those nights, I know you did, I know you did, I know you did.

I love you. Love me again too.

Martin x'

I have this letter stored on Neil (during a subsequent visit to Julie's house, I conspired to photograph it) and am looking at it onscreen now. The note is not so sad in itself but because, in one corner, my mother has written to herself 'I love you too Martin', and because several of Martin's words are smudged by, I imagine, a tear stain. I recall, also, that this was the one and only letter I discovered in my mother's entire collection with any romantic content at all, and that the single piece of notepaper had been much handled. The envelope was stamped January 1999.

In her 1998 diary, I found some further evidence. There was one entry in mid-November in which she complained about Tom's absence, and recorded her decision to accept an invitation to go to the theatre. The invitation was from 'a new young teacher with manners' who had, in less than a term, become 'a favourite with the Head'. My mother must have been flattered by the man's interest, and had justified responding because of her growing resentment towards Tom. A further short entry, at Christmas time, concluded with the simple phrase 'Martin rang'. The 1999 journal, a separate book with even fewer entries than the previous year, recorded nothing in March/April, round about the time I was conceived, except a bout of flu and depression which led to several visits from the doctor.

Despite the content and date of the letter, I was convinced that Martin had to be my father. I scoured the house to see if Julie had kept any school newsletter or prospectus from that period, but I couldn't find anything.

I also tried to project forward as to how, when my mother returned, our conversation would proceed, and how I might introduce Martin's name without giving away my illicit search. If I had been sufficiently angry this embarrassment might not have been a problem, but I wasn't: however large my mother's sin, I did not want her to know I had been rifling through her letters.

That evening, a Wednesday, I was taken out by some old school-friends. We went to the Mankind, a pub by the river the other side of Godalming, and played MoonFusion for hours against a team in Seoul. We lost. I couldn't concentrate, and, that difficulty apart, I was hopeless at netgaming. All day Thursday I pretended to myself that I was reading a controversial book on the failures of the United Nations (which I did, eventually, use extensively for a mini-thesis), but in reality I was brooding, and becoming increasingly unsettled by Tom's revelation. I telephoned Alfred, on holiday from Manchester University, in Lagos, but chickened out of talking things over with him.

CHAPTER 4

IN WHICH I CONFRONT MY MOTHER — TO NO AVAIL

Julie returned on Friday night. It was still pouring with rain. She had rung the doorbell without thinking, I suppose, because she couldn't be bothered to find her key. By the time I had hopped my way through into the hallway, she was already inside, standing on the mat, a sweet picture: her glad-to-be-home-but-weary face, her damp glistening hair, fastened up as usual in a tidy bun, her overlong mottled green raincoat dripping, and a suitcase dropped down by her side.

'Sorry,' she said. And, for a moment, I thought she was apologising for her adultery.

'No taxis?' I asked rhetorically, knowing that, although both of us would normally walk from the station less than half a mile away, we would often buy a ride in bad weather or with heavy loads.

Twenty minutes later, we were sitting in the breakfast room where she had brought a tray of tea things. I listened to the details of her journey with curiosity, not duty, for she kept her anecdotes short and did not ramble. She was a good teacher, I am certain, one that holds an audience with confident and interesting delivery, as opposed to a poor one who tries to do the same through discipline alone. But, all the time, I was thinking about how and when I was going to confront her. She's tired after the journey, I told myself, I'll wait until tomorrow. Then she quizzed me on what I'd been doing. I looked away, hesitated, said nothing. And then the words came out.

'Tom was here, he got drunk and told me something.' Words come out, we don't exactly choose them (not unless they are part of a prepared speech or presentation). And then we hear them, think about them, and then rally round to make sense of them with expressions, or more words, or actions. This was my brooding, jumping out of me.

'Tom was here, when, why?'

'He phoned for a chat, and when I said you were away, he said he was nearby and so popped in. That's all.'

'And?'

'And what?' I was afraid, trying to back away from the confrontation.

'You said he told you something.'

'Yes, sort of. It's a bit difficult. It can wait until the morning.' She had her elbows almost vertical on the table, and her chin rested in her hands. Her face was in the shadow created by her head from the ceiling light above. This was my mother, and I felt closer to 12 than 20. I looked away. Silence. I used silence a lot as a child. It was a defence against inquisition. Tom could never deal with it, and lost his temper. Julie, though, was more artful. She used patience, and soft-speaking, and, what? ... Yes, an expression which made use of a gentle encouraging nod, a slight sideways tip of the head, and raised eyebrows. I glanced towards her, saw this expectant look, and said the simple words I'd rehearsed.

'Tom says he's not my father.' The human face is a marvel. We train it to express some emotions, and yet it expresses so much else involuntarily. How can I explain the physical changes in that moment as I watched my mother take in those few words? A narrowing of the iris, as her brain switched attention from vision to thought, a tensing of the forehead, a drawing in of her cheek muscles, with a consequent loss of the slight smile she tried to hold in company. Certainly, the colour drained out of her skin, turning her very pale.

'Tom says he's not my father. I want to know if this is true, and, if it is, who my real father is.' This was another rehearsed statement. In my projection forward to this conversation, it was easiest to imagine my mother would say nothing immediately, and therefore to prepare a follow-up. I may have repeated the question too quickly, too urgently, for Julie then reinvigorated herself instantly, and responded sharply.

'He was glossy, he was talking tosh.' She got up and began to clear away the tea things. Denial. I had not expected a denial, and was momentarily phased. Could Tom have made it all up? Why would he do so? No.

'What else did he tell you?' she called through from the kitchen where water was running. 'Has he taken up Buddhism?'

I shouted back, not in anger yet, but loud enough so she would definitely hear me.

'He's had us – him and me – checked out with DNA analysis. It's 100% sure, Mum, a 100%.' I heard the water stop running. She padded back into the room, and sat down. I said nothing. I watched her thinking for a few minutes. I was in a state of high excitement, although I kept myself motionless and cool, waiting, fully expecting a momentous revelation. After a long silence, she spoke in a low distant voice, not to me, but to herself.

'I don't know, I don't know what happened. I had suspicions. But I don't know.' She got up again, heavily this time, taking the teapot with her.

The pitch in my own voice and language rose to follow her.

'You must know. It's not that fucking difficult to work out who you were sleeping with nine months before I was born. Or is it?' She stopped in her tracks, astonished to hear me use such language.

'I can't help you,' she said and walked out of the room.

I resorted to loud crude sarcasm next.

'So you weren't screwing anyone else at the time, you were completely faithful to Tom, and I was a miracle.' I collected one crutch and hopped after her. I stood in the doorway of the kitchen. 'Were you sleeping around, or weren't you? You must know, come on Mum, you teach sex education, you know how it happens. Who's my bloody father?' I wasn't given to swearing, or vitriol, or even anger most of the time, but on this occasion my normal behaviour patterns gave way to some combination of those I'd seen employed by Tom or *Eastenders*' characters. I stood there screaming while my mother, her back towards me, did the washing up.

I stopped soon enough. It was as though someone else was doing the shouting. I doddered back to the other room, where I sat down, and calmed myself. I considered whether I should ask her directly about Martin. Yet this was too risky. Firstly, she might simply carry on saying nothing; secondly, as I've said, I could not bring myself to let her know I had been through her private things; and, thirdly, my illicit behaviour could create a diversion for her and attenuate the righteous force of my demands to know the truth. I decided to make a more rational appeal. She returned to the table, looking at me with a rare sense of vulnerability.

'Mum, you can't not tell me. I have a right to know. Was there someone else?'

'Not really.'

'Not really?'

'There was a young man once, when your father was away, but, ...' she paused, appearing uncertain and confused.

'Yes,' I said encouragingly.

'But ... but I can't tell you any more. I don't know any more.' She paused again, having become vague and very distant. After that she closed up completely. Despite my insistent, but now calm, questioning, she would only repeat that same phrase, 'I can't tell you any more', with the strangest inflection on the last two words. Then she went to bed.

I quizzed her again in the morning, but when she refused repeatedly to answer any of my questions about the past, or to acknowledge my right to the information, I left. I packed my rucksack (with some difficulty), called a taxi, and took a combination of trains and another taxi to get back to my Bermondsey flat. Tom rang while I was waiting at one station or another to tell me to go easy with Julie. It was just like him to be late with good intentions.

What did my mother mean by 'any more'? This taxed me for a long time afterwards. Did she mean she was not able to give me any further information, or did she mean that she no longer had any answers, that she was confused about the past. I never found out. Stranger still, I never discovered whether she even knew what had happened to her. She had certainly blanked out the truth in some way, but whether this was an involuntary unconscious initiative, or whether she deliberately pushed the information so far back in her mind and made the conscious decision not to access the knowledge, is hard to know. I incline to the latter view.

I am undecided whether to conclude this story now, or to leave it for another chapter.

CHAPTER 5
I PERUSE SOME EARLY FAMILY PHOTOGRAPHS

A peppery omelette was brought in for me some minutes ago, and while eating I launched a database of early snaps that are now fading in and out on the screen. Some of these are so grainy, a tell-tale sign that they were scanned or snapped digitally in the period when computer memory was constrained by size and expense. They exude a glorious sense of generalised, not personal, nostalgia: I know who these people are, but they do not touch any live memories. Other photos from later on in my life are more meaningful in an emotional way, but they must wait their turn. For now, I might pause on one or two of these pictures.

Here are Tom and Julie outside a registry office. He is in a white suit, tightly fitted, with a compact pink rose in one lapel. He looks like a dandy. He may have had tendencies in that direction but, although a vain man, I thought of him as well-dressed rather than over-dressed. Perhaps, if circumstance had given him more freedom, he may have gone foppish. Julie is in a pink dress, and looks like a bridesmaid.

In another photo, confetti is falling around their shoulders, and they are surrounded by family members. Alan, to one side, is looking amused and holding a box, from which a teenage girl is reaching for a further handful of confetti.

Julie's mother, Eileen, is there on the other side. She was a stern but fair woman, also a teacher, and for many years the head at a large primary school in Reading. She was a keen potter. I never saw much of her. Tom used to tell me, when I was older, that she was more interested in her pupils and her pots than in her own children or grandchildren. She could never bring herself to approve of Tom, whose charm always fell flat with her. It is possible we saw her more when I was very young, but after our move to Guildford, and after her retirement to Parsonville, a custom-built retirement village near Bournemouth, she never came to visit us. As a family, we went to see her twice a year at most, although Julie alone went more often.

Eileen's husband and Julie's father, Oswald Hapgood, had died of a brain tumour when Julie was only ten. There was also a distance between Eileen and her son Alan, which grew wider as they got older. Eileen was a traditional Tory: in her dotage she would reminisce about Margaret Thatcher, the Conservative prime minister in the 1980s. But Alan, despite her best efforts, went left, then green, and didn't start the journey back towards the centre until well into middle-age. My mother, by contrast, could never be bothered with politics, other than when it affected education policy.

Percival, Oswald's bachelor brother, stands at the back of the photo. He was a grey fellow. Oddly, he came to life when pulling crackers or playing tiddlywinks. In conversations, his contribution was often confined to nods and shakes. He tried to interest me in fishing once, not long after his retirement. I believe he spent time in a mental home. I remember his death, or rather seeing his dead body, the first one I ever saw in the flesh. I was 12.

Tom's father and mother, Barry and Evvie, are in the photo too, looking pleased with themselves; or is that relief in their eyes and smiles? I never knew Evvie, she died soon after the wedding. Barry emigrated to Malta.

Here is a favourite photo of Tom, Julie and me in Monte Carlo in May 2003. Tom is sitting on the bonnet of a bright red racing car, I am on his lap in bright red shorts, an orange t-shirt, and a baseball cap sporting the name Ferrari. Julie is standing next to us laughing at something Tom, or the camera holder, has said. She is wearing a light yellow frock, and a straw hat, and is looking her prettiest. This is how I picture my mother whenever I think of her as a young woman in the time before I had my own memories. She had this photo enlarged and framed; it was displayed in one room or other in the St Albans, Guildford and Godalming houses. There are two anecdotes about that holiday. I was told both of them a few times.

Julie's eyes would mist over when she looked at this photo – this is later, after Tom had left – and she would drift into a nostalgic mood.

'That was the best holiday we ever had, not because of the place or the weather, but because your father had never been more loving or caring. I had not been to Monaco, but he knew it well from business trips, conferences and exhibitions mostly. I was dreading the holiday, you were so young. I knew there would be multitudes of people and we would be pushing and shoving our way through the streets, amid the noise and smoke and smell of those noxious and obnoxious cars. But something magical happened. On the very first day he showed us around the botanical gardens with wondrous views across the town and beaches, and he held both our hands. As I was gazing at the succulents, the prickly ones, the curly ones, he was chattering on about the race as though my interest in it really mattered. He was the Tom I first knew, all childish and inspiring, all charm and innocence. The next day, the day of the main race, we negotiated the teeming crowds without any problem. He was determined you should have the best view of the race, and so he kept you on his shoulders most of the time. He bought us expensive ice-creams, took us to the aquarium, and played with you for hours on the beach. I remember – I know this sounds funny – falling in love with him again.'

I should note, although I'm racing ahead all of 80 years, that Lizette broke her hip in those very same gardens. It was a horrible injury which brought our retirement mini-journeys to an end.

Tom's story about the photograph was told to me for the last time that New Year's Eve when he came to visit while Julie was in Edinburgh. He saw the photo half hidden behind a pot on a windowsill in the lounge.

'That's a Ferrari, son. It came 8th – or was it 10th – in the 2003 Monaco Grand Prix. Do you know who drove it? Damn, neither do I. I forget.' He stopped to laugh. 'But how did I get the photo, that's the puzzle? You can't just wander around and sit on those cars – they cost millions.'

'No idea, Dad, how did you get the photo?'

'Oh I know you know, but it's worth the telling.'

'The re-retelling.' He snorted, and ignored me.

'After the race, it was heaving with people in every direction, all going back to their hotels and yachts. I didn't want it to be over, so we walked a kilometre or more – you were a great little walker, long strong legs even then – until we came to the track area with the grandstands and the pit areas. But of course we couldn't get in, there was a huge wire mesh gate and several two metre tall guards. Vehicles and pedestrians were entering and leaving constantly, and all were having their identity checked. Inside, one could see mechanics and drivers and advisers and owners and promoters milling around in the after-race milieu. I so wanted to be in there. I went up to the friendliest looking guard. I had to pull you hard because your mother was standing firm and holding onto your other hand. I had no idea what I was going to say.'

'Let me guess,' I said. He snorted and ignored me again.

' "Ferrari here," and I pointed at you, "is three years old and he's never seen the real thing." This was in my best Franglais. "We only want to have a quick look at the cars, five minutes that's all. We'll be back I promise. Look I could leave you my credit card, my bag ..." There was a smirk of contempt on his face. And then, I'm not sure why, I said he could have my wife too. Julie looked shocked, as if it might not be a joke, but the guard smiled. Then he was diverted for a minute by a car leaving. As luck would have it, one of the passengers was old Limey Bimmerson from Exxon. I was embarrassed to be a punter and not on the inside of the show, but he leaned out the window, all friendly and smiles. "Hiya Tom, great race eh, Chet's down there somewhere in hospitality, this your wife? Hiya. Say hi to Harrison." Harrison was my manager at the time. And then the car whisked him away. The guard had witnessed the exchange, and came back over to us. He knelt down and looked you in the face. "What's your name son?" Good English. This would blow it, I thought. You said ...'

Aren't parents the limit. At this point, Tom stopped and looked at me, so I could contribute to the pathetic story.

'Neil.'

'Neil. Yes, you little bugger – not so little now – you said "Neil", and I wanted to kick you across the other side of the road. Not that you could have known any better. Julie saw my face cringe, and bent down to gave you a hug. The guard simultaneously stood up to his full two metre height and laughed his head off. "I am so relieved," he said, "that your son is not called Ferrari; go on, but be back in ten." I bustled us through the gate before he could change his mind. Getting to the car itself was easier, we slipped under a rope, dodged round the back of a garage, and sweet-talked a mechanic. Even Julie was impressed.'

Here's another photo, more interesting in its way, for what it says – all too obviously – about my background. A group of mostly primary schoolchildren are standing or crouching together in several rows on a park lawn. All are wearing wellingtons and bright yellow pull-over bibs with black lettering saying 'Reading clean-up week'. Julie, a shy-looking 12 year old, and a lanky 14 year old Alan are the only two holding, what look like, walking sticks but which are surely litter guns. Between them, in the middle of the group and centre stage, is Eileen, in her prime. Eileen's dedication to clean parks led, possibly, to Julie's keen attention to green issues as a mother and teacher, and to Alan's career in environmental organisations. And the combined influence of all of them certainly affected the direction of my own career.

One more. It is a standard school photo. I am seven, though you could mistake me for eight or nine, given my height. I am wearing a dark blood-coloured school sweatshirt, and grey trousers. Across one side of my head is a wide white bandage, stretching from the middle of the forehead, skirting round the eyebrow, and down to the left ear. This was one week after the most frightening experience of my childhood (not counting Tom losing his temper with Julie or with me). I was cycling along a narrow dirt track near our house. When I came to a large builder's lorry which had stopped and was blocking the track, I tried squeezing myself and my cycle between the side of the lorry and a hedge. I was halfway along when the lorry started to move. The rear wheel, which was huge, caught the back wheel of my bicycle and crunched it to the ground. I leaped for my life to the side, into a thorn bush, bashing my head on a thick branch stump, and tearing my clothes. Only after the cycle crunching did the driver spot something wrong in his wing mirror, although he should have checked before starting off. My wound did not ache that much, but it bled a lot, and looked severe. It is the feeling of shock afterwards I remember most, the fear of what might have happened. The driver shouted at me, as though it were my fault, but a foreman appeared. He proved to be a surprisingly gentle man, and walked me home carrying the cycle. Kudos came my way at school, and then, after Julie wrote a couple of letters to the construction company, a cheque arrived. Tom helped me buy a new bicycle – one with suspension.

CHAPTER 6

IN WHICH TOM TAKES ME TO THE CINEMA

I see I have avoided making a decision on when to finish the story about my conception. No longer. I have decided to do so later. These photos have put me in a different frame of mind, and I am thinking about my young life and schools, especially Witley Academic. My earliest memory, or the one I have fixed on as my earliest, is of a broken window, fear and Tom shouting. I do not believe I was ever hit hard, although Tom visited violence on me in other ways, chiefly by shouting and punishments which involved my muscles aching. Otherwise, I recall the feeling, not the face or personality as such, of a few playmates and teachers: Brittle Charlie who cried a lot; Quid who got his fingers stuck in bottles; Clarissa who came round to tea, because Julie liked her mother; KZ who knew how to find cricket balls at the recreation ground; and Mr Subramani, a teacher beloved by all, except my mother who may have been slightly jealous of his innate empathy with children, and my adoration of him.

Mr Subramani, who came from Birmingham (he called it Brimmingham for no particular reason), told us about the world. Some days he brought in a newspaper, showed us the headlines, and then explained how and why the news was important, but without talking down to us. This was the period when the conflict between the Christian and Arab worlds was only barely simmering, and when a general view prevailed that, so long as the United States and its allies spent billions on their war against terrorism, nothing as bad as 11 September could ever occur again. Years later, thinking back about Mr Subramani I came to believe he must have thought otherwise, he feared for humankind, and decided he would do what he could to educate for tolerance and understanding.

But, at the age of eight, when Tom found himself a new and better job, I was wrenched away from the school in St Albans to another one in Guildford, a commuter town south of London. There were good and bad things about the way that happened. We moved in the summer, so my 'forever' goodbyes at the end of the school year were lost among all the summer farewells. I would never see my best friends again, and I was inconsolable – until I saw several of them at the swimming pool two days later. There were lots of arguments in the week we moved, with all the packing and unpacking, but it was exciting to explore the new, bigger house and garden. There was an old rusty barbecue standing on the terrace out of view from any of the main windows. I acquired a box of matches, a potato, a frozen sausage and a chocolate bar. This makes me sick thinking of it even now. I used paper and a few fallen twigs to cook them. I didn't eat much of the black uncooked potato or raw sausage, but the melted chocolate dribbled down my clothes and gave me away. I blame this humbling experience on the fact that neither Julie nor Tom lavished enough attention on me in that manic few weeks. Worst of all, and hanging over me all summer, was the knowledge that I would be a marked boy at my new school, Boxgrove, since my own mother would be working there, as deputy head.

It was probably at this time – our move marks the most likely dividing point – that Julie withdrew from her intensive involvement in teaching me at home. I cannot testify as to what impact she had had on my education so far for I was too young. I do recall long sessions of reading, of writing, of talking about topics, and not being able to watch TV as much as my playground buds (was the term 'bud' in common parlance then, I can't remember). There is laughter and fun in my memory of these times, but emotional colours of delight at achievement applauded and of disappointment at failures noticed are stronger. Julie could be stern, but I was always seeking the laughter and the smiles, and the only way to do this was with neat writing, correct answers, good work. (As an annex to Part One of this volume, I am including extracts from Julie's emails to her brother Alan. I am unable to provide much intelligence on my early life, or on Julie's role in my upbringing, so these extracts seem an essential addition to my Reflections.)

At Boxgrove, there was no Mr Subramani. I had 'grown-up' conversations with my mother about the conduct of our relationship at school. She never learned to ignore me entirely, but she did her best. There was bullying of sorts. Without deliberately setting out to become a schoolboy guardian angel, I shamelessly used both my size and the threat of my connections to neutralise the bullies significantly. I became respected over time for never once actually enlisting my mother or any other teacher to defend myself or others. There were lessons and clubs. I competed in the pool with Josh, who invariably swam faster than me, with Little Manfred for top place in English, and with Veronica for bottom place in Music. I played chess as if it were as simple as draughts with Big Manfred. A school trip to Snowdonia was all midnight feasts, rain, and queuing up to partner Josh on his netgames console.

Tom was away as often as not, and when not, there were rows. Julie would end up crying and lock herself in the bathroom. I would rush up to Tom and punch his arm. He would push me away, onto the floor or against the wall. There would be a snort, a rude comment, and then he would bang the front door. Julie would re-emerge, with make-up on, and a smile. When I asked why Tom was so angry, she would never tell me. As I grew older she would generalise about how adults have complicated personal and relationship problems that can be difficult to resolve.

'But if you love each other and try hard enough, then you can solve them,' I would say naively.

'Yes, my little wise man, yes. I hope so,' my mother would reply. What I noticed, in retrospect, about my mother was that somehow she was getting bigger, stronger. Perhaps this was to do with a confidence in her deputy head position, or, perhaps, after marrying someone older, she was finally finding her own character, her own way.

'Yes, my little wise man.' A phrase I consciously repeated on occasions to my own children, but I'm sure never to the same effect as Julie with me.

At weekends, Tom had a knack of turning me against his interests. Cards. He knew so many different card games – from cribbage to canasta, from poker to piquet – and he made me play them all long before I was even able to hold a handful of cards in order. Mostly, he took control of both hands, and got very excited in explaining how they should be deployed. But, whenever he expected me to show skill or knowledge, I was a dumbo. I gave up trying very early on, he was too demanding. He had a particularly nasty way of calling me 'stupid' or 'idiot' that made me squirm.

Lizette, the last love of my life, whose final absence now gives me time to spend writing these Reflections, was a wizard at Melbourne Bridge. I tried to learn, I did try, for her. I enjoyed the complications of stylised bidding and back-bidding negotiations but I failed to rise above novice level, or escape feelings of tedium.

And, thankfully, Tom ensured I would never be very keen on cars or motorbikes or speed. He filled up winter weekends with non-stop sport on the screen – Julie never agreed to me having, what was quaintly called, a television in my bedroom – and dragged me to motor races or rallies whenever the weather was clement. By the time he left, when I was 12, I had developed both defensive ('too much homework', 'a friend's party') and offensive ('I don't want to go – I hate motor racing') means of avoiding these day trips.

I say all this, yet surprisingly I loved him greatly and missed him whenever he went away. He brought me presents, that was one of his secrets. He was always telling me anec-dotes about people he had brushed shoulders with in the oil industry, or places he had been, or some new theory he had read in magazines about space and space exploration. I don't believe I was ever interested in what he had to say, I simply wanted him there, talking to me. But the best times with him were the trips to the cinema. He was the movie industry's ideal punter: uncritical, star-struck, and unable to relax in his seat without a giant pack of rainbow popcorn.

I can define three stages in my relationship with Tom through our movie-going habits. While he and Julie were together, and I was but a child, he took me to the cinema once a month, from the age of about five, in St Albans, then in Guildford. After every film, he would ask me to compare it with the last one or two we had seen, and then give it a rating. As I grew older, I asked him for his rating too. There was one film, *Trumpet Boy*, to which we both awarded top marks. It made such an impression that it both haunted and enchanted me for years to come. I have never forgotten the plot and some of the visuals. The flick itself aged badly and only achieved cult, as opposed to classic, status. The director, a Mexican, Pedro Antonio de Malancas, known as Pam, having been feted in Mexico, was seduced by money to go to Hollywood, where he made *Trumpet Boy*. He was dubbed as a new Stephen Spielberg (the director of *ET*). I met Pam once and we did a good thing together – but I must attempt to maintain a semblance of control and chronology over the order in which I set down my memories, and write about this in a later volume.

I was ten when Tom and I went to the Odeon in Guildford to see ... I forget what. By mistake, or Tom's artifice, we settled in the wrong auditorium. No one had checked our tickets on the way in, and no one claimed our seats. When the film started and Tom pointed out that it was classified a 15 (or was it 14 by then?) it could have been a documentary and I would not have cared. *Trumpet Boy*, a computer designed and animated flick from beginning to end, was set in the near future on an island country, Reefland, in the Caribbean, with extensive poverty and ill-health, and rampant crime. The plot revolved around a group of teenagers who begged, borrowed and stole to set up computer and internet facilities for other teenagers. As the movement flourished across the country, so the confidence and ambitions of the teenagers grew. Along the path towards their, eventually successful, overthrow of the corrupt government, they faced – as one would expect – many physical, moral and emotional dilemmas. At the time, the computer generation of teenage characters was praised as impressively realistic, and the media was full of debate about whether actors were needed any longer. Within a few years, though, the films from that era were already looking wooden and crude. For me, Manuel, the 15 year old pickpocket and trumpet player, with long purple hair and a large brown mole on his cheek, who reforms, leads the revolution, and becomes president for a few weeks, was and is as real as any actor-performed film character I have ever seen.

Stage two – this sounds like a committee report – in our movie-going habits lasted until the Bangkok trip. After Tom left, and while I was living at home before going to uni, we used to meet once a fortnight, unless he was away, on Friday or Saturday and go to the cinema. I would sleep over at his pad in Bramley, and then return to Julie later in the day. This was the phase in which my own tastes matured, and I was able to persuade Tom to come with me to see films which were more serious or even subtitled.

Stage three is all the rest of the time. As an adult, I never saw very much of Tom, but this mutual enjoyment of the cinema kept our relationship one notch above dutiful. It was not uncommon for me to receive an email inviting me to see such-and-such a film that same evening or the next, and for me to refuse because of work or family commitments. On occasions, if I saw an opportunity a few days hence, I would email him about a specific film, and we would meet, eat some popcorn, watch the film, and drink a beer after. He told me, not long before he died, that he wanted Vincent (Mush) Mallow to play him in a film of his life.

CHAPTER 7

IN WHICH FLIP APPEARS AS SOMETHING OF A HERO

From Boxgrove in Guildford I moved to the private school, Witley Academic (situated approximately 12 kilometres from Guildford and six from Godalming) and not before time: by the age of 11 I had outgrown primary school in more ways than one. Tom was earning a good salary, so he could afford the fees, and Julie acknowledged that, despite endless rounds of educational reform, there were still some private schools in a class of their own. Witley Academic, one of the original Academic schools (there were to be 100 before the company was broken up under the Fuller-led coalition in the early 2040s), was not in the premier division, but it was in the second, and more importantly, it was nearby and I could get there on the train. Most of my buds moved on to schools in Guildford, and I wanted to go to one of those too; but I didn't, and, if I had, my life would have been very different.

Second only to nearby Charterhouse School, which we passed often and which was definitely a premier division school, Witley Academic was the largest school I had ever seen, even though it had been downsized from its 20th century incarnation as King Edwards when hundreds of boys and a few girls had boarded in addition to a large daily intake. Some of the buildings had been sold off to computer and service businesses, and some of the land had been transformed into a housing estate. Nevertheless, in my day it boasted two playing fields, its own full-size chapel, a large library, a swimming pool, a roomy gymnasium, language labs, well-appointed science and engineering laboratories, and domestic science kitchens. Every classroom was fitted out with computer screens, and the pupils had their own lounge rooms, with special areas for different age groups.

Flip. I cannot think of Witley Academic without Flip coming immediately into view. Flip, aka Philip Liphook, was an inspiring history teacher, albeit one with a strong prejudice towards the ideal of European integration, who taught me for seven years. He wore a ragged beard, a black teacher's gown, and suede shoes with stains. Yet, despite his dishevelled appearance he managed to make a positive impression from the outset.

'I have one rule, and one only. Can you divine what it might be?' Sniggers and silence and more sniggers. 'Is it: no talking when I'm talking? No. Is it: never be late with home-work? No. Is it: no drinking in class? No.' More sniggers. 'Well come on then.' I can hear him now, his voice booming through the room. 'Well someone ask what it is then. Yes, you, what's your name?'

'Horace ...'

'Speak up, you're not here to learn to be a mouse.' We heard this more than once or fifty times.

'Horace Merriweather.'

'Yes, Mr Merriweather.'

'What is your one rule, sir?'

'Thank you for asking, Mr Merriweather. Your name, by the way, opens up boundless possibilities. My rule is that I tell at least one joke every lesson.' More sniggers, a little wary this time.

'Now then, help yourselves to the exercise and text books in the corner. We must press on. The Romans won't wait for us, will they?'

Immediately after that lesson, I joined a loose collection of dazed pupils who were divided as to whether our teacher was a crank, an idiot, a fake, or all three. Horace was there at the centre of the argument full of very firmly-stated but wavering opinions. I kept my own counsel for a while and then sneaked off to find out the truth from one of the older pupils. I re-turned to the group bursting with the news that Liphook's nickname was Flip and that it was true he never failed to make a joke in every lesson. But my class-mates had moved on to telling jokes of their own, and no one was interested in my news.

Flip's rule or promise, whichever way you look at it, proved less difficult to adhere to than we had imagined. He did tell a lot of bona fide jokes. He would stop mid-sentence to say 'that reminds me of a joke', and then he'd tell it, and we would roar with laughter. Frequently, the joke would be linked in some way to the subject matter which led us to suspect it was all part of the prepared lesson, but equally frequently the joke would be related to the morning's news, or a question from one of us. There is no doubt he had a comic gift for timing. When the joke was over, he would give us 15 seconds to recompose ourselves before expecting perfect attention. And, usually, he got it. Even without the set jokes, Flip could never get through a lesson without making us laugh. His style was so full of quips, gentle facetiousness, sarcasm, mimicry and puns that it was a wonder we ever learned much, but we did. We loved him, and wanted to excel.

Forty years later, at the gala show and presentation to celebrate the school's 500th birthday in 2053, Flip was nearly as old as I am now, but he could have passed for 60 not 90. His beard and hair may have turned white, but who could tell the age of the man underneath. He was among a long line of staff and ex-staff receiving special medals from ex-pupil Terrance Spoon for their service to the school. I was in the main hall due to my friendship with Horace Merriweather who served, albeit briefly, in Spoon's inept mid-40s right-wing government, and who had done much to aggrandise the anniversary programme. He saw it as a way to revive the flagging fortunes of the school. This event and others in the week-long celebrations, were broadcast and archived on Euronet Solar, which is how I come to have it stored on Neil, and am watching it now.

When Flip arrives on the stage, the audience in the Great Hall erupts with applause and then cheers. It is as though we have all stored up so much appreciation and thanks for the man and have not been given a chance to express it before now. The applause continues as we watch Spoon place a commemorative ribbon and medallion over Flip's head. The two of them exchange a few words. After several attempts, Spoon manages to quell the uproar by raising his open-palmed hands and moving them lightly backwards and for-wards.

'That's an applause to die for,' Spoon says. A ripple of laughter. 'Should we give Mr Liphook, or Flip ...' loud cheers '... the floor?' Louder cheers, which evaporate as Flip moves a step forward indicating his intention to speak.

'Not too many mice here today then.' Uproar. 'Thank you Mr Spoon, Headmaster, and thank you all. I take pleasure in seeing so many here today, I genuinely thought you would never survive in the real world – mollycoddled as you were in these buildings.' Laughter. 'Which reminds me of a joke.' A spurt of laughter, then a respectful hushed silence, and more silence. 'No it doesn't.' Said in a different way or with a lack of confidence, or without the wrinkled grin just visible under the white wiry hairs, this could be a bathetic statement. But it isn't. The camera pans around from Flip's face to the audi-ence, and I can see we are all on our feet cheering and cheer-ing again, as if it is the funniest joke we have ever heard. And, in its way it was.

'I was going to tell you the one about the history teacher who so loved his job and his pupils that at the age of 89 he couldn't resist coming back for one more fix of the old school. But I don't need to. You know that one and all the rest, and thank you so much. Until the next time.' Everyone is on their feet clapping. One camera rotates round again (there are many familiar faces) and this time I can see myself in the shot. Horace, who is seated a row in front, is leaning back, whisper-ing to me.

'A1 star,' he is saying. 'No, A1 Star plus for Flip, there is nothing I enjoy more than seeing Terrance upstaged. He so, so hates it.'

That's Arturo next to me, he was already in his 30s, sur-prised to be there, and amused by the whole show. Why didn't Diana and Guido come? I forget. Diana and I must have already started to draw apart by then. 2053. Yes, that was the beginning of the end for us as a couple. I'll check the dates later.

CHAPTER 8

IN WHICH HORACE AND MELISSA APPEAR NAKED

Needless to say, Flip must have had a great and beneficial influence over my educational achievements since I excelled at history through the 16 exams and achieved a distinction in the 18 exams. He also ran a debating club and, for sixth-formers, the Brideswell Society, although Horace and I and several others were allowed privileged access to this before we reached the sixth form. The debating club, volleyball, the pool, homework in the library were among the activities that, most days, kept me at school long after lessons were finished.

It was through the debating club in the second year that Horace and I became firm friends. For several sessions in a row, all we did was listen to older pupils pontificate on subjects both interesting and deadly dull. It was only Flip's energy and encouragement that kept us coming. Then, about halfway through the year, he invited Horace and me to propose the motion 'Life will be better tomorrow' against two girls, one of whom was Gemma (who matured into a beauty and paired up with Alfred for a while). We set to our task with youthful enthusiasm, preparing and rehearsing our speeches as though our lives depended on it. I suggested we try and anticipate what the girls might say, so we would be better prepared for the concluding speeches, but Horace wanted to wing it.

A good crowd turned up, our classmates and a fair sprinkling of seniors who came to mock. Horace, hands on hips to give himself maturity and more presence (hence the nickname Hip, like mine consciously similar to Flip), was fluent, witty and concise. By contrast, I was given to protective stooping, and verbose complicated arguments. We won by a close vote. On dissecting our performance afterwards, we came to the joint conclusion that it was Horace's inspired, but not entirely relevant, reference to 'hope' that gave us victory: 'And what happened to hope. We are but teenagers, how can we not believe life will be better tomorrow?' We may have won that debate but we were wrong – so far as I can judge from today's standpoint. Yet, if Horace were here now and we were asked again whether we wanted to support or oppose the motion, I feel sure we would both, without hesitation, opt for the same stance again.

For the next 18 months or so Hip and Kip were often to be found together in the library researching on the net, or deep in discussion about some topic or other. Although we rarely lost a debate, sometimes it was too close for Horace's comfort. Criticism of my speaking style began to creep into our conversations, and this led me to object to his lack of depth and over-reliance on rhetoric. Witley Academic, as represented by Flip, inflated us without our knowing. But, whereas Horace's confidence was all brimming on the surface, mine was not. In the middle of the third year, I told Horace I no longer wanted to continue public speaking, but that if he could find a new partner who was happy to work in a team of three, I would do research and put forward ideas. There was no shortage of volunteers to pair up with Horace, but, to his credit (because I'm about to describe a debit and our falling out), he discussed with me who he should choose. Initially, Jeff Zimmerman was sceptical about the unusual arrangement we proposed but, when he saw the strength of our friendship and our commitment, he soon fell in with the plan. In practice, the system operated well: Jeff and I did the research, all three of us collaborated on the final preparation, and Jeff and Horace delivered the goods.

Now I must backtrack a year and reflect on a difficult subject. It was a Thursday. I had been messing around in the pool. I had changed, and was in a hurry to leave and catch my train. But, as I came out of the boys' changing rooms, I dropped some coins, one of which rolled across the corridor to the dead end wall next to the door to the girls' changing rooms. Two senior girls were chatting in the doorway, propping the door open. From my crouched position on the ground, I could see through into the dressing room. Several girls were half dressed or drying themselves with a towel, but one girl was entirely naked, standing upright and facing my way. I could see all of her except her head. This was the first fully naked girl – plump breasts and fair curly pubic hair – I had ever seen in the flesh. I froze. I stared. She walked forward a step, a beautiful step nearer, and as she did so she called to the other girls to close the door. One of them then turned to re-enter the changing room, which let the door swing free, and the other moved to exit. Momentarily, I was able to see the face of the naked girl, Melissa. In the same moment, before the door closed, she saw me. She did not blanch, or turn, or try to cover herself, she grinned, and the door shut. The girl remaining in the corridor then saw me scrabbling around on the floor for my coin and told me I should get a pair of binnocks.

That was the start. I have tried to analyse over the years whether my sexual preferences would have been any different if that episode had never occurred or if Melissa had shrieked and turned instead of smiling. Twice in the course of my life I have mentioned it to analysts of one description or another without the revelation leading to any firm understanding as to its relevance. During the following months, I overcame mighty feelings of guilt and embarrassment in attempting to achieve a repeat of the experience. The problem was invariably the same: the entrance to the girls' changing room was at the end of a corridor and there was no legitimate reason for a male to be there. On countless occasions, when the corridor was empty, I positioned myself strategically in a crouch outside the door, with a loose coin on the floor behind me. I moved as soon as anyone exited either changing room, or saw me along the corridor. Yet, even when luck was with me, and the first person to emerge came from the girls' changing room, I never had both a good line of sight and something to see.

It was only when a girl in my own form called me a 'pervert' one day apropos of nothing in particular, that I woke up to the extent of my foolishness. I never entirely stopped hoping for another vision, but I scaled back my furtive spying efforts. Instead, I channelled my energy into bypassing the school filters on the internet computers which were designed to protect us from pornography and other undesirable material. I focused on the art-related netsites, particularly those linked to photographic galleries or magazines, which I found the most rewarding.

As for Melissa, I loved her, and lusted for her, but from a distance. She knew, and she knew I knew she knew. In the evenings, I was physically incapable of leaving the swimming pool, if she were there. I would watch her secretly, waiting for her to walk along the side. If we were to pass in the canteen or a corridor, she would straighten her back, push out her chest, lift her chin, and flick that long fair hair back to fix my attention, and only then would she look at me with such pride and power that I always lowered my eyes. I imagined a smile of satisfaction on her lovely face as she walked away. But this was not so. I know for sure, because, astonishingly, Melissa became my first lover, and she told me otherwise.

I explain all this because it needs explaining but also to demonstrate how clear I was in my own mind from the age of 14 or so that I liked girl's bodies and, by extension, girls. Horace, by contrast, developed a taste for lads. This appeared to happen to him without me knowing or suspecting. There was one day in the week, in the autumn term of our fourth year, when our last lesson was physical education. This meant that when the lesson was over there was no hurry to change. For some reason, Horace (who detested all sports except golf, and was never to be found in the gym or changing room outside set classes) and I chatted for longer than usual – no doubt about a forthcoming debate – before dressing. By the time we entered the shower room, it was empty apart from us. When Horace came so close that our shoulders touched, I moved away. Then I looked round, I saw him holding his penis in one hand. It was erect. Maybe there were activities I had missed out on, but so far in my young life, I had not shared my erections with anyone, nor had I seen anyone else's.

'Give us a rub, Kip.'

'Get off.' Yet Horace was my best friend, and it wasn't easy to say no to him.

'Come on touch it, you'll like it.' I moved further away again, into the corner of the showers, and he followed. He stretched out one hand wanting to grab my penis. I pushed him way.

'No, I don't want to.' This was Horace as I had never seen him before. He pressed himself forwards, pinning me against the tiled wall.

'Come on Kip, what's the matter. You afraid.' He was trying to rub himself on my thigh. It may have been partly in jest, but I did not see the joke. I pushed him off and forced my way past him. I stopped before leaving the showers, and turned to say something, but he was too busy – with himself.

Horace prostrated himself before me, metaphorically that is, for days after, but I wouldn't listen to his protestations or to those of Jeff and one or two others who interceded on his behalf (without, I should add, knowing why). Our row, or rather my unilateral decision to end the friendship, was the talk of the middle school for several weeks. It took me months to recover. Horace was able to resume where we had left off as if nothing had happened. For my part, I was never able to fully trust him again. Looking back, I can see that it was only because I developed a respectful wariness of him that I was able to remain a close friend for so long.

CHAPTER 9

IN WHICH MY PARENTS FINALLY SEPARATE

Logically, I should move on now and talk about another
important Witley bud, Alfred, and volleyball, but that's a
happy story I want to employ as a bookend to this early
chapter of my life. For the moment, I need to take the train six
stops from Witley to Guildford, London Road station, and
walk seven minutes to 121 Larch Rise. I usually caught a train
around 6pm. Julie would know my schedule, and I would
usually message her if I changed my plans. Occasionally, but
not often, Tom would be at home when I arrived. Julie prepared supper for around 7pm, allowing Tom (if he was there)
and I to catch *Eastenders* while Julie cleared up in the
kitchen. This sounds unfair, but Julie preferred to keep the
kitchen neat and tidy, especially during the week when we
were all busy. She complained if we interfered. I did make her
a cup of tea most nights, when she settled down to mark
homework or listen to the radio. I'm not sure what Tom did
around the house. He brought in more money than Julie, and
he undertook handyman jobs when pestered. This was the
general ordinary pattern for a year or so after I started at
Witley Academic.

Shouting was not an uncommon occurrence in our house,
as I've said, but things got worse in 2012 and came to a head
in the long warm summer of 2013. Tom had a short fuse. Julie
had a way of moaning about petty things which were not
important, and, as I grew close to adolescence, I developed a
defensive habit of remaining silent, mute, which provoked and
challenged both of them from time to time. The worst arguments by far, though, were those between Julie and Tom
which ended with Julie weeping and locking herself in the
bathroom, and Tom storming out of the house. Julie would
tell me that he was out getting drunk. When these arguments
occurred late at night, I would sense them first in a dream,
with loud voices drifting through from far away and scaring
me. Then I would linger for an unknown length of time, in the
state between sleep and waking, desperately attempting to

resist consciousness. As I describe this now, I realise the sensation is not dissimilar to that I used to have, as an aging man, of not wanting to recognise the signal of my bladder and the need to make the effort to rise and go to the toilet. (Now, in bed, I am permanently plumbed, without the fear of psychological or practical inconveniences, and so, when I wake in the night it is for other reasons.) As the volume of their voices – his crunchy, over-reliant on swear words, hers crisp, exasperated – ratcheted up, so I would bury my head under the pillow and press its sides into my ears. If a serious quarrel erupted during the day on a Saturday, I would travel into school; and, if on a Sunday, I would find a friend to visit. If I was lucky, Alan would be available.

I should mention my uncle Alan – Mr Abominable Snowman – at this point. Our moving to Guildford had coincided more or less with his temporary return to WWF's recently-expanded Godalming offices. He was always a busy man, never without a full diary, but he clearly had a soft spot for his sister and me, and so we saw him once every few weeks. Mostly, I enjoyed our walks on the North Downs, or along the Wey, or to the Waverley Abbey ruins or through some arboretum, with a visit to a teashop afterwards. Now and then all of us (including Tom) would take Sunday lunch in a pub. These meetings would often end in Tom and Alan arguing (I mean Tom arguing and Alan being calm and patient as ever), and me getting very bored. When Tom was away, Alan would come round and eat supper with us. More often than not, he would have a story to tell, about nuclear pollution in the Kola Peninsula, or developing the wetlands in Moldova, or a parrot in Borneo that had been saved from extinction, or the crooked empire of the oilserfs. There was a pattern to these evenings. While Julie cooked and prepared food Alan and I would talk, and then, through supper, the conversation would include Julie and start to lose me, so that as soon as I had finished my meal I would slip off to watch a screen. Then Alan would read to me for a few minutes before lights out. Later, once I was established at Witley Academic, it was not unusual for him to turn up at the school, and give me a lift home, or take me to his flat in Farnham, 20 kilometres away, for tea and cake and a chat. He also drew me into a team of volunteers which helped carry out environmental works on the marshy commons nearby. This was mostly cutting tree saplings, building and repairing board walks, and draining ditches. It was tiring work, to which I was not especially suited, but rewarding.

At the time, I did not know the underlying cause of the arguments between my parents, nor did I brood on them. In their own way, both Julie and Tom had tried to comfort me so many times when I was younger, that I no longer believed them. But I was not so numbed that I didn't cry, secretly, often. I would long for Tom to go away on a business trip, so the arguments would stop, and then I would long for him to come back, because I missed him. Unfortunately, I have no record of our emails from that time. It is my impression that we wrote a lot, and that this was fun, something I wanted to do. I rehashed Flip's shorter jokes and amusingly described the worst excesses of other teachers, and Tom talked of 'big deals' and 'big money' and 'very important people'. I would boast about his whereabouts to my friends ('my Dad's in China') and show them composite tourist pics (of him standing in Tiananmen Square, or climbing the Great Wall). Life was undoubtedly better when Tom was away: not only did I love him more then, but my mother and I got on so much better.

I do not wish to dwell too long on the summer of 2013. It was the time of shocking revelations about the extent of Western state surveillance operations, chemical weapons in Syria, riots in Egypt and the shocking murder of the singer Vi Hoop by religious extremists.

Tom's hopes of moving to Singapore or somewhere in the Far East was one open sore. Julie's wish to have a second child, and Tom's refusal to consider it, though, was the deep and underlying problem that had been festering between them for years. Both Julie and Tom confirmed this to me at different times and in different ways. I am sure Julie would have muddled through until I had gone to college but for Tom's increasingly brazen adultery. I suspect that Julie chose to ignore the signs, so long as they were not obvious.

But that summer the evidence became far too strong, too pungent. Tom had picked up a venereal disease, which, under doctor's orders, he had to tell Julie about. Then, a few days later, there was a nasty letter, a rant, addressed to Julie from Tom's current mistress in London. She had also been informed about Tom's problem, and naively, stupidly, imagined Tom had caught the disease from his wife. However generously Julie assessed the situation – and I am using Tom's analysis here, the one he gave me on the Bangkok trip – she had no choice but to leave him.

It was a horrible, horrible day, the day the letter arrived, Thursday 15 August. There was intermittent shouting and screaming, mostly by Julie. She wouldn't allow me to go out (presumably because she was already expecting to leave) and so I was forced to wear my earphones much of the time. Tom, in real distress, asked me twice to intercede on his behalf, which provoked an almost physical assault on him by Julie, for once completely aloof to what I might think of her. This in turn enraged Tom who began bellowing for his right to talk to his son. I went out to the garden, where I was embarrassed to find I, and the neighbours, could hear the shouting. Then it stopped, suddenly.

An hour later, Julie and I were driving down the motorway to Parsonville. I think she hoped for sympathy from her mother, but she didn't get it. They argued non-stop too, only not in raised voices. One day later we were heading back to Farnham, to camp out at Alan's flat. Alan himself came and went for a few weeks, and then moved to live in Switzerland. I was more sad about my uncle's going away than about my parent's separation. We went back to Larch Rise of course. Before long, though, the property was sold. Julie and I moved to Godalming, and Tom rented a property in Bramley, five kilometres east of Godalming. (Some years later he bought himself a modern semi-detached monstrosity much closer to London, in Epsom.)

CHAPTER 10

IN WHICH I PLAY VOLLEYBALL AND RECRUIT ALFRED

Another summer, two or so years later, was memorable for me in another far more positive way. In late July, some of us from the Witley Academic volleyball club were recruited for ball collection and other duties at the European volleyball championships being held for the first time in the UK at the Guildford International Sports Complex. The two main auditoriums had been refurbished to provide championship grade courts and changing rooms, comfortable seating and top-notch media facilities. There were three matches a day on each court for the mini-league phase during the first week. I fetched balls for two matches most days, and watched the third one. This was thrilling, not only because of the volleyball, which was of a standard I had never imagined, but because of the buzz of activity, the teams, the coaches, the support staff, the officials, and, most exciting of all, the media people.

I personally was interviewed by journalists from two broadcast companies, one from Croatia and one from Italy, about what it felt like to be a ball-boy at one of the most exciting matches of the year. It was a quarter-final between Italy and Croatia, and one of those titanic struggles that live in everyone's memory for years. At the time, I was standing too far back and was too focused on my job, watching and waiting for the ball, to follow the game and the drama closely, but so much was talked about the match, and written, that I soon absorbed the details: Italy lost five points because of a scoring error (almost unheard of at international level); and one of the Croatians sustained a serious ankle injury. There was also a very rare disqualification, the referee having finally lost patience with the Italian captain who, having sought clarification after clarification of the umpiring decisions, would not accept the loss of a point that gave the Croatians the fourth set.

There was also some of the most exciting volleyball you could imagine. The camrecord of that game was used for many years by coaches all over the world. How do I know?

Because I was in it, and whenever in my adult life I met someone who had played volleyball at a high level, I would bring the talk round to Croatia-Italy 2015, and more often than not they would say their coach had shown it to their team. The recording has another place in my story, but I must come back to it at the right time.

How is it possible that after my whole life long, I can still sense a frisson of the excitement of being involved in that week? There were two rest days when I should have stayed at home with my mother but she was sulky and depressed, so I lied to her about being committed to certain tasks. Instead, I spent the time watching the practice sessions, requesting autographs and then asking as many questions as players or officials or journalists would answer. I even knocked a ball around with one or two of the more easy-going international players. My one disappointment was not being selected to help with the final when Croatia beat Spain, nor being allowed to watch in the auditorium, although I did see it on the live relay in the second auditorium. I did ball duties for one of the semi-finals, but I don't recall who played, and I can't be bothered to search for the information. England, of course, disappointed. It was only 20 years later in Estonia, under the inspired and committed American coach John Buffer, that England finally made it to a European final. They didn't win then either, but it was a high for English volleyball.

All us from Witley Academic that had been involved in the championship were deeply inspired to do better. Club nights became more disciplined, we started to spend time watching coaching films, and our instructor signed us up to play a number of friendly matches against other schools and groups. A year went by, we all got taller and slightly better; and then I recruited Alfred.

Alfred Ajose. He was a great man and a good friend. He died in Zanzibar during the Grey Years. I had an email from him the day before the accident, but I don't want to think about that one message now. I am remembering him as a young man of 14 at Witley Academic, one year younger than me, but eight centimetres taller. I had seen him in the play-ground, usually at the centre of a small band of other coloured pupils, and I'd heard he was the son of a Nigerian diplomat. He attracted serious attention, though, when he pinned a remarkable poster on the canteen noticeboard. It accused one of the teachers of unacceptable behaviour and of bad teaching, and it was signed. Alfred was immediately suspended; but, extraordinarily, he was reinstated without further punishment within a few days, and the teacher in question was dismissed. Later, I discovered that it had been the teacher's overt racism that had provoked Alfred into such risky action. Our headmaster must have been a wise man, for, having initially ignored protestations made by Alfred in private, he finally realised the truth of the matter; and decided that Alfred's actions had been more brave than subversive.

It was a direct result of Alfred's notoriety that I found myself talking to him in the lunch queue. Because of his height, I suggested he join the volleyball club. To begin with, he proved awkward and gangly, as if unsure how to control his long limbs; and it took him nearly three months of training to gain a place in the team. I like to think that he persevered, despite being talented at many things and being much in demand, partly because he enjoyed training with me, but more importantly because I promised him he would be good. That I proved right about this was to leave him with an exaggerated impression of my intuition and foresight.

We both reached our full heights early. He achieved 190 centimetres, a useful size for a hitter, by the time he was 15, and I topped 180 centimetres, reasonable enough for a setter, by 16. For two years in a row, we won the national schools championship. My setting was certainly recognised as contributing to that success, yet it was Alfred's consistently accurate and uncanny hitting that took our team to the top. It was not only his practical skills that helped us to win, but also his captaincy. He knew instinctively when and how to be angry or sympathetic. He knew who would play worse if moaned at, but better if encouraged; and he knew who would raise his game if the fate of the team was suddenly thrust on his shoulders. Whereas our excellent coach taught and trained us, worked out our moves, planned our strategies, chivvied us along between sets and in time-outs, when in the thick of play on court, it was Alfred who gelled us.

And, as for the slapping of hands my father had referred to, that was how we expressed our joy at a good move, the combination of a good retrieve, a good pass and a good hit. Even as middle-aged men, departing from important meetings, Alfred, by then a more solemn person, and I would slap hands, perhaps in recognition of a result achieved, or more likely so as to revisit the intense pleasures of playing and of friendship in those days of youth.

EXTRACTS FROM CORRESPONDENCE

<u>Julie Fenn to Alan Hapgood</u>

October 2001

I must thank you for this computer. It has taken a while to get used to the new operating system, and the up-to-date software, but it's marvellous. Tom wanted to fiddle with it, but I told him sternly no – it's mine. He seems to have accepted that.

Will we never be rid of war. Everyone is waiting for the invasion of Afghanistan. I can't bear to listen to the news. I'd rather not write about it.

Neil has grown up so much in the last few weeks. He has such a range of facial expressions, and he can now use two and three word combinations. One of his favourite words is 'juice', he says it with such precision, it makes me laugh with joy.

Sometimes we sit together and say the alphabet. This has become a special game between us. He sits on my lap facing me. We look each other in the eyes. I say 'let's do the alphabet' and a smiling glint comes across his face. 'A', I say, and there is a long pause; he looks slyly at me, testing, watching, waiting; I say nothing and finally he says very softly 'A'. Then on we go through the letters of the alphabet, he can say most of them very well. If I say it loudly, he does too; if I whisper the letter, he whispers it too. When we get to the end, to 'Z', and we always do, for I never let him not finish, I give him a big kiss and we're both happy.

I was trying to think how I might possibly want him different, but he is perfect, adorable. Do all parents think this about their children? I can't believe so.

Alan, I don't like you being overseas in these turbulent times. When will we see you next?

August 2002

Tom and Neil and I have been in the Peak District for a week. I organised to stay at a B&B in Matlock Bath. The house was all pine, spick and span: pine furniture, pine doors, pine toilet-roll holder. The landlady gave us a front sunny room. Tom complained, accustomed as he is to five star international hotels. Breakfast on day one was a mite traumatic: I worried that Neil would spill egg down his front and on the cushion which the landlady had provided; I was concerned at the great fork he wielded in his left hand; and I worried about the volume of breakfast he stuffed away. But what a treat for him – chocoflakes, orange juice, egg, sausage and bacon, toast – all for breakfast. It's so long since you've been home, I bet you've forgotten the glories of an English breakfast.

On one walk we passed some lavender beds and I picked off a bit so we could all smell. Neil said, 'I like rosemary too; but I don't like black pepper'. When we saw a very old crippled man sitting on a bench by the river, Neil pointed to him and asked, in a very loud voice, 'Is he dead?'.

I have finally taught to him to shower, so that now he no longer cries when the water flows over his face. He grins and bears it. He does cry when soap goes in his eyes but I can easily divert him by asking him to shower my hand, or by pointing to his funny feet. Yesterday, he took Karshula (the name he has given to the panda you gave him) into the shower, which is a good sign.

May 2003
I haven't heard from you in a while, are you well? Is Monique in with a chance!

Neil has come along a treat. He is a beautiful child, with a charming spirit and an abundance of fun and joy in him. I think he is clever, but he has a general intelligence not any specific ability. He certainly displays a good memory and is already behaving in a conscious and calculating manner, mostly to the good. I must admit to being unbelievably in love: nothing has changed, tears come when I watch him sleeping.

Do you remember me telling you about the Peak District holiday? I have to pay for that now: Tom is insisting we all go to Monte Carlo for the Grand Prix. Why do I feel a headache coming on!

June 2003

All morning Neil was pretending to be a frog, and making strange frog-like noises. After lunch, he became a snake and is now crawling from place to place making sss sounds wherever he goes. Comfort toys have become important for him, and he invariably goes to bed with one of the pandas you've given him. But Karshula remains his favourite.

Yesterday, though, we had a difficult time. I became upset and angry because he wouldn't recognise words I knew he could. He tried to pretend he didn't know them, and when I insisted he did, he started crying. Instead of comforting him, which I usually do when he cries, I shouted at him. And then, when I asked him to re-read some words we had already covered, he suddenly couldn't read those either. And I got angrier. There is no doubt my behaviour was counter-productive. I was doing precisely the opposite of what I was setting out to do. Why am I telling you this?

Against all my expectations, we had a lovely time in Monte Carlo. How the rich do live!

I had a long talk on the phone with Mum. She's finally got a date for her hip replacement – October. It would be nice if you could manage a visit. She's become rather grumpy of late.

July 2003

I have stopped the word lessons with Neil due to the difficulties I told you about before. They carried on, and his reading appeared to get worse. I have to make a real effort to remind myself he is not doing it on purpose in the way an adult does something deliberately. I must make it fun for him, or else there is no point. Meanwhile, he is proving to have an excellent aptitude for numbers so we do quite a lot of arithmetic and geometry. Before lights out last night, I showed him a photo of his nursery group. He names all the children and teachers for me. Then I ask him which of the children is the roughest, he says Jack; which of the children cries the most, Emile; which of the children laughs the most, Truman; and which of the children is the cleverest, 'me'. He chuckles. I read him a Noddy story. Minutes after turning the light out he is fast asleep.

August 2003

You wouldn't approve. I don't think I do. We went to the zoo last weekend. It was Tom's idea. Neil had a splendid time running from cage to cage and looking at giraffes, elephants, owls, flamingos, penguins and gorillas. We had a long chat about gorillas, and I explained how friends of yours were helping to make sure they could live safely in the wild. But many of the animals looked in poor condition (emaciated, fur hanging off, apathetic) and the cages and pens were far too small.

I have been through the alphabet several times with Neil in recent days, and he now knows all the sounds of the letters, so I can say any one and he will say the right sound. Before a story this evening, I spelt out the sounds of C A T until he knew what the word was and then I said we were going to replace the C with an R, and we did the sounds until he got RAT and then we did the same with H and HAT. When I asked him if he could think of any more rhymes, he said 'BAT' straightaway. I am more and more convinced that the secret of good teaching, especially with really young children, is to keep their interest, to keep the subject fun. All these years, I've been a teacher, I suspected that was true, but I never really knew it. I do now.

Have you been reading about this Kelly business? I'm so confused I don't know what to think.

September 2003

We went to Malvern for a week. I hired a cottage this time, after Tom's complaints about the B&B. It was more work for me. One evening, we left Tom to watch the television and took a picnic up on the hills. It was such a lovely spot as the sun descended slowly in the west leaving its shine across the valley. Neil said it was like being in an aeroplane – The Malvern Aeroplane. And later he drew a colourful picture of it.

December 2003
I am glad you are coming home for Christmas. Will you stay with us for a few days, Neil would so love to see you. Mum is up and about, with a renewed lease of life. I pity her local Countrywide Campaigners group, she'll be launching all kinds of new efforts now.

Do you remember *Thunderbirds* and *Dr Who*. They are both showing again on television. Neil adores them.

September 2004
Neil has started school full-time, and he loves it. After his first day, I waited for him in the playground and when he didn't appear I walked into the classroom to find him hiding from me – he didn't want to go home. For a second, I felt acutely embarrassed.

September 2004
Neil became very upset this weekend because of Tom and I arguing and shouting. I am surprised how well he manages to exert pressure on us to make up. He moves from one to the other cuddling us, and if one of us refuses to do whatever we were going to do together (be it sit down to lunch or go out for a walk) he makes it very difficult to stay angry. Once, not this time but earlier, Tom was sitting down for a meal and I was getting the food out of the oven, and we had all calmed down. Neil quizzed Tom asking him, 'Do you think Mummy is a wonderful mummy?' I heard Tom answer, 'Yes, I think she is wonderful Mummy.' Then Neil said, 'But is she a wonderful Mummy to you?' Tom didn't answer. Then Neil said, 'But do you think she is a wonderful woman?' He said it so urgently, so sweetly, so tenderly, that I stopped what I was doing and gave them both a hug. He's growing so tall, I wish you were here to see him ... us more often. I've attached a photo.

October 2004

We are reading another Dahl story – *The BFG*. It is wonderful and captivates Neil. He has remembered and learned a number of good jokes and adores hearing new ones especially those that make a play on words which he understands. Here is his favourite from a new joke book I bought him yesterday: Who is the boss of the hankies? The Hankie Chief. He told and retold the joke a dozen times to us in the car. Other favourites are: Where do cows go on holiday? Moo York. What do frogs drink? Croak a cola. And he made this one up today: Knock knock; who's there? Car; Car who? Karshula!

January 2005

Dear Uncle Alan – thank you for the wildlife book. I like all the pictures of the pandas. Have you ever seen bamboo? I have, in our garden.

January 2005

Oh, I can't bear to watch the news these days, so much suffering in so many places, so much loss ... I hope you are OK.

Neil's birthday passed in a feast of presents, activities, cakes and colours. He was a darling all day. Not long after dawn, he came into our bed all soft and quiet. When I asked him if he wanted to open his presents, he smiled coyly and said 'yes'. He started slowly trying to examine each one but after a while he found it impossible not to speed up, there was always another present to run and get: a construction set (racing car designs!), which is far too old for him; a Thunderbirds model to make; some clay modelling material (from guess who); a box of magic tricks; and the book you so thoughtfully managed to courier in good time.

Yes, Mum came to stay over Christmas and was so annoying that when Tom shouted at her, I gave up a silent prayer of thanks. It's not only her sergeant major ways, it's the fact that she can't stop preaching to me about politics. It's difficult to know whether to blame the Tory party members like Mum, or the Tory party itself, but it seems to be so far to the right, it'll never find its way back towards the middle ground. Commentators are already predicting the Lib-Dems could do much better at the next elections, and that would be good for schools.

April 2005

Tom is away for three weeks, in the Far East I think. I don't care.

I have moved on to the multiplication tables with Neil and he is making good progress. I am anxious, not that he learns the answers necessarily but that he sees and knows the patterns, that he understands how seven times three is the same as adding up three seven times or seven three times. I have also been teaching him to count in twos and the difference between odd and even numbers. Why do I tell you all this?

Blair looks like getting back in. I won't begrudge him victory if he does, though I'll vote for the Lib-Dems as usual. Mum's fuming, she thinks I, personally, am to blame for the failure of the Tories.

Guess what? I've been made deputy head, did I say. It means more money and paperwork, but slightly less teaching.

I was sad to hear you and Monique have split up, but I do understand how difficult the distance made things. Won't it always be a problem for you, unless you decide to slow down, settle down?

August 2005

We went on our own to Snowdonia this summer. Tom was away again. I loved being out and about on the hills. Neil is a real trooper. He never complained once on our walks. When we came to forested parts, he was full of half-serious fears about ghouls and goblins, all stemming from the Tarquinade stories you read him last time you were here.

May 2006

While Tom was trying to mix a cocktail on the sideboard this evening, Neil climbed up on one of the chairs, and asked him if he could have a climb. He used to do this a lot, but he's bigger and heavier now, and Tom has been trying to discourage the toddler behaviour. A few days ago, Tom claimed a success in that Neil had climbed up onto his shoulders, Tom had remained absolutely lifeless and silent, and Neil had eventually climbed down out of boredom. This time, however, there was a twinkle in his eye and he was trying to suppress a grin. 'Don't look in my pocket,' he said to Tom. Tom turned to shrug him off, and Neil said, 'Oh darn it' or similar (he's full of family cartoon expressions such as 'yippee' and 'yummee'). Tom then saw that he had a mini-book in his trouser pocket and pointed it out. Neil played up to him with a guilty smirk. We all laughed when we twigged that his ingenious plan was to take a book up with him so he wouldn't get bored at the top.

Sometimes I love him so much I want to weep and weep with happiness, or take him in my arms and never let him go. Maybe that's why – you did ask – I cannot get too anxious about the absence of any real relationship with Tom. Don't be fooled by the cute domestic scene above. We had a row a few minutes ago.

January 2007

Mum gave Neil an expensive fountain pen for his birthday. He broke it within 24 hours; and when I got angry with him he went mute. I'd never seen him like that before. Later in the morning, he came up to me and said, 'Mummy, you know you said I was under a cloud, well there it is,' and he pointed above his head, 'and now it's raining, and now the cloud's gone away. Is that all right Mummy.' Sweet child. I made him write an apology to Grandma.

Is it really possible that peace will come to Palestine now – it's difficult to believe. And what terrible floods in Malaysia. Is this the sort of event you've been warning about?

From Hungary to Russia! I loved your descriptions of Siberia (I have read them to Neil, and he wants to go. Beware, you're becoming a hero. He needs to see you more often or else the reality may be disappointing. So do I.) But are the environmental problems so bad, you make it sound heaven and hell all rolled into one?

March 2007
Neil continues to grow up into the most delightful boy. He has intelligence, strong features, and at certain angles, he looks like you. He is sporty and competitive, but not too much; he is never bored at home and responds as well to being given things to do as to finding things to do on his own (mostly reading). Recently, he has learned to ride a bicycle and to tie his shoelaces – but not at the same time.

I've been reading a fascinating new book called *The Snowball Effect or Parenting made Difficult* by Julia Derwent, an American Professor. I don't know how fresh the ideas are, but I've never read anything similar. She explains in layman terms what we know about the complex interactions between nature (genes) and nurture (environment), but then argues that early random influences – in the first year or two or three of a child's life – can have a much more profound influence than has ever been recognised. In essence, she argues that an event which appears benign in itself at the time can lead a child into behaving in a certain way, which then leads to the original event or pattern to be repeated and the reinforcement of the behavioural response – thus, the snowball effect. She cites fascinating studies of twins brought up together, showing how some develop very different characters, a fact which cannot be explained by their genes or their environment. She also sees a link between this analysis and several childhood development problems.

She suggests, very controversially, that over-attentive parents can sometimes lead very young children into certain kinds of resistances, to foods, for example, or learning to speak or read, and that these resistances can then develop and enlarge, like a ball of snow rolling downhill enlarging itself. She does, though, pull the analogy up sharp and insist that once formed a child's behaviour patterns cannot be broken up and remoulded like a snowball. Quite the reverse.

The book only came to my attention because of the media furore, but I know from personal experience with Neil how close I came to forcing on him too much teaching at too early an age. God knows what damage we teachers do in class, although, according to Derwent, much of a child's character is already determined by the time he or she starts school, even if, according to the snowball effect theory, this might not yet be apparent, and any characteristics that are likely to change significantly during school years will do so in response to peer pressure rather than what teachers, or parents for that matter, do or say. She has quite a lot to say about this too.

I do go on so, don't I.

Your birthday is coming up, are there any books you need/want?

Oh, and I nearly forgot to tell you, Tom proposed we move to Singapore for a few years. Over my dead body, I said. He stormed out.

June 2007

I am making an extra effort at present with Neil's teaching at home. There have been personnel changes at his school which leave him less interested in class work. But he enjoys his home lessons. However, I will not be able to keep up this level of attention as Neil grows older, nor will I have the knowledge to keep his learning well directed. I am pinning my hopes on moving him to a better school, possibly next year, but we may also move if Tom decides to change jobs.

Have you ever been to Brazil? I can't remember. There was this glorious ten part series on the television. It's just finished. I watched it with Neil. The first programme on the Amazon hooked us, and then there were others about the Cerrado, for example, the country's history, and carnival – why are we so boring in this country, Neil wanted to know.

We spent a lot of time on the commercially-oriented internet site, and, guess what, Neil persuaded me to order him lots of Brazilian posters. I helped him take down crinkled torn photos of the moon that Tom had pinned up years ago, and put up the new ones. But, by the next weekend, Tom had bought a huge poster of that Spanish driver – whatever his name – who won the Grand Prix circuit last year, and another one of the car he drove, and helped Neil rearrange all the posters to make room for them. Neil tries to be fair about these things.

So, stranger, you are finally coming home for good. I'll believe it when I see it, when I see you, here.

October 2007

Uncle Alan. Mummy says you should be coming home by now. I hope you are not cold in Siberia. Mummy says you might be interested in my Dodge Book. 1) Get away from homework. Build a passage out of the window, and rope down. If there is no window try and burst the door in. 2) Excuses to teachers for not doing homework. I dropped it in the bin on the way to school. The wind blew it out of my hand. I did it, but when I turned it over it was gone. I used a piece of wood as paper, but Dad threw it on the fire. I suddenly went deaf at exactly the moment the teacher told us about the homework.

Next time you go to Siberia can I come, Mr Abominable Snowman?

PART TWO

Brussels, Bangkok and Brazil

The Lover's Triangle
'First, there's me
Heroic, handsome, strong and gentle
Then there's you
Angelic, graceful, bright and loving
And then there's Dick
Cunning, interfering, mind-controlling Dick'

The Ballad of Unwin Johns and other poems
by Unwin Johns (2025)

CHAPTER 11

In which Melissa exhibits and then fades away

There is a photograph on the screen now, the original of which I first saw in May 2020, a few days after Gillian had dispensed with my services, and several weeks after concluding the search for my father. It is not one selected from the database of 19th century prints which I personally owned at one time or another, but from the much larger database on Neil of prints which I have copied, from books, catalogues and netsites. I showed this photo to Jay, my youngest son, when he came to visit yesterday, and asked him whether I should write the story about Melissa. Either he had forgotten or I had never told it to him before. Consequently, I was able to rehearse what I intend write. He listened patiently and gave me his advice. Otherwise, he was full of gossip about the outside world, family and friends.

As I lie here this evening, I am thinking about how much I love Jay, about how kind and generous a son he has been, and I worry that I won't ever have much to say about him in these pages, at least compared to my other more wayward children.

On the right of this photo, a pretty young woman, a girl, dressed in a white robe or sheet, lies semi-reclined on a chair, her head and shoulders resting against a large white pillow. Her dark shoulder-length hair is tucked behind an ear, and her eyelids are lightly closed. Her mouth is ever so slightly open. She looks neither asleep nor awake, daydreaming perhaps, or in a coma, or dead. Behind her stands a maid-servant adjusting the pillow. She is bending slightly over the top of the girl but is looking above her head and across the room, towards an older woman, the mother perhaps, on the left of the photo, who sits directly opposite the girl. The older woman is wearing dark clothes including an oddly ornate bonnet, which hides all but the edge profile of her concave face, pointed nose and thin lips. She looks neither angry nor sad, but resigned. High curtains provide backdrops to these three people on either side of the photo, but, in the middle, where a cloudy sky can be seen through a sash window, there is the dark and featureless shape of the back of a man, the father perhaps.

The photograph, a composite albumen print by Henry Peach Robinson from 1858, is called *Fading Away*. It was created from five different negatives, which goes some way to explaining how Robinson, in the High Art style of the time, was able to make the characters stand out from the photograph, thereby giving a similar effect to that created by the pre-Raphaelites in painting.

There is another of Robinson's photos, *In Wales*, which I did possess for a while. Here it is, in the other database. It is less famous than *Fading Away*, but it too reminds me of Melissa. A smiling girl sits on a log or rock in long grass. She leans forward, elbows on knees with hands clasped together near the handle of a picnic basket. There is a pond in the background. She is wearing a shapeless white cotton hat, with the sides curled up, so similar to the one Melissa was wearing that day ...

It is through Alfred that Melissa and I became friends. He launched a steamy affair with Gemma, a tall slinky brunette given to stretching the dress code more than most, after a Christmas dance. In the following months, he began to miss the occasional volleyball training session. Then, one Saturday, he failed to turn up for an important match, which we lost. Until that moment, none of us had yet come to appreciate how completely we relied on him for our success. Individually, several of us, including our coach, appealed to him not to let the team down again. But I told him he had such a great talent, that to squander it would be a terrible waste. Subsequently, Alfred confided in me that he had been much touched by my appeal. Soon after, he was back at training and playing with full commitment.

He must have come to some arrangement with Gemma for, thereafter, she came to support our home matches and travelled with us to away matches. As the season was drawing to a close, in spring 2017, she brought a friend to one game – none other than Melissa. My play suffered, and I was substituted off court for two sets. This hurt my pride, yet her smiles towards me on the bench were simple and friendly; not even I could interpret them as a taunt. Thankfully, the substitute setter didn't fare too well either, and the coach put me on to play for the last and deciding set. As we lined up Alfred put his long arm around my shoulder and whispered in my ear.

'Concentrate, man.' Afterwards, Alfred, Gemma and Melissa sat around chatting in the school coffee-house for half an hour. I didn't say much. Not only was I disappointed with my own performance, but Melissa's presence and her warmth confused me.

Two or three weeks later, after a match, Alfred and Gemma organised for us all to go into Godalming for moussaka and retsina and then conspired to leave Melissa and me together. She was full of chatter and comment and sex appeal. But she also had an unnerving habit of starting a new topic of conversation while I was trying to respond to something she had already said. As I came to recognise this as a nervous habit, so I became more confident, and she relaxed in equal measure. On this first contrived date, though, Melissa did all the leading. She led the conversation, she led me to her home in nearby Busbridge (her mother and younger brother were away, with the mother's boyfriend), and she led me into her pink and yellow candy bedroom.

I do not recall what we talked about, I was still trying to fathom out why she liked me. Moreover, I was too intent on monitoring myself, trying not to say or do anything that might divert her interest, and debating with myself whether and when I should confess either or both of my shortcomings: being a virgin and being condomless.

After closing the bedroom door, she went silent. She sat down on the bed (a lemon chenille bedspread), and I sat down next to her. I was shaking internally and externally, and my heart was beating as loud as the music in the Greek restaurant. I wanted to say 'I've been in love with you since I was 12' and 'I can't believe this is happening' and 'you are so beautiful', but every sentiment I considered seemed tacky or immature. Instead, I resorted to silence, a tactic that has stood me in good stead throughout my life in many different situations.

'You remember that time, the time you saw me?' I nodded. 'I thought about it for days and weeks afterwards you know.' She was very serious. 'I liked it. I liked knowing you had seen me. It gave us a special bond. Did you feel it too?' Then I had to say something.

'I watched you in the pool.'

'I know. I know. Whenever I saw you, I thought of you looking at me, and I liked it, I wanted you looking at me. But this is the weirdest thing, I wanted you looking at me naked.'

This was it, in essence, although I may have added an adult tone to her words. We kissed passionately for a few minutes, and then Melissa slowly took off her clothes. She stood naked in front of the bed, watching me watching her. I came in my trousers, and rushed off, red-faced to find the bathroom. By the time I returned, she had carefully rolled the chenille cover back, and climbed inside the sheets. Although I joined her in the bed, I knew the best part was over. My body was too big, my arms and legs were always in the wrong place; and I didn't know what to do, or when to do it. Melissa attempted to fit me with a condom (rather expertly), but I remained too limp.

We were to have three more such encounters, every one split into two disjointed parts: foreplay and attempted copulation. It is my impression that we both preferred the former. Melissa's undressing and naked parading took longer and became more elaborate on each occasion. By contrast, my efforts in bed remained both gauche and gawky. I was getting the better part of the deal, and Melissa would surely have tired of me shortly. But fate intervened one very sunny June Saturday – the day of our final volleyball match of that season.

Under orders from her mother, Melissa had been told to look after her 13 year old brother, Rob, and a classmate of his. This had unsettled Gemma's plans for a picnic after the match, but the two girls decided to proceed in any case, and to pack enough food for six. So it was that, around 4pm, we left the grounds of Witley Academic, crossed the busy main road, and walked the half mile or so along an overgrown footpath to Sweetwater Pond, and a flat grassy bank with a copse to the side providing shade.

Alfred and Gemma disappeared into the trees, and the boys went to mess around by the water, leaving Melissa and I to unpack the two picnic baskets, and then to lie quietly on the grass. I wanted to embrace Melissa, or touch her, but she had carefully and persistently declined my attempts to hold hands or kiss anywhere outside the privacy of her house. With one hand reaching over towards her, I shyly pushed the white cotton sunhat from the top of her head, and was thinking I might lean over to kiss her. All of a sudden the boys were screaming with laughter. I looked up to see Rob holding a very long, thin, metal rod he had retrieved from the pond's edge on the far side where some builders' rubble had collected. He was waving it around, and splashing it in the water. A few seconds later, Melissa's phone rang. She stood up and walked the three metres towards the pond, to where her bag lay. At the same moment, Rob swished the wire over his head, as if it were a fishing rod, in order, I suppose, to create a bigger and better splash. The sharp end of the rod whipped backwards, straight for Melissa's head, and into her temple. It stuck there for a moment, and then sprang out. Melissa fell to her knees and crumpled on the ground, lifeless. There was no blood, and, apart from the hole in her head, which could only be seen close up, there was no evidence that anything untoward had happened.

For an instant, I wanted to think Melissa might be play acting, but my mind couldn't hold on to that explanation for long. She had crumpled to the ground, too effectively, too realistically. As I moved over and knelt down by her body, I shouted out as sternly as I could for the boys to stop playing with the wire. Her face was lifeless, empty. I shouted out again, this time for Alfred. Within a few seconds we were all gathered in a circle around Melissa's body. I think we all assumed she was dead. Gemma was the most active of us, bending over to see if she was breathing, and then dialling 999 on her phone. Strangely, Rob was the least emotional, he stood there frozen, just staring at the pond. Paramedics arrived in 20 minutes, the police in 30. Half an hour later, we were at Royal Surrey County Hospital. Melissa was not dead, but in a coma.

The parents of Rob's friend arrived first. Within the next 20 minutes my mother, Gemma's parents and a colleague of Alfred's father all arrived. It was some hours, though, before the police tracked down the mother of Rob and Melissa. By then, doctors, nurses and police had all talked to us. By the tone of their questions and the various discussions we half heard, there was no doubting that the adults understood this was nothing more than a tragic accident.

I never talked to Melissa's mother then, or ever, although I was to have two series of uncomfortable encounters with Rob later in my life. Poor boy, Melissa apart, he was certainly the most affected by the events of that afternoon. Subsequently, he became one of the 'losers' or 'inevitable costs' of the liberalised drug regime in the early 20s. I don't recall how exactly, but, in some way, the tragedy also accelerated the trajectory of the relationship between Alfred and Gemma, which ended, either before or during the summer vacation period.

As for me, I recovered surprisingly quickly. I confided in my mother, Julie, that Melissa had been my girlfriend, and allowed her to comfort me. I persuaded myself that Melissa would recover fully, a projection which clearly made it easier to get on with the rest of my busy life without feeling guilty. Initially, I took the train and bus to the hospital every week, staying only a few minutes. Yet this schedule soon slipped. Four weeks of that summer I spent abroad in Brussels, and, by the autumn, I was down to one visit a month. Melissa showed no signs of recovery, and no signs of dying either, and I simply became accustomed to the situation. Every now and then, I was arrested, so to speak, mid-phrase or mid-action by something triggering the memory of the wire whip arching through the air, slotting into the side of Melissa's head, staying there for a second, and then jerking out. When Melissa was transferred to a hospital in west London, my visits became less frequent. Later, once I was established at the London School of Economics, I made diary notes to be sure of not forgetting to pass by the hospital every two or three months.

And so, finally, for it has taken longer to tell this story than I planned, I come to May 2020 and Henry Peach Robinson's famous photograph. For me, it was a routine visit to the private room where Melissa lay, permanently. I planned to stay only ten minutes, and to read, as usual. That said, I was finding it difficult to concentrate because of a growing preoccupation with Gillian's offhand behaviour (a subject I shall come to soon). But this morning I had time neither to read, nor to get maudlin about my relationship with Gillian, for a consultant called me to his office. He explained, gently, that it had been decided, in full consultation with Melissa's family and various doctors, to turn off the life support systems within a week. I said I was sure it was for the best, and walked back to her room to say goodbye. She was propped up – similar to the girl in *Fading Away* – her eyes closed, her face white, her hair combed and shorter than before, and her life long, long gone. I kissed one cheek, said farewell, and left.

Half an hour later, after walking aimlessly the mile or so to Kensington, I found myself entering The Photography Place. The venue survived no more than 15-20 years, but, for a while, it was a lavish modern library and exhibition space dedicated to pre-digital photography. One gallery was showing a collection of Robinson's prints, including *Fading Away*. The picture took hold of me in a barely explicable way. It seemed to catalyse my emotions about the accident, fermenting feelings which, though never fully expressed, were unleashed by the news of Melissa's impending death. I stood there, staring at the framed print, seeing Melissa, realising that I would never see her again; seeing her standing there in the shower room, laughing; seeing her prancing around in the bedroom, unbuttoning her blouse; realising, finally, I would never see her again; seeing her lying there on the grass, her eyes shut, her lips widening into a smile as she feels me sliding the soft hat from her forehead; realising, finally, finally, that I would never see her again; and seeing her there, lying silently among the white sheets and recalling the touch of my lips on her cheek but an hour ago; and realising, absolutely, that Melissa, unlike the girl in the photograph, was dead. Dead.

I cried for a short while, and then purchased a postcard reproduction of the picture. Odd and heartless as it may sound, the catharsis in front of Robinson's photograph served as a finale to my actions and feelings for Melissa, discounting Rob's several later re-appearances, and the occasional emotional refrain that would come whenever I saw a copy of *Fading Away*.

CHAPTER 12

IN WHICH I FIRST COME ACROSS WILLIAM CAXTON

The end of the school year was always a busy time, and year six, which finished in July 2017, was no exception. The volleyball season had ended the day of Melissa's accident but, by then, I was heavily involved in the Brideswell Society, a forum for topical lectures. My responsibilities, initially confined to promotion of events around the school, had widened, thanks to Flip's confidence in me, to include direct liaison with speakers. Ronald Shuttleworth (who would shortly change his name to William Caxton) was our star speaker. He held the position of junior minister for communications in the first successful (but not popular) Liberal Democrat-Labour coalition government. From my point of view, though, he proved to be a most difficult guest.

To begin with, Caxton's private secretary replied to the invitation I had written in Flip's name asking for a lot more information, about previous speakers, the school's population, and the expected audience size. A week later we received a curt rejection note; but then, a few days after that, Caxton himself telephoned Flip, said he had changed his mind, and offered to speak on a different day from that planned for the lecture. Flip agreed, and I was left with the task of rescheduling the programme. As if that wasn't enough awkwardness, Caxton offered one title for his talk, and then altered it with three days to go. He insisted on a named bottle of red wine and another of water, and on having a private room available should he need it. One of his secretaries informed me that the minister would not be available to answer questions after the lecture (because of time problems and the sensitivity of the issues), despite the very clear guidelines I had sent him for Brideswell Society events. Then, before I had a chance to ask him to reconsider, an email arrived, announcing that he would, after all, be prepared to answer questions for ten minutes. This was my introduction to the character who later rose to such heights and dubbed himself 'The man of the people'.

There can be no doubting Caxton's genius, although I'm not convinced any one biographer has yet managed to explain it adequately. I have reserved, in my mind, a part of the next chapter for Caxton, and for my – what shall I call them? – dealings with him, and so shall skip lightly over the day of the lecture itself. Suffice to say, he spoke passionately (although not convincingly to my young mind) about the need for freedom of speech, for open net access, and for minimum net regulation. Policing of the net had developed into a major political issue five years earlier, but this government, which was fast drawing to a close, had shunted the issue to one side. Caxton's views, which led to his resignation prior to the 2018 election, in fact fitted far more snugly with the subsequent Conservative Alliance administration that ruled our country so poorly through to the year I joined the civil service (don't blame me, my vote went to the Lib-Dems in the 2018 elections). But, by then, of course, Caxton's media empire had begun to flourish.

Two things struck me when Caxton walked into the foyer area where the headmaster, Flip and I were waiting to greet him and his two assistants (one old and male, the other young, female and attractive): his youthfulness, he must have been 30 or 31, and his short height, 165 centimetres or so. Those physical attributes apart, he bowled me over with his energy and intensity. After the introductions, he turned his babyish face towards me square on, his chin forward, his head angled upwards, a posture which gave him a permanent air of confidence and/or superiority. He never had any doubt that he was at the centre of a circle in which everyone else was on the circumference.

'You're Fenn.'

'Yes, sir. Neil or Kip Fenn.'

'I was mightily impressed with your organisation, the clarity of your emails, your responsiveness. Thank you.' He took a quick look around to assess whether anyone was pressing him to do something, before asking, 'What's your subject?'

'History.' Quick as a flash, he had a question for me.

'Who was the most influential politician in the 20th century?' I hesitated, went red, and looked over towards Flip.

'Don't look at me, mouse,' he said, but in a kindly way.

'Depends who you are, I might say Ghandi, if I was an Indian, or Mandela if I was African, or ...'

'But you're not, are you. You're British.'

'Yes, sir. And European.' I looked up and saw the whole group was waiting for my answer. Caxton glimpsed at his watch, a tiny gesture but one which provoked me.

'I won't say Hitler or Stalin because I can't choose between them, and, besides, I expect you mean influential in a positive way, so I'll opt for Jacques Delors, though I reserve a final answer until I have a precise definition of what you mean by 'influential' and 'politician'. Do you want me to say why?' There was a momentary silence, before Caxton gave me a slow soft clap, and a 'bravo'.

'No, I'll pass on the sophistry,' he said, gaining a chuckle from both his assistants. Before I could recover my composure, we were walking across the quad towards the packed main hall. Later that evening with Flip and others in the Chiddingfold Arms, I recounted the exchange to Horace, who earlier had petitioned Flip unsuccessfully to be included in the reception party. I don't think I had ever experienced Horace so transparently jealous of me.

CHAPTER 13
IN WHICH TOM HELPS ME TO A SUMMER JOB

A few weeks later I was on my way to Brussels, thanks, I am happy to recall, to Tom who otherwise had not played much of a parental role through my teenage years, apart from providing money, and taking me to the cinema. Earlier that year (2017), I had been advised at school to consider work experience jobs in the summer, and then, a few days later, I had gone with Tom to see the zany Italian comedy *Hold on to Your Boss*. Pacciotti went on to make better, more respected films, but never one so genuinely and ingeniously funny. Afterwards, in a pub by the Thames, I'd asked Tom if he could help me find a summer job. I didn't expect him to make the effort, let alone to achieve anything. He was good at promises, Julie commented more than once, but not at fulfilling them. On this occasion she was wrong. He messaged me one afternoon at school: 'Surprise in store. Collect you at gates at 5. Reply only if you can't do.'

When I saw him with a new car, a Retro Zephyr, I brushed off any expectations for myself. He drove us to a tea-house in Compton describing every feature of the vehicle in loving detail as if he were a car salesman. It was only when we were sipping cappuccinos and munching muffins that he did truly surprise me. It transpired that he had contacted a good customer of his in the London office of Euroil plc, an international oil/gas exploration and production company, who had then sent out a general email to colleagues. The manager for European policy/planning in Brussels, Sterling J Wood Junior, no less, had responded saying he would be undertaking a study exercise in the summer, and could do with some basic help. It would be database inputting mostly, Tom told me, some filing and research.

'But hey, what can you expect at your age,' he concluded.

In addition, Tom had established that I would have use of a company studio flat for no cost. Although my mother Julie expressed concern about me living away from home, and overseas, for four weeks, she had no legitimate objections –

the euro, Eurostar, and the (failing) Euronet meant that Brussels was, in practice, down the road, or round the corner.

Altogether I spent three separate months working for Sterling at Euroil, a month that summer, a month the following summer, and a month in August/September 2020, at the start of the year I took off from university. I'm not sure what my original expectations of Euroil were, but the reality did not live up to them. On my first night, Sterling took me for an expensive fish meal in the St Catherine area of downtown Brussels. He talked, like my father, about the majesty of the oil industry, the riches it had brought to the world, and the constant need for vigilance against loony environmentalists. I listened mostly. I judged (rightly as it turned out) that there would be no advantage in trying to impress him with my own ideas or learning. I understood that I had 'cheap labour' written all over me.

Initially, the office was busy with 15 or 20 staff, but many of them, including Sterling, soon departed for vacation. I was left in the charge of Sterling's personal assistant, a middle-aged Flemish woman called Hilde. My main job was to revise a three year old directory of people in the various Union institutions and of interest to the oil industry. This meant trawling the Euronet and the wider net, emailing and phoning people, and, on my own initiative, redesigning the directory layout. In the evenings, I went to the cinema, walked around the city and through the parks, or stayed at home to watch news or write emails. One weekend, I travelled to Holland to join Alfred at a volleyball tournament, and on another weekend Julie insisted I meet her in Bruges for sightseeing.

A year later, after my 18 examinations, the general pattern repeated itself. This time Sterling, who again took me for a meal and again disappeared on vacation within a few days of my arrival, really did have a study for me to work on. Earlier in the year, there had been several unsuccessful attacks by Muslim extremists on gas export pipelines in Algeria and Turkey. This had prompted the European Parliament to call for more emergency natural gas storage capacity in the European Union (EU) to be funded through an EU-wide energy tax, which itself would help to curb demand. The European Commission (the EU's executive civil service) had tabled a proposal in June which the oil/gas industry disliked intensely. In preparation for the lobbying that would take place in the autumn, my task was to trawl through European Parliament votes on energy taxation and oil/gas issues during the previous ten years to identify any Members of the European Parliament (MEPs) who might have shown an inconsistent policy. Sterling and Hilde prepared a basic list of relevant laws and showed me how to find, from them, other relevant laws and resolutions. Beyond that, it was simply a matter of accessing the voting records and making lists.

Socially, life improved during this second trip. I went to the same annual volleyball event, but this time Alfred had pulled together a better team, and we won our mini-league; and winning is definitely more pleasurable than coming second or third. One night I went to a cavernous club, Noir Two, with the friend of a school-friend. He brought his girl-friend and a friend of hers, which made for a cosy foursome. My blind date proved to be a live wire, but too hot for me. I was too shy to ask for a date or to make a follow-up call to my original contact.

Unexpectedly, my uncle Alan showed up one day with a Czech girlfriend called Tamara. They took me to an Arab restaurant. We sat on the floor, ate with our hands, drank light tea and puffed on a waterpipe. They listened attentively to all my news, demonstrating, by their enquiries a genuine interest in me and my life. The rest of the time we discussed and argued about global problems, especially those concerned with oil and climate change. That was a special evening.

Otherwise, I spent too much time using the studio computer, not least to access pornography. Although fluid communications were common, they were not yet universal. We had one such connection at home, but my private computer in the bedroom was an antique. In any case, Julie deliberately entered my room at all kinds of times, and for odd reasons, making any illicit activity difficult. During my first summer in Brussels, I had resisted the temptation of using the studio computer to seek out pornography, in case whoever maintained the machine might discover my trails. But I was a year older at the time of my second visit. Moreover, by then, I had been to Bangkok.

I see I have already referred to Bangkok several times; but, now I am here, at the point where I should expose Tom, I'm not so convinced there is much to say.

CHAPTER 14

IN WHICH TOM TAKES ME TO BANGKOK

In autumn 2017, Tom came up with the idea of taking me to Thailand for Christmas. He had a seminar to attend, he said, and could trade in a business class ticket for two standard class seats. It would be a well-earned break for me, in my final year at Witley Academic, he argued, and was an opportunity not to be missed. Julie hated the idea. She and Tom argued furiously on the phone; and Julie employed her whole emotional armoury to persuade me not to go. All to no avail. None of my friends could understand Julie's arguments when I tried to replay them.

I have visited Bangkok a few times, yet that first extraordinary but excruciating trip stands out, like a neon light on a dark night, like a naked girl in a roomful of businessmen. There was the metropolis itself, a non-European city, with its US-style skyscrapers, Asian-style cycle rickshaws, appalling infrastructure and teeming human life. I had never seen human society so cheap, so dirty, so crowded, so colourful, so noisy, so animate. I recall, in particular, the magnificent Grand Palace with its radiantly coloured tiles and its many murals of town and country scenes; the exotic floating markets along the Chao Praya selling foods and flowers and artefacts which may as well have been transported from Mars for all I knew; and the drama/dance troupe we saw perform a traditional Thai legend at the New National Theatre. The story told of how royal brothers, wearing glittering costumes and tall golden hats, escaped from a sea giantess. Several singers and musicians, playing xylophones and small metal drums hung on a string in a horseshoe frame, accompanied the action. I observed a similar show in the new National Theatre decades later, and I don't believe it had changed in any significant way.

The snake farm, located on the outskirts of the city, impressed me too. Tom was at his seminar that day so I teamed up with a group of four Bristol University students. It was evident from their banter that they'd come to Bangkok as sex tourists and were only filling in time. We saw cobras, one enormous king cobra with its head held high, yellow-ringed snakes and vipers. The information has never been of the slightest use to me but I know to this day that the venom taken from poisonous snakes by squeezing the sides of their heads is injected into horses to incubate antidotes. Come to think of it, there must be more efficient ways of doing it now. And then there was the food. I had eaten Thai food at the Chiang Mai on Guildford High Street, but it was the street fare – pancakes with coconut, fried pork pieces and boiled rice, banana and sweet potato – which was so different, so exotic, so tasty.

For three of the six days, I had a fabulous time. Then came the fourth evening. Tom wanted to go to a night club and I wanted to go to the cinema. This sounds strange, but I was never a typical youth, interested in loud music and parties. Tom, who was fast closing in on 60, often acted and behaved younger than me. We had argued a few times already, but over minor things (such as the clothes I'd brought and my mislaying of the room keycard) but when I said I didn't want to go to the club he blasted my head off, perhaps because he was partially drunk, or (I worked this out later) because he had planned the experience in advance and was taken aback by my unexpected stubbornness.

'Fuck me if you aren't intent on spoiling everyone's fun. You know what you are, you're a boring old fart, and that's saying something for an 18 year old going on 14. Who paid for this holiday, anyway, who fucking organised it?' I took a deep breath, and gave in silently.

So far, I had avoided the extensive red-light districts. Tom had not steered me towards them in our walks together, and, on my own explorations, I had a strong sense that I shouldn't be interested in what was on offer there, and that the whole sex scene was sordid, dirty. The club Tom chose was not, by its location, obviously part of the sex scene. Neither did I twig the truth immediately on entering the place. I believed all the teenage girls dancing amidst the multicoloured flashing lights were genuine clubbers, and that the groups of men sitting in the shadows were their boyfriends or singles on the prowl. I began to feel uncomfortable when Tom suggested we step onto the dance floor as several other men had done. I rebuffed him tetchily – we had never gone dancing together before. When he insisted, and fearing a replay of his earlier rage, I followed him shyly but irritably. My mood transformed, though, when a pretty girl soon drifted into dancing with me. She was no older than me, but must have been 40 centimetres shorter. Apparently, she failed to notice I was awkward, tense, had spots on my forehead, and my cheeks were redder than the spotlight in one corner.

'American?' she asked.

'No, British.'

'My name, Choolee, you?'

When we returned to our table, the girls followed. One of them immediately draped her arm around Tom; Choolee was less forthright but sat close enough to be touching me. A topless girl emerged under the red spotlight and rolled herself gymnastically around a stainless steel pole. I stared at her trying to work out what was happening. Then, when Choolee put a hand high up on my thigh, my body went rigid. Some combination of confusion, anger and fear must have shown in my face, because a cheery-looking Tom tried to reassure me.

'Relax, relax, it's all part of your education,' he said.

It was a set-up which went horribly wrong. Tom, no doubt, had meant well, but had failed to allow for the normal insecurities of a young man, let alone the powerful nature of his sexual insecurities. I couldn't cope, I simply could not cope with what was happening. I froze emotionally and physically, which explains why I didn't race off into the night. After 20 minutes or so of me doing nothing, saying nothing, Tom told me to go with Choolee. I allowed her to direct me through a curtain, along a dingy corridor and into a plainly decorated room with no more in it than a double bed. I do not know how long I was there, but whatever Choolee did (and she did a lot of things) an erection would not come. She remained friendly and smiling throughout, and never stopped trying. I came to realise later, thanks in part to Gillian's detached behaviour in the bedroom, that a diversion – a conversation, the television, almost anything – might have helped.

Choolee led me back to the disco room, kissed me on the cheek, and disappeared for ten minutes. She was back on the dance floor before Tom returned, beaming. When he asked me how it went, I replied with a meaningless phrase such as 'fine, thanks', and when he pressed me, I said I did not want to talk about it. And, in order to forestall further conversation, I thanked him for the experience.

This episode affected the rest of the holiday in two ways. Firstly, I used up all the rest of my free time separated from Tom in exploring the red-light district. I discovered I could enter a brothel to gawk and gape through a wide glass screen at a dozen naked or near naked beautiful teenage girls. They might be sitting and wriggling, or dancing and gyrating; whatever, the view was exciting, and free. But, then, for a negligible amount of money, I could buy the privacy of a booth with a one metre square screen and choose from a multitude of high quality porn flicks. A pack of tissues was available on the floor. For slightly more baht, I could watch, through a peep hole, a real live woman take off her clothes, and parade every bit of herself as though she was alone.

Secondly, Tom's behaviour, which clearly implied that he was accustomed to using prostitutes, gave me the right, or at least opened up the possibility, to question him about the failure of his marriage to Julie. I distanced myself emotionally from him, and felt older, wiser, and more determined to uncover the full extent of his guilt. Tom proved surprisingly willing to talk about the details, which is how I came to know as much as I did. Most of that which he told me had the ring of truth and fitted with what I already knew (though it was still to be another two years before he told me the biggest truth of all – about my paternity). My parent's story was a common enough one: in the beginning, the sexual side of their relation-ship was adequate, although Tom did all the running, until I came along, and then Julie lost interest and shut him out;

Tom strayed, and there wasn't enough else in the marriage to keep them together.

On returning to the UK, my relationship with Tom remained strained. I did not see him for six months or more. He called to congratulate me on my exam results, and we then agreed to meet for a film and meal. This was the week before my second trip to Brussels. As I've said, that summer I spent too much time discovering the possibilities of a powerful computer and open access to the net, discovering, in fact, that the net was a voyeur's paradise. From then on, I was able to indulge this puerile habit without inhibition.

***

My consultant, Dr Rupert Lipman, came by a few minutes ago with a gaggle of doctors and Chintz, one of the nurses.

'Fine, Mr Fenn, everything is fine. We are re-tuning your pill menu slightly, think nothing of it,' Lipman pronounced. He looked over at the wallscreen, 'That's a pretty picture, where is it?'

'Copacabana,' I said, 'photographed in 1890 by Marc Ferrez.'

'Nice beach,' he remarked, none the wiser, and walked off followed by his entourage. Only Chintz remained.

'You mean Copacabana in Rio de Janeiro?' she asked.

'Yes. It was a wild and unpeopled place once.'

'Wow,' she uttered appreciatively.

'I own the original of this picture,' I bragged, knowing the boast would not mean much to her.

But, I'm running ahead of myself, I was only trying to jog my memory in preparation for what I should write tomorrow. No, that is not strictly true, I was drifting. This is a mammoth task I have set myself. It is so difficult to know what to write, what to leave out, who to mention and who to ignore. I should précis my early days at the London School of Economics (LSE) university, and move on as swiftly as I can to 2020, and the period after Tom's drunken New Year's Eve revelation.

CHAPTER 15

IN WHICH I EXPERIENCE STUDENT LIFE AT LSE

I had been drinking moderate amounts of alcohol since I was 15, I had spent half an hour with a prostitute, and I had voted in the 2018 general election, but my adult life only truly began later that year, the day I moved into the Bermondsey flat with Bartock and Philli, a couple from Matlock, Derbyshire, who had taken on the lease and advertised through the LSE notice-board. Philli, like me, was aiming for a history degree, and Bartock, who later dropped out to start some venture or other, was studying commerce. Patrick, who took the other spare room, came from Belfast, and never ceased to keep us amused with tales of his attempted seductions. Philli suggested we should meet once a week for a meal which she would cook, so long as one of us brought a bottle of wine. It was a good idea in theory, but in practice there was never a night all four of us were in – or wanted to be in – at the same time.

I never found much in common with any of the three, and increasingly became irritated with the size of my room, the traffic noise outside, and the inane domestic nattering of Philli and Bartock. After two terms, I moved into another larger flat, also in Bermondsey, with two friends from the international history department: Peter de Roo, a highly intelligent soft spoken Dutchman to whom I am eternally grateful for intro-ducing me to Diana (my second partner); and, confusingly, another Peter, Pete Sampson, a formidable debater who ended up a professor at Keele (and through whom, coincidentally and decades later, I met my third partner Lizette). I became friendly with de Roo, even though he was doing a postgrad degree and was three years older, because of volleyball, and with Sampson because we were taking similar modules.

Student life was everything I had discussed with my buds at school and more. The social whirl, for which I was not best suited, carried me along to costume parties, pop and jazz concerts, pretentious arty happenings, cheap meals in newly discovered guzzleshops, and relationships on every level.

I tumbled into two affairs at the same time, neither insti-
gated by me. Dark and mysterious Trisha would make firm
arrangements and never show, or turn up in the middle of the
night weeping for no apparent reason, demanding that I hold
her tight and long. By contrast, Annie, another history under-
graduate, took a more serious view of life and friendships,
which required much discussion about every aspect of our
affair, not least my apparent impotence. I was as useless at sex
as I was at deception, and I hoped they would both finish with
me when they found out about each other. Instead, I became a
war zone for two or three months (not because of any desir-
able attribute in me, but because I was a territory, any territory), until I could take no more, buried myself in the library
and refused to answer any calls. Interestingly, though, of the
two it was Trisha's self-centred egotism that came closest to
rousing my natural sexuality, while Annie's determined
attention to my problem – like Popsicle's later – failed mis-
erably.

Volleyball remained an important part of my life until the
second year at LSE – until I twisted my ankle in December
2019. At the summer tournaments in Holland with Alfred, I
had met some high-level players from London Docklands, a
club which had won the national league three times in the last
seven years, and I had been invited to train for the second
team. After much biking backwards and forwards to Roth-
erhithe, where London Docklands was based, and months of
strenuous practice I did achieve selection. In my second
season, during the autumn of 2019, I trained vigorously and
performed well; then came the injury during a second team
match against the Reelers. Although it had been exciting to
train with some of the best volleyball players in the country
(more than half of them foreign), I was not committed enough
to stay with the punishing coaching schedule, and there was
no chance of making the first team. Thus, thereafter, I restricted my playing to the uni club which operated at a less
competitive level, and where I was a bigger fish in a smaller
pond. (By contrast, Alfred went on to greater things: he helped

Manchester University, a rival of London Docklands, win its way into the national league; and, later, he played in more than 50 internationals for Nigeria.)

Whereas the social buzz sounded the loudest and always clamoured for attention, it was the intense low-level hum of LSE's intellectual life which attracted me more. I gravitated naturally from the Brideswell Society at Witley Academic to the European Society at LSE with its lively debates and sponsored trips to Prague or Warsaw; I attended the Grimshaw Club lectures on occasions, and I took a keen interest in the Green Action group, even if sometimes I felt frustrated at the juvenile level of its politics, and the silliness of its activities.

It was to the Schapiro Government Club, though, that I was drawn most strongly. It had declined badly in recent years. A self-serving clique of quasi-fascists had staged a committee coup some years before my arrival, and the club had never recovered. But, I had enjoyed running the Brideswell Society, and the Schapiro was an opportunity to do the same thing and more, without any adult interference. I inveigled both my flat-mates – the two Peters – to help out.

To begin with, we simplified the name to Government Club (without Schapiro), and then set about finding controversial or interesting speakers. I contacted Flip who put me in touch with ex-Witley Academic notables.

One of our best early events, and the one which put the club back on the map, and, more importantly, brought in a flurry of subscriptions, came about as a result of an appeal to my uncle Alan. Amazingly, he delivered, so to speak, WWF's international negotiating director Ingrid Kallström. Not only did she speak with authority and humour on her topic, *Lobbying for Sustainable Balance*, but, according to Peter de Roo, she was 'drop-dead gorgeous'. I couldn't disagree. The two of us, Peter and I, had the privilege of taking her to the student bar for a drink; and the Government Club made front page news in the next edition of *The Beaver*, LSE's student paper.

In my second year, Peter dropped back to concentrate on his studies, but Pete Sampson and I, and a few fresh liberal faces we had recruited, took the Government Club to new heights. Its renewed popularity (and, not forgetting the status of the international history department professors) meant we could attract the occasional junior government minister and key figures from the European institutions.

I have no intention of trawling through our programme, even if I were able to recall it. I vaguely remember one excellent event which made the national media: a large audience justly booed the Conservative Alliance transport minister for his, only half-humorous, suggestion that students should travel less and study more for the good of the country.

However, I do wish to mention, in passing, that Pete had an important influence on the club (and indirectly on me) because he was a mover and shaker in LSE's Net Society. This led the Government Club, in association with the Net Society, to present more events linked to internet and communications issues than might otherwise have been the case. For example, we bagged a top level European Commission official for one talk, and he explained frankly the political reasons behind Euronet's failure; and, on another occasion, we had difficulty keeping a straight face while Georgia's deputy ambassador justified his country's hosting of renegade net service providers with waffle about human rights and freedom.

CHAPTER 16

IN WHICH I DRAW CONCLUSIONS ABOUT MY PATERNITY

But now I must move on again to more personal matters. I am
trying to keep order – first my father, then Gillian, then
Brussels, then Brazil.

My father is easily dealt with. The doctor did it; the cad, or
the rapist, whichever way you care to look at it. I'm not 100%
sure, but I'd bet my inheritance to Jay on it. I had spent one
year and one term at LSE by the time of that fateful New
Year's Eve with Tom. For a while, I did wonder whether, if I'd
returned to Bermondsey before that night and allowed friends
to ferry me to a party, I'd ever have discovered the truth. I
suspect Tom would have told me, eventually, one way or
another.

I returned to uni that January uncharacteristically depressed. I worked solidly, as usual, and continued my various
activities, but all too often I shut myself in my room seeking
out diversion on the net instead of engaging with Pete and/or
Peter. On occasions, I caught myself in a trance-like state
during lectures, or, more dangerously, while cycling: a mile
would pass by without me being able to recall the state of the
traffic or whether I'd stopped at a junction. I made a series of
querulous calls to Tom, without discovering any additional
information. I visited Julie with the sole purpose of stealing a
copy of the letter I've already mentioned; and then I tracked
down its author.

If Martin Beale, the man who'd written my mother's tear-
stained letter, had no longer been a teacher, I might never
have found him, but there was a trail, from colleague to
colleague, a longish one, which, over several weeks, I managed
to follow. I started at Julie's old school, where there was only
one teacher who had been there more than ten years. I asked
her for the name and subsequent workplace of the person who
had been there longest when she started work there. This was
the trickiest link in the chain.

Three connections later I found someone who had known
a young teacher, one 'who fancied himself a bit too much',

called Martin Beale. He had transferred after three years to a larger primary school in nearby Wheathampstead. I phoned several schools and asked to speak to the longest serving teacher, and thus found that Martin Beale had moved on to a school in Bedford. I rang him there, and impressed on him the urgency of my mission, but without explaining what it was about. He agreed to meet on the Saturday morning and suggested the Ale and Coffee Lounge, not far from the central station. The Ale and Coffee Lounge!

Throughout the journey to Bedford I was preoccupied with trying to calculate the chances of Martin turning out to be my father. If he were, as I think I expected, then I knew I should be preparing myself for a pretence of interest in him as a person. But, if he were not, then I should be preparing myself for an anti-climax, a serious disappointment. But my mind jigged to and fro across the scant information available unable to reach any conclusion. I did not know what I thought, or believed, or hoped.

I saw him, complete with dark specs and a black duffel coat, entering the glass door, before he saw me. As he surveyed the Lounge and various shoppers relaxing on the large sofas, I noted a sense of disappointment nudging forwards into my consciousness. It originated, I worked out quickly, from his height, or lack of it. He took off his glasses, caught my eye, and walked over to greet me. We shook hands. He removed his coat. A waitress came and took our order.

'Julie,' he pronounced after only a short burst of fluff talk. 'I'd be lying if I said I remember her well. But I do remember her. Dark, not pretty but not plain either, fussy. You want to know if we had an affair, I can't think why else you'd trudge all the way to boring Bedford. Well, we did.' He turned his head from side to side to see whether the waitress was coming. 'And yes, I did know she was married. Her husband was never around, or so she said.' He peered over towards a corner where a group of children were being boisterous.

How short a time it takes to dislike someone. Any traces of disappointment, engendered by a recognition that his modest height meant he was less likely to be my father, were truly vanquished by his undisguised aura of conceit. I didn't much care for the neat-cut beard either, or the ostentatious specs lying on the tabletop. I grasped the nettle with both hands, as they say.

'When did it finish, I mean when did your affair end?' He looked at me full on, so that I would be able to see him pretend a light was dawning behind his squinting eyes.

'Oh I see.' He spoke slowly, with a put-on drawl. 'You think I might be your father. How thrilling.' I tried to keep cool and reasonable.

'You had an affair at the end of 1998, I know that much.'

'And what does Julie say?' Oddly, I had not prepared myself for someone who might be prepared to lie or joke about the matter, and I hadn't thought through an answer to this question. I ad-libbed.

'She's dead; she died last year. Cancer.' This stunned him momentarily.

'I'm sorry.'

'I only want to be sure when your affair finished.' He looked at me again as if getting ready to tease me further.

'How old are you?' And then I realised that he knew, he absolutely knew I was not his son. How else could he be so flippant. In case he pressed his point, I prepared to tell him I was 19 not 20.

'Please, if you can, tell me when your affair ended. That's all I want of you.' The waitress arrived with our coffees. He sipped off the cream and licked his moustache.

'As far as I can remember, and it's a long time ago now, we only ever had sex two or three times all towards the end of 1999. I had to call it off after that. She was too uptight, and she kept coming to me in school time asking for another meeting.' Prick. I began to imagine his spotless duffel coat covered in café au lait.

'After you called it off, you never had sex with her again? Maybe she came on to you, for example, some months later and you were unable to resist the temptation?' (Did I really speak about my mother in that way? It is how I remember it.)

'No. And, besides, I always, always used a condom.' That second 'always' rankled deeply. Inwardly, I was shaking with rage. I rose to my feet slowly, collected my coat from the side arm of the sofa, and threw a five euro note on the table to pay for the coffee. Then, as I was turning to leave the table and make for the doorway, I gave way – in my mind only, not in reality – to a display of soap opera emotion. I lashed an imaginary arm across the surface of the table swiping Martin's half-full cup of coffee and a bowl of sugar onto his lap.

Locating the doctor, William Jessop, could not have been simpler. He was listed in the St Albans telephone directory. Why did I seek him out? He was my only other option. I never considered him as a possibility for my father, but the fact that Julie had consulted him around the time I was conceived (according to her bare diary entries) opened up the possibility that she may have confided in him. One Thursday, the only weekday without a lecture or seminar, I rang his surgery and persuaded the receptionist to book me 'on a personal matter' for five minutes after his last appointment. It was a solitary practice taking up the ground floor of a large double-fronted house in Hemel Hempstead Road. Old and scruffy posters adorned the corridor and waiting room walls; grey wiry stuffing edged out of torn seat covers; a threadbare patterned carpet had lost its colour many years ago. I didn't have long to wait. As I entered the untidy consulting room, Dr Jessop busied himself with a computer screen and a few papers. I had prepared an imperfect pitch.

'Sit down, boy.'

'I'm sure you won't remember me, but we did meet once, when I was about 12, and my mother was your patient. I was told you personally delivered me at home. Apparently, my mother insisted on a home birth.' I tried an innocent smile. He carried on typing, barely looking up. 'This may sound a strange request, but my mother – that's Julie Fenn – died recently, and before she died she talked to me about a special friend she had in the spring of 1999. And I'm trying to trace this friend, though I don't have his name.'

'Why come to me?'

'This is the strange bit. In her agenda for the same period, she notes several appointments with you, and the one word 'depression', and so I was wondering if there might be a connection between this special friend and the depression. I put two and two together, and probably made five. It sounds dumb saying it out loud.' He looked up and over towards me with an aging face, ruddy and burdened by a heavily wrinkled forehead, not at all how I remembered him. I glanced down, in an attempt to maintain my ingenuous act. 'Is there a chance you could look in your records to see if there's anything you can tell me.'

'Don't need to. I remember Mrs Fenn, and she never mentioned any of her friends.'

'Why did she need to see you?'

'Depression, as you've said. Though you know as well as me, I'm not supposed to tell you.'

'I thought, since she was dead ...'

'Well you thought wrong.'

'There's nothing you can tell me. Did you treat her?' He appeared to drift away in his thoughts for nearly half a minute. Then, when he spoke it was with an artificially bright tone.

'Hypnosis. Worked a treat. Now, boy, if that's all. I have to rush.'

That was it, the end of the trail. He gave me the clue, and left it up to me. He knew what he was doing. A few weeks passed before the whole story fell into place, thanks to Gillian. We had been dating for a month or so, and when one evening I opened up this unsettled bit of my history, she suggested the doctor might have used hypnosis to seduce my mother. She vaguely remembered reading about such a case, and proposed a newspaper archive search. Within five minutes, we had found the following article.

'*Doctor acquitted of hypnosis rape* – 15 March 2009.

A general practitioner was yesterday cleared of raping a woman placed under hypnosis during a home visit. Dr William Jessop, 48, from St Albans, Hertfordshire, was acquitted of raping Mrs X a 33 year old patient, who the judge ordered cannot be named, in November 2005.

The woman said in court that she been very stressed about her failure to re-establish sexual relations with her husband after the birth of their first child. Dr Jessop suggested hypnosis therapy, and, after one session in his consulting rooms, he visited her several times. On each occasion he administered pills to aid the hypnosis. She had no memory of sexual contact with the doctor.

When the woman gave birth to her second child in September 2006, she assumed her husband was the father. But, two years later, she saw a photograph of Jessop's own children in his surgery and was struck by the likeness with her son. Without her husband's knowledge Mrs X paid for a paternity test, which proved that Mrs X's husband could not have fathered the child. Mr X discovered the truth, and the couple separated. Mrs X then went to the police.

Dr Jessop claimed that Mrs X had "thrown herself at him" after one session, and "very stupidly" thought it would do her harm if he refused. He denied that he had administered any pills. Ishmael Coulter QC, defending, brought forward expert witnesses who claimed it was impossible to be raped under hypnotherapy without being aware of it. Mrs X said, "I have no other explanation for what happened." '

What can I say about my response to this revelation? I understood, without any reservation, that Tom was my Dad and would continue being my Dad, and that my genetic father meant nothing to me. I reasoned, therefore, that I would be able to forget the matter and immerse myself again in work and my clubs, and spend more time with Gillian. Yet, my mind would not let the matter go. My thoughts festered around each of the three individuals involved. Should I confront my mother with the facts? Should I be angry that she had refused to face up to whatever it was that happened, her indiscretion, his rape? Should I be sympathetic and allow sleeping dogs to lie? Should I tell Tom? What good would it do? And should I go back to Dr Jessop for an *Eastenders*-style confrontation and force him to admit his guilt, his paternity?

No answers came into focus. No, no answers came into focus, not then, not ever. Instead, the questions agitated for a while, for too long, before slowly sinking into my subconscious. From there they took but occasional excursions to the surface, at different times during my life, without ever finding closure, as an analyst might say.

***

Rudy, Peter de Roo's son, came in to see me this afternoon. He's not been to Willow Calm Lodge before, and probably won't come again. He does not cross the sea to England very often, he said, but tonight he is playing his saxophone at a reunion gig with some old friends. He looked very tired, worn out. We talked mostly about Guido, my son and his friend, although I was delighted to hear news of Rudy's own son, Arnout. He's now in his 40s, a successful music producer, and father to two young boys. In my memory, though, Arnout is but a toddler, a scamp, racing around with Jay at Guido's wedding.

It would be a pleasure to tune in to Rudy's Coltranesque playing (Rudy gave me the broadcast coordinates), but I must press on to write about Gillian, Gillian Tilson. A whole lifetime later, my feelings and thoughts about her remain confused. I loved her. I'm sure that is true, when all is said and done. And, there is no doubt about this in my mind, she had a profound influence on who and what I became, possibly the most profound of any person after my mother. She also caused me much suffering. I am, though, clear about the difference between the emotional anger, with its sharp and short-lived pains, I suffered when we were young, and the intellectual resentment I harboured towards her later because of the way our children turned out.

CHAPTER 17

IN WHICH GILLIAN BUSTLES HER WAY INTO MY LIFE

Gillian was partial to making new year's resolutions, and the start of 2020 was no exception. As on many other such occasions, she decided she needed more exercise, and would take up a sport. She started in January with basketball, gave up in February, and, on the advice of someone in the basketball club, tried volleyball. The LSE volleyball club had a system for involving beginners at the start of the academic year, but for the rest of the time, any newcomers took pot luck.

In early March, Gillian showed up to a mixed training session, dressed in tight shorts and a bikini top, as if ready for a session of beach volleyball, knowing no one, knowing not a move or rule, and perfectly convinced she was in the right place at the right time. Had she been prettier, one of the club's Don Juans would have volunteered quickly to give her some coaching. Yet, somehow, it was I, still taking things easy with my ankle, who ended up talking her through the basics, and giving her practice with a ball. We all used to meet up in the bar after training, and Gillian bought me a beer by way of thanks for my help. She plied me with questions about my course, and told me all about her media studies degree. It is my impression that Gillian short-listed me that evening. She was single at the time, and looking for a partner; and she found me. She was tall, clever, serious and, superficially, strong. I was tall, clever, serious and weak. I do not mean to imply she was consciously looking for these qualities in a boyfriend; nor would I be able to explain how she knew so quickly that I might be suitably subservient.

Gillian never came again to play volleyball but we met for lunch in the canteen a few days later. She decided the time and the place. Oddly, I recall that she interrupted my order at the serving counter and changed it. When I hesitantly challenged her decision to deprive me of my favourite meal, she launched into a three or fivefold justification of her action (health would have been one, changing routines would have been another, letting go control might have been a third). It all made sense. She usually made sense, in the moment, or, if not, it was difficult to see a lack of sense when she delivered so many different ideas in fast succession. She had a certain gift of the gab (which may have come from her actress mother or from maternal Irish grandparents), which is not to deny that, when she tried, she could also argue very logically about issues of the day.

Having quizzed me over lunch, she then asked if I wished to accompany her to a ball. This involved hiring a formal dinner suit (with Gillian's help), parading, dining and dancing with Gillian at the event itself, and then engaging in drunken sex of some kind at her flat in the early hours of the morning. After that, she treated me like a long-standing boyfriend, and acted as though we were a fully-fledged couple. It felt good, and I fell for her completely. The over-riding impression I have of those early times with Gillian is of her intense interest in me, who I was, my family, my background, my interests. I only had to hint at an important unresolved practical problem, and she wanted the full story, and was bubbling with ideas to help.

This brief affair, which lasted less than three months, served – I can observe in retrospect – as a dress rehearsal for how we were to be later, only the performances at this early stage were bland, unpronounced, amateur. I allowed her to dictate my social life (apart from club activities) because she was good at society and socialising in general, and I put up only gentle resistance to her attempts to control all the little aspects of our times alone. Some of these were amusing, in which case I negotiated for the hell of it, but others were irritating in which case I ignored them. When Gillian sulked for hours over a trifle, I never for a moment imagined her mood was real or profound. I could usually win back her good favour by making some compensatory compromises. When I couldn't, then I would find myself distracted all day thinking about her, and about what I could have done, or should have done to please her.

Later, I was able to look back and see a pattern and how Gillian might have unconsciously expected me to be more submissive than I was. That was one problem, which may have led to our early separation. And then there was sex, or not.

During those two months, Gillian and I slept together regularly, three times or more a week, mostly at her flat. Yet it was hit and miss whether we would make love. We never kissed or cuddled out of bed, and nor did I ever make a pass at her. She took a business-like attitude. I believe it was vital for her to be in a couple as a way of earning social position, and sex was part of the job description. I don't think she ever expected to get much pleasure, nor do I know whether she ever did. If, after a few minutes of basic foreplay in bed, I didn't get an erection, she turned over, without a murmur, and went to sleep.

Her disinterest in my performance proved a useful aphrodisiac. I discovered that with a few drinks, a pleasant evening behind us, and the television on, I could put in a passable performance. This did not mean the sex was passionate or erotic by prevailing standards, but at least we did fornicate from time to time – much to my mental relief. Emboldened by this step towards sexual normality, I once tried talking to her about my impotent tendencies (not about my voyeuristic ones). She tried to listen, I must accept that, but she found it too difficult. I think it truly distressed her to talk or think about sex, or anything too intimate. Although her behaviour in the bedroom was unaffected by the confession, my insecurities returned with a vengeance. When Gillian finished with me – by email – on the pretext that she had no more time for a relationship because her exams were approaching and she needed to study 'twenty four seven', I partly blamed myself for being tactless.

The tears I cried a few days later in front of the Henry Peach Robinson photograph, *Fading Away*, may have been more in response to this email, than to Melissa's final passing away.

CHAPTER 18

IN WHICH I RETURN TO BRUSSELS AND EUROIL

Gillian's defection, Melissa's death, and the never-to-be-answered questions about Dr Jessop all conspired to undermine my psychological well-being, and consequently my work. When the end-of-year exam and project results were posted, my personal tutor called me in for a 'private chat'. I also talked at length to Julie, and exchanged several emails with both Flip and Alan, before deciding to take a year off. Tom helped too, by contacting Sterling at Euroil who agreed that, after my usual month of working in August, he might be able to employ me on a more permanent basis.

For a third summer, then, I found myself in Brussels. Sterling did not bother to dine me this time, and Hilde foisted another boring database task on me. I remained at the company flat for only two weeks, then moved myself into a furnished one-bedroom pad in Ixelles. I signed up for a crash course in French, which led to some pleasant evenings out with other students.

In order to overcome the tedium of the long office hours, I read, discreetly, through the Euroil archives. I started with those available on the company's employee site, where I located a store of public and not-so public documents (some of them written in the time of Euroil's predecessor companies): annual reports, outdated merger and acquisition studies, new market analyses, declassified techno-commercial field statistics and so on. I flicked through the titles of scores of such documents, and occasionally skimmed the conclusions. I dawdled longer over the environmental studies, not the location specific ones but those which looked at pollution problems more generally. For me, the most interesting sections – perhaps because of the influence of Ingrid Kallström's talk we had organised for the Government Club – were those dealing with the lobbying of regulators, and the counter-actions aimed at defusing the successful impact of environmental lobbyists. There were hundreds of documents related to the global warming issue, and I found a few case studies clearly written by oilserfs ('oil-is-still-the-future enthusiasts' as they became known – *Encyclopaedia Universal* informs me – in consequence of some highly successful Greenpeace advertising in the US during the period of the Alaska demonstrations). Some of these concerned the introduction of laws in Europe on unleaded and sulphur fuels in the 1980s and 1990s, the costly fight against banning the gasoline car in California, and a revealing story on how to ensure financial efficiency for decommissioning operations in Nigeria.

Among multinationals, Euroil, which eventually rose to challenge the giants Exxon and Shell, boasted a relatively clean reputation. Nevertheless, I had half-hoped to uncover a scandal, a buried secret, a forgotten illegal activity. This youthful zeal had several drivers. Firstly, there were the talks I had attended as a member of LSE's Green Action group. Secondly, around this time, there was a highly successful television drama series, which ran for several years, called *Charm*, after the name of the fictional multinational Charm. Many of the story lines concerned environmental or safety issues. Although different parts of the company with different characters were involved in each new plot, invariably the bad Captain Jake was skulking in the background trying to save the company money, helping a local manager to sack an over-conscientious employee, or bribing an official to open up a new opportunity. And, in the foreground, good Adam White was doing his best to clean up the unexpected and messy consequences of Jake's actions. Thirdly, I shouldn't forget Alan's subtle but persistent influence. He was always ready to polish every phone or email discussion with a green shine.

Having tasted the official documents on the Euroil netsite, I recklessly snuck into Sterling's office one lunch-time when Hilde, for some reason, had left a set of keys dangling from the filing cabinet lock. I rifled through several files and found one, benignly titled 'Future NGO campaigns' (NGO being short for non-governmental organisation) but with 'Confidential' emblazoned across the front cover and every page. I pulled it out, closed and locked the cabinet, and made my way to the print room to make a copy. Before I could replace the report, Hilde came back early from lunch. I was obliged to return to my desk concealing the original file. I waited, in a state of heightened tension, for half an hour before she disappeared to the toilet. I raced into Sterling's office. Thankfully, the key was still in the filing cabinet lock. I replaced the document, hopefully in the right place, and was exiting the room when Hilde returned. I flustered, I floundered, and I made some excuse about looking for a pencil sharpener. I imagined her glancing over my shoulder and seeing the other keys on the ring still swinging.

That night, in the privacy of my rented pad, I keenly looked over the prize: a copy of an NGO9 'Confidential Memorandum of Understanding' listing future strategy aims and, what I thought were, secret policies. It had been reported, earlier that year, that the newly-formed NGO9 (the nine most important environmental organisations worldwide, including WWF and EEB) were planning to concentrate their actions and avoid unnecessary overlaps, but, as far as I knew, no detailed policy objectives had emerged. Yet, according to my document, there did exist an extremely detailed plan of action. I reasoned that Euroil must have obtained the paper from a mole, and that he/she worked in the WWF since the document had a faint WWF watermark running along the bottom of each page. It did not take long for me to decide what to do. I placed the copy, with a short note, in an envelope labelled 'private' and 'urgent, to be opened only by Alan Hapgood', and then put that in another envelope addressed to Alan at the WWF offices in Kiev.

My efforts were inconsequential. When I met up with my uncle Alan, months later, he explained reluctantly that, although the document had apparently been partially restricted (hence the 'confidential' tag), it had been deliberately leaked – long before I got sight of it – to governments and to industry.

The day Sterling came back from vacation he called me into his office and told me I would not be needed beyond the end of the week. I asked him why, and he told me that company policy prohibited him from employing anyone who was an active member of a radical environmental lobby group. How did he discover I had been a member of Green Action? After catching me with a guilty look in Sterling's office, had Hilde taken the trouble to scrutinise the LSE club netsite and the members' lists? I never found out. Then and there, I did try to explain to Sterling that Green Action, despite its name, was no more than a student talking shop. He shook his sterling silver-top head, and looked down at his papers. As I walked passed Hilde's desk, I made some ridiculous comment such as: 'I'll be more careful where I look for a pencil sharpener next time.'

CHAPTER 19

IN WHICH I HAVE MY FIRST TASTE OF EUROPEAN POLITICS

I spent only three days unemployed in Brussels before Lionel Wilcox MEP, took me on as a personal assistant. My incredible good fortune happened in this way.

I had already developed an interest in the European Parliament, partly from the Euroil project I had undertaken two summers previously, and partly from my general interest in politics. I went straight from Sterling's office to my desk and compiled a list of the few MEPs who had given presentations to one of the LSE clubs. I also emailed my old history teacher, Flip, asking him, as a favour, for the names of any MEPs who had spoken to the Brideswell Society in the last five or ten years. Flip replied overnight with four names, Wilcox being one of them.

On my first day of unemployment, I took the long way round to the European Parliament's palace of glass, so as to walk in the bright sunshine through Parc Leopold. From the reception area, I rang the office of each MEP on my list, making the most of whatever connection I had established, and asking for a moment of the MEP's time. It sounds naive, but I got three interviews in two days. Two MEPs were friendly and helpful, but said they had no position available.

And then I met with Wilcox who gave me five minutes at the coffee bar. When he asked what I knew about internet regulation, expecting me to shake my head, I was able to say something reasonably intelligent thanks to the talks Pete Sampson and I had arranged for the Government Club. Firey made a point of noting my lack of languages, my (young) age, and my inexperience, but he did, though, take a telephone number. The next day he called and offered me a temporary research assistant job. His offer: 'Long hours, a minimum wage, and a boss who shouts, or so they say.' My response: 'Sounds great.' I learned later that he had emailed Flip for a reference.

Firey, as he was known to friends and the press because of his red hair and occasional loud outbursts in committee meetings, had been an MEP since 2004, the year the first batch of ex-communist countries joined the Union. A Liberal Democrat, representing the southwest of England, he worked energetically, unlike some in Brussels, and made his mark as the rapporteur on the original Euronet Regulation proposal. Apart from a limited number of positions (such as committee chairmen, party spokesman, institutional liaison etc.), the best an MEP could hope for then was to be appointed rapporteur on an important legislative proposal. A rapporteur was responsible for guiding negotiations internally in the European Parliament between the political groups, and then for arguing the Parliament's agreed position in complex negotiations with, what was then known as, the Council of Ministers, the grouping of Member State governments.

In retrospect, the Euronet – a regulated competitor to the free internet – came to be seen as both ambitious and innovative, even though its initial incarnation was castrated at birth by insufficient funds and political will, despite the Parliament's best efforts, led by Firey. It is not my task here to give a history lesson, but, as I became deeply involved in this issue for some years, I need to shade in some background.

By 2005 or so, many politicians and several left-wing governments had begun to look more carefully than before at certain aspects of the internet. Various influential academic studies had emerged in a flurry which appeared to point, if not conclusively then with very strong argument, at the internet as a serious threat to the fabric of Western society. As many had suspected since the start of the internet (my mother for one), it was demonstrated, by these studies, how the internet allowed criminal activity to flourish. The internet was a lawless land where terrorists, of whatever kind, could meet and discuss plans, where racists could congregate and reinforce each other's ideas, and where a flourishing trade in the abuse of human beings could be promulgated under the guise of international au pair agencies and exotic marriage or adoption bureaus. What concerned most Europeans, though, was the free availability of pornography, and not only soft-core top shelf images, but pictures and films of every imaginable and unimaginable type of perversion.

The original Euronet was launched in 2013. By the time I joined Firey's office only 7% of European citizens used it exclusively, and, on best estimates, only about 1% of total net activity by Europeans took place on the Euronet. Nevertheless, when the second world net summit was convened by the Union in 2018, a wide consensus had emerged for stronger and more effective regulatory action. The European Commission again tried to lead the way by presenting ambitious proposals to improve and strengthen the Euronet. Firey, by now a big fish in the Central Group, which held a majority in the European Parliament at the time, was the natural choice for rapporteur. I had been taken on, in addition to his normal staff of two, a part-time secretary Bronwen, and his main adviser Brian Veitch, to help with the donkey-work. I was given a week of light duties to allow me time to read up on background and essential documents, and thereafter, for the whole year, through to the following June, I learned the meaning of hard work. But it was an enthralling time.

Bronwen, with a Danish mother and an Irish father, and an exquisite sense of the comic, was a laugh a minute. She had excellent administration abilities, and kept us all in order. I learned much from watching her operate. Moreover, I should note, she scared Firey. The first time he shouted her down (this is before I arrived), she wasted no time in clearing her desk and marching out. A grovelling apology from Firey, an increased salary, and a promise of never-ending respect eventually attracted her back. Brian, by contrast, enjoyed Firey shouting at him. It gave him a position of superiority, and usually led to Firey accepting some fine point that Brian had otherwise failed to get across. As time went by, I began to appreciate how well Brian would choreograph these arguments, leading Firey into, what would usually transpire to be, the right position. There was, regrettably, one unwholesome side to Brian. While studying for a postgrad degree in European politics at Humboldt University in Berlin, he had developed an addiction to salami full of garlic. People who knew him always chose to sit at a healthy distance, and those who didn't would shift uncomfortably on their chairs if Brian leaned too close. Bronwen plied him with mints, but he binned them complaining of rotting teeth. He never had a woman friend – to my knowledge – in all the time I worked with him, although I heard, years later, that he married a Polish journalist, and became some sort of adviser to the Euronet Agency (long after my involvement with it had ceased).

The Commission's plan contained a plethora of legislative ideas. There were further attempts to provide extra control over the internet's activities, by tightening the legal base for legitimate services providers, and by strengthening possible sanctions against countries hosting renegade net service providers (NSPs). In addition, there was a major revision on the guidelines for authorised addresses on the Euronet. The key issue, though, was finance. The Commission argued that the Union should levy a tax, through the NSPs, on every customer, and use the income to fund a Euronet Agency. To avoid citizens subscribing in their millions to non-Union based NSPs, the Commission proposed an equivalent tax, to be raised through the telecom operators, on all access calls to NSPs based outside the Union territory.

Not only were these proposals highly political but they were all very technical. Firey's team, including me, spent the whole of that autumn seeking advice. We talked to companies, industry organisations, national and Union-wide regulators, consumer organisations, technical consultants. Often my job was to provide a half-page summary of a meeting with the key relevant points; or else it was to brief Firey, if Brian was away, on what questions/arguments to put before a forthcoming visitor. They both came to respect my way of simplifying issues down to core principles and consequently sought out my views from time to time. More mundanely, I was responsible for researching any and every whim of Brian's, and, in liaison with Bronwen, for arranging meetings and coordinating agendas. By end November, Firey and Brian had decided to propose a radical reshaping of the Commission's proposal, to divide the one Euronet into three: a basic Euronet, a business-oriented Euronet, and an academic Euronet. They confidently asserted that, despite the Euronet's less than glorious past, public finance and political backing were now ready to fall into place.

Armed with Brian's dazzling and detailed analysis, smoothly transformed into a bullet-point presentation by me, Firey spent several weeks persuading his Central Group colleagues to support such a big change to the Commission's proposal. By January 2021, we had finalised a draft report and amendments, but it took six further months of negotiations and discussions before the full European Parliament formally agreed its position on the original Commission's proposal. But, as I will recount, the dossier subsequently became stalled when the EU's Member States could not agree a position among themselves; and it would be many years before the new Euronet became operational.

A week after the final Parliamentary debate and vote, I left Brussels to return to London for ten days before flying to Brazil. Firey, Brian and Bronwen all tried to persuade me to stay but I wanted to press on and finish my degree. In any event, I was assured of a (minimum wage) position when my studies were complete, if I wished to return to Brussels.

Leaving Firey and his crew was tough enough, but there were other reasons I would miss Brussels. I thrived in the political atmosphere of the European Parliament, it was so full of important people, pretty women, characters of every nationality; and barely a week went by without one issue or another making media headlines and creating highly-charged gossip in the corridors. I recall listening to President Andrew McFeather make an absurd plea to the European Parliament to tone down its criticism of human rights violations in the US, vis-à-vis the Mexican immigrants, as if his very presence would be enough to influence the position of MEPs. He didn't last much longer. There was the day the Parliament voted, by two votes, to reject Turkey's accession to the Union. The vote had been turned by a German documentary, released via the net the night before, showing beatings of Kurds in Turkish prisons. The ensuing riots in Turkey against the government – for failing to gain EU membership not for the prison revelations – resulted in over 200 deaths across the country. For several days, the corridors went noticeably quiet as MEPs contemplated the consequences of their actions.

Best of all, I was there in March 2021 when the great African leader, Ojoru, then only 25 but already deputy president of Nigeria, delivered his historic mantra. Advance copies of a fairly standard speech had been distributed to the MEPs and to the press agencies, and the great chamber was only half full when he started speaking for his allotted ten minutes.

'In Africa, we are the most impoverished peoples in the world, we are the most uneducated, we are the most diseased. Why? Why is this? Why is it like this now? Why has it been like this for so long? Why will it be like this in the future? Why are your peoples so much less impoverished, diseased and uneducated? In Africa, we are the most impoverished peoples in the world, we are the most uneducated, we are the most diseased. Why? Why is this? Why is it like this now? Why has it been like this for so long? Why will it be like this in the future? Why are your peoples so much less impoverished, diseased and uneducated? ...'

By the third time round, the chamber had filled up with astonished MEPs, officials, visitors and me. We listened in total silence as he repeated exactly the same set of sentences 21 times, and by the end he was crying. He bowed, sat down and wiped his eyes. The European Parliament president remained silent for what seemed an age, then thanked him, and resumed normal business. The mantra was repeated on every newscast and in every newspaper around the world for days, and African issues were catapulted, overnight, to the top of the agenda in every international organisation. Ojoru, as is well known, went on to work tirelessly for African unity. He transformed the African Union and almost single-handed made it into a forceful presence within the United Nations. Alfred knew him well, and introduced me to him once – which turned out to be a key moment in my story. Much later, I should add, Alfred lost faith in Ojoru, and accused him of having a god complex.

CHAPTER 20

IN WHICH I VISIT BRAZIL AND LUST AFTER GABRIELLA

There is more I could say about my year in Brussels, but I am moving on – to Brazil. I had had a dream about visiting the country since as long as I could remember, so, with both money and time at the end of my artificial gap year, there was no good reason not to see it through. I will admit now, although I resisted the suggestion at the time, that I was influenced by the Hollywood flick *Gabriella* which had been released a few months earlier. It was a great movie, and became a romantic classic. It also introduced me to the 20th century Brazilian writer, Jorge Amado, and I defy anyone to read Amado's books and not want to go to Brazil.

I took advice from a Brazilian I had met at the European Parliament staff volleyball club in Brussels not to miss out on Recife. Alan insisted I visit an ex-girlfriend of his in Rio. Otherwise, I planned to visit Salvador, Ouro Preto and the Iguaçu Falls. I bought a detailed guide book, a pair of sunglasses, and an Earthmate V, which, incidentally, was a beautiful machine. The first of its type, I believe, weighing in at under 300gm, which combined sophisticated computer, phone and net facilities, a cam, Galileo services, and long-serving batteries that were easily rechargeable with solar power or, less easily, with body shake.

As so often in life, the higher the expectations, the deeper the disappointment. Bleary-eyed and jet-lagged I wondered aimlessly around Recife in a heat and humidity new to my experience. An intense disillusionment filled me to the point of depression. Recife was no more than a big ugly city, dominated by concrete skyscrapers. Here was infinitely more squalor than beauty. I only had to walk a few metres from the tourist centres to be lost in a favela and be accosted by beggars or ragged urchins – the like of which I had not seen even in Bangkok – and to find alleys of pure garbage. And the only beauty I could see was of two kinds: the beaches, and a few tourist sites with preserved colonial – i.e. European-built – buildings.

Chiselled into a wooden plaque, hung on the wall above the reception desk in my pousada, was the well-known epigram: 'Brazil: the country of the future, and always will be.' In truth, the country had been making steady progress for nearly 30 years and had been a member of the G8+5 for a decade or more.

Day two was no better. I received a message that my grandmother, Eileen, had died. This sad fact led me into several email dialogues with Julie and Alan. But then, while resting my weary feet and drinking a cafezinho or three, my Earthmate, which I had naively placed on the table for a second, was snatched, in front of my very eyes, by a boy no older than nine. I raced after him instinctively, but he ducked and dived through the alleyways; I lost him within seconds. On my return, the barman shrugged his shoulders. I made my way to a telecoms office so I could phone Alan. I had to queue for access to a phone. As I began to wait, I thought if Alan or my mother wanted me to come home, I'd catch the next flight. But, after a few minutes, and by the time the phone was free, I realised I was terrified of being asked to return and attend the funeral.

On the third day, a breeze blew in from the Atlantic and brought a light shower. It refreshed my mood. I made my way to Olinda, and found the romantic images I must have been expecting: the baroque churches, exquisitely beautiful, the picturesque colonial houses (I rapidly let go of my prejudice against colonial architecture), and the sun-washed plazas with distant views of the sea.

The following day I took a bus to Salvador. The journey lasted most of the day, but could have gone on forever for all I was concerned. I was sat next to the most beautiful girl I had ever seen. She was, she is, my Gabriella, although I confess, here and now, that later I confused the images of Gabriella and Conceição, who I shall come to, both in my conscious memory, and in my storytelling to friends. I have Gabriella's photo before me now on the screen, as she was then, 16 years old. Back in London, I had an enlarged print of this photograph framed and it hung wherever I lived – until Gillian gave it to a jumble sale.

Gabriella is standing at a petrol station, although there is no petrol pump or lorry cab visible because, subsequently, I airbrushed them out. She is wearing a loose, white tank top, barely covering her sharp full breasts with nipples erect behind the thin fabric, tight white jeans, with a lime-green belt and silver buckle. She is looking directly at the camera, brimming with innocence and temptation, her long jet black hair in front and behind her shoulders, but half covering the left side of her youthful, sultry, beautiful face.

We talked in fragments of English and phrasebook Portuguese for the first stage of the journey, enough for me to be so bold as to ask to take her photograph at a service station stop. Back on the bus, we swapped places so she could sit by the window. The seats were comfortable and she soon dozed off, her body slightly twisted towards the window, and her head leaning against an air cushion she had brought. I did not fall asleep, or look out of the window across her. Instead I stared at her, which I could do without fear of embarrassment, at her face, but mostly at her tank top and the breasts behind. As the journey progressed so one side of her top was pulled sideways incrementally, exposing millimetre by millimetre more of her left breast. This was sexual ecstasy without a climax.

I only mention Gabriella – rather than using these paragraphs to give some history of Brazil (with talk of Vargas, Tancredo or the future leader Neco the Prosperous) or to discuss deforestation and the plight of the Yanomami – because I was primed, as it were, as a result of that coach journey, to fall into the arms of Conceição. She was lounging with a group of boys in a bar round the corner from the cobbled Praça Pelourinho, in the centre of Salvador, where I had stopped for a beer before pressing on to try one of the cheap pousadas mentioned in the guide book. The group appeared lively, and I saw no reason to rebuff the friendly questions put to me in pigeon English. After a while, Conceição, who was very slim and dark and wore sunglasses, promised to find me a cheap place to lodge. I went with her, somewhat warily, to a pousada which proved both cheap and pleasant. When later she offered to show me around, I accepted. After eating and drinking too much, I allowed her to come back with me to the pousada and try – without success – to use her experienced hands in relieving me of my lust for Gabriella. I expected to pay her in the morning, but all she asked was to stay with me, to be my guide and interpreter.

To cut the story short, Conceição attached herself to me for a total of five days. She proved to be both fun and sexy, which, I suppose, is I why I didn't try harder to detach myself, though she proved a useless guide, and a drain on my resources. She giggled a lot, and she had this cute habit of giving me a childish wave whenever she left my side, even if it was only to go to the bathroom.

There is much in Salvador to detain the tourist, but I only wish to mention the sculptor Hector Julio Paride Bernabo (or Caybe as he was known) and his wood-carved panels in the city museum. Each one, inlaid with imaginative patterns of other woods, metals and ceramics, depicted an animal and some aspect of the macumba. Six decades later, I was to see them again, in the national museum of modern art in São Paulo.

From Salvador, we bussed to Ouro Preto, the fabulous town built on the back of the gold rush in the 18th century, and reconstituted in the 20th century with tourist gold. I like to believe Arturo was conceived when Conceição and I had sex on the squeaky iron bedstead in the traditional pousada near the Mine Engineering Museum. There was a spectacular sunset with the last of the sun's rays streaming through our window onto the bed. Conceição had succeeded in giving me a full erection which she then put to its proper use. I must have been overwhelmed with passion or gratitude or stupidity, for I neither worried about AIDS, nor about her getting pregnant. We were to copulate only one other time, but it was in a dirty hotel, which rented most of its rooms by the hour.

By the time we arrived in Rio, I had decided it was time to separate. I contemplated ditching her furtively, but was too timid for such deception. Instead, I made up a weak story about wanting to spend time alone, and then I gave her more than enough money to return to Salvador. And, because she said she wanted to write me letters, I gave her my mother's address. I didn't have the gall to invent one on the spot. At the bus station, she waved goodbye, in her silly childish way, as if I would be seeing her again in five minutes.

Thanks largely to Monique, an ex-girlfriend of Alan's, I spent two glorious weeks in Rio de Janeiro. Originally from Tunisia, she had lived much of her life in France before working for WWF in East Europe. For several years, she and an Alan were a couple, but then she moved to Rio to campaign on rainforest issues. She insisted I use the spare room in her tiny Ipanema apartment, and she introduced me to some of her younger friends. I played volley on the Leblon beaches, climbed Corcovado, danced samba at gafieras, bought trinkets at various markets, got drunk on caiparinhas, and engorged myself at churrascarias.

A few nights, I scurried off to the Copacabana clubs, unsure whether I felt more guilty for enjoying the sex shows, or for having employed the services of a prostitute for a week. Through a Brazilian friend, I came to understand later, long before Arturo appeared, that by British standards Conceição was less a prostitute and more a sort of good-time girl, one who offered short-term faithfulness in exchange for being looked after money-wise.

Two blocks from Monique's apartment I chanced on an exhibition of Marc Ferrez's panoramic photographs from the late 19th century and early 20th century. At the turn of the century, when Rio was already a sprawling city, the old photographs showed Copacabana as a wild natural beach with only a couple of buildings set back from the sand dunes. Furthermore, although a cable car could take you to the top of the Sugar Loaf, there was no Urca suburb as now exists clinging all around the base of the Sugar Loaf and Urca hills, since the rock face plunged straight into the sea in those days. I purchased two large books with beautiful reproductions of Ferrez photographs. Somewhere along the way of my life, I lost them, but not before all the photographs had been scanned into Neil.

Monique also took me to stay for a weekend with charmingly bohemian friends in Parati, another colonial delight similar to Ouro Preto and Olinda, impressively preserved in Brazil's darker years with United Nations money. There, I was spoilt with Brazilian delicacies, where everyone spoke English after dinner so I could take part in the conversation, and where I went scuba diving in waters as clear as glass.

I experienced an unforgettable night at Maracana when Argentina beat Brazil in a world cup qualifier. I queued, jostled and pushed for four hours to buy a ticket (with the help and companionship of the porter at Monique's apartment building – if I'd been alone I would never have persevered). Over 100,000 fanatics squeezed into that stadium, and I saw it as a miracle of modern society that war did not erupt then and there around me, such were the passions of every individual, and the tensions and releases of tensions in the stadium as a whole. With heated arguments, fights and scuffles, and everyone moving aggressively through the crowds to get away, it was another miracle we escaped uninjured.

And, before I flew home from São Paulo (an infinity of skyscrapers, a monstrous place then, and no less so when I went for the last time in 2081), I visited Iguaçu, which involved long boring bus rides (no Gabriella diverting my attention, no Conceição making me laugh).

CHAPTER 21

IN WHICH I HEAR OF 'ENDEMIC SOCIAL TERRORISM'

On my return, after family visits, I went to see Pete Sampson. Excitedly, he said he had signed up with Wilma Johnson at the LSE history department to do a PhD. In time, Johnson was to become one of the department's most famous professors, not only through her warm media-friendly personality but because government after government called on her advice. She developed, according to Pete, a fresh approach to the analysis of modern history by following the geographical and chronological routes of religions and sub-religions and sidelining the role of nations.

Pete, who painstakingly taught himself to read Russian, found her methods suited the study of Central Asia during the communist period, about which very little detailed history existed in English. He travelled extensively in the region during the five years of his PhD – part-funded it must be admitted by his family – and became something of an authority on the subject. His decision to remain at LSE was very good news for me, not least because he had stayed put in our old Bermondsey home, and was ready to take me back as flatmate. Not long after I had reinstalled myself, Peter de Roo moved out to cohabit with Livia, a Cornish girlfriend, and we replaced him with someone whose name I cannot recall. I know we charged him a high rent so as to reduce our own. He was annoyingly good at word games, I seem to remember, so that Pete and I would conspire to beat him at speed scrabble, which we played very occasionally.

Although I had looked forward with anticipation to my final year at LSE, in reality I found it a frustrating and unsatisfying period. Student life felt stodgy and constrained as opposed to spontaneous and liberating; and there was a tired second-hand sheen dulling everything I did. Attending lectures, studying student texts, and writing essays were all tediously irrelevant compared to the work in Brussels. History itself, a subject once so enthralling to a teenager, thanks wholly to Flip, had become no more than a supporting act to the main show which I now considered to be international affairs, government and politics. I was granted leave to focus my degree dissertation on the origins of the European Union in reference to the history of inter-regional organisations, and this gave me considerable intellectual pleasure, not to mention an excuse for two week-long research trips to Brussels during which I was able meet up with Brian, Bronwen and others.

Pete Sampson had maintained firm control of the Government Club while I was away, and fully expected me to continue running it with him on my return. I did, but with far less youthful enthusiasm than in earlier years. There were, though, several younger members of the committee who more than made up for my absences. One of these was Tommy, a short tidy man of Indian heritage, who later worked for me at the IFSD. He was one of the most loyal, hard-working and enlightened individuals I ever knew. He fought ferociously, for example, throughout his life against religious or national prejudice in the Indian subcontinent. I recall him being drunk one night in The Madonna, after his first public contribution for the club, and telling me how he had been called TomTom at school, and how he used to stand around in the playground patting his head repeatedly.

My Brussels contacts proved a helpful network through which to find and attract high-class speakers, who served to pull in large audiences and new members with minimal effort. One evening we took over the wallscreen room to watch the launch hour of William Caxton's new free broadcast station, The People's Channel. Most commentators gave it no chance against the main channels (including the BBC, Sky and Four if I recall correctly) and the galaxy of other odd free channels that came and went as regularly as the seasons. We felt no need to take it seriously. In the debate that followed, for example, two political students parodied, with scintillating wit, the case for complete liberalisation of television advertising, especially to children.

There was one speaker we did not have to find – Triti Madan. She stands out for me, even more so than Ingrid Kallström, as the most impressive thinker the Government Club presented in my time. In a short, friendly letter, addressed only to the 'President of the Schapiro Government Club, LSE, London', she explained that she was the professor of international politics at the University of Mumbai, that she was coming to England to visit her daughter's family for Christmas, and that, because she had been a student at LSE and very much enjoyed the Schapiro Club, she would be pleased to give a half hour talk on her recent, 'slightly controversial', work which had been published in major academic journals. We exchanged a few emails, to set a date and time. She attracted a huge audience thanks to Tommy, who made a special effort to promote the event. Our advertised offer of free mulled wine after the discussion might have helped too.

Madan, who must have been consciously and/or unconsciously inspired by the reports of Ojoru's mantra nine months earlier, quantified the extent to which civil unrest was growing and continued to grow, barely noticed by the West unless Western civilians were caught up in an incident. Although governments worldwide and international bodies continued to blame religious fundamentalists, this was no longer a credible position. From one side – 'internal disorder' she called it – poor citizens were being inundated with Western values, through multinational advertising, films on street-screens and product placements on popular international radio broadcasts, and yet were utterly unable to realise the dreams being sold to them. From the other side – 'external disorder' – climate change had clearly begun to unsettle and disrupt both urban and rural populations in all kinds of ways (floods, hurricanes, earthquakes) thereby critically exacerbating the problems of governance in many countries with unstable politics.

None of this was new thinking, yet the traditional Hindu dress combined with the middle-aged motherly features and a crisply pronounced near-perfect English, gave her message such poignancy that we were transfixed in listening. But then she moved on to speak eloquently and forcefully on the need, not to double the flow of funds from the developed to the undeveloped world, but to increase it fivefold: at least to 2.5%, the level of Islam's Zakat.

She suggested it was already 'very, very late' to consider a proper and adequate redistribution of wealth around the world, in parallel to the way that wealth is redistributed within a nation through taxation and government spending. The tides of resentment in the affairs of man, she said, are under-estimated time and time again, and they are at times so huge that no dam, no army can ever stop them. Governments, peace organisations, individuals all stand for years and dec-ades like King Canute trying to resolve the wrongs and re-sentments built up un-recognised for decades, or even centu-ries beforehand: witness Northern Ireland, witness Palestine, witness Kashmir, witness Syria.

The same effect, she argued, is happening in a global, less precise way, and only a substantial sharing of wealth will stem the rising tide of hostility felt by the poor of this world against the rich. Why not, she concluded, consider how much money you – the West – spend on beauty products, on pet food, or, apparently less decadently, on incremental medical research. So much of your medical research is taken for granted, un-questioned, yet what does it achieve? According to my detailed research, the average annual medical research budget of the United States improves overall life expectancy of an American citizen by five days. The same amount used effectively for health training or education or hospital infrastructure in India could increase life expectancy by five months. Ignore this reality, she said, and I predict 'endemic social terrorism'.

I had never heard the phrase before, and nor had any of my colleagues, but we would certainly hear it again.

CHAPTER 22

IN WHICH GILLIAN AND I SAY WE LOVE EACH OTHER

Gillian came back into my life during the autumn. We had eaten lunch together once in Brussels, when she was visiting for some vague purpose, possibly to see me. On her initiative, we had had a long camphone conversation during the summer, swapping anecdotes about our lives. I welcomed both these encounters at the time, but afterwards I found myself thinking about her for days, and missing her high-octane companionship. She had messed up her finals, blighted by nerves or a personal problem she never revealed to me, and only scraped through with a mediocre degree. Nevertheless, she had a job in the print media, sub-editing for one of the Sundays. She liked the people and the kudos of working on a national paper, but the work itself bored her. Despite her best efforts, she had been unable to make the switch to a reporting position.

One Friday morning, while drinking a lukewarm tea in the canteen, I received an email with the title 're: End of the affair'. She was asking me to meet her later that day at the 'usual place' and promising to pay. The 'usual place' was a guzzleshop called Mintoffs where we had snacked frequently during our short time together. Suggesting that she would pay was a joke since it was the cheapest halfway decent place to eat outside of the college. The message disturbed me, confused me, excited me. Why had she called it 're: End of the affair'? Was it a mistake, a joke, or a discussion topic? Gillian did not make many practical mistakes; nor did she joke very easily. The latter possibility seemed the most plausible. And was it our affair she wanted to discuss, or another affair, in politics, show business, film fiction, there were plenty around?

Mintoffs was heaving, and sweaty. Some of its customers had got caught in a heavy downpour. Gillian was at a tiny table squeezed up against the mustard-painted wall, shifting a shoulder as she tried to avoid dribbles of condensation. She looked downcast, with wet unkempt hair, darker and less curly than when dry. I stopped for a moment, before approaching, and wondered if I was making a mistake.

Gillian did not beat around the proverbial bush. This is one of the many things I admired about her – her directness. Yet, in time, I came to realise it stemmed more from a lack of confidence than strength. Although happy to talk on a practical level about people's problems, she did not appreciate her daily life being disturbed by personal or intimate matters, such as difficulties in her relationship, or illness, or, as I was to discover, the complications of children. And so, when such a difficulty finally welled up to a point of needing resolution, she tried to get over it as quickly as possible.

With a vulnerable sheepish look, and while brushing her wet hair to one side with the back of a hand, she confessed that she had made a mistake. She realised, she said very plainly, that she loved me and wanted us to give our relationship another chance. Without waiting for any reaction from me, she went on to ask forthrightly if I still loved her too. I could smell bacon butties, which reminded me that we had yet to order. Did I love her? It was not a question I could answer spontaneously, honestly, passionately, in the way I might have been able to to Melissa, or dishonestly but lustfully to Gabriella had she asked. But, I don't believe she was asking me that. Later, after a little soul-searching, I understood better. In that moment, I think I knew instinctively that she was asking me if I loved her in the way she loved me.

'Yes, Gillian, I do love you.' What I meant by this was that I needed her, wanted her to be a part of my life, and that my life was incomplete without her. Romance and sex did not enter into the calculation of her question or my answer. Gillian required nothing further, all the rest was taken for granted. Instantly, we were an item again. That night we went to the cinema in Kilburn, and I stayed at her newly acquired mansion-block flat in West Hampstead. Once in bed, Gillian turned out the light and we kissed for the first time in nearly 18 months. Desperately not wanting to disappoint her, or myself, I directed my imagination to the picture of Gabriella in my head.

But I did. When she rolled off to the side, I thought she would fall asleep in minutes. Instead, she leaned across to switch the side light on, and then got up, naked, and walked around the room as if looking for something. I lay on my back and watched her. I watched her stretch to peer above the wardrobe, I watched her from behind as she bent over to look under the wardrobe, and I watched her stand in front of me not noticing that I was eyeing her up and down and smiling. Customarily, she wore a gown after the bathroom and so I had never seen her standing, let alone walking, naked before. She may not have been pretty but there was something very handsome about her face, and she kept her body fit and trim. Under the bedclothes, I was visited by a longed-for erection. Eventually, she pulled out, from one plastic bag underneath another one in the corner, a lacy bra. I could see her hands tremble as she tried to fix the clasp behind, and her body was all tense. She was nervous.

'What do you think?' she asked.

'I liked it,' I said, in the past tense, meaning the display, not the brassiere.

In the morning we breakfasted as though there had been no break in our affair at all. I was reinstated into Gillian's social life immediately. This had evolved since her student days, in terms of the quality of her dinner party invitees, food and conversation and with respect to her interests: she was on an opera kick that autumn, and had joined a swimming-for-fun club. Mostly, when together, we ate out or went to the cinema, and then spent the second half of the evening arguing about the acting/plot or menu/decor. In this way, we were great mates, inciting each other to increasingly irrational arguments. The only difference was that when we were with friends she behaved the same, and I closed up, preferring to listen rather than speak. We never had a problem with money, which – to hear the tales of friends – was a boon. She paid more than her fair share. This was practical since she had an income and I had debts. To show my appreciation of her generosity, I would buy her cheap but colourful flowers.

We never talked about intimate matters or feelings, so I never knew why she had left me, nor whether she had been in any other relationships. But we did confide in each other about our work and our hopes, and once or twice strayed close to language that implied a long-term future for us as a couple. There was also an unspoken assumption, especially in the way Gillian referred to 'us' in conversation with others, that we would live together one day soon, when I was no longer a student.

I should add that there had been no change in Gillian's bossiness. We settled further into a pattern, whereby I let her dictate our private life almost entirely. I told myself it did not matter, and that my partner's behaviour stemmed from an over-zealous care for me. I did, though, dislike it intensely if she treated me the same way in public, with friends or strangers in hearing distance. When this happened too obviously, I held my peace until we returned home, and then I let loose, raising my voice and letting out a torrent of abuse, half-consciously imitating Tom. On the whole, Gillian tended to ignore these outbursts, so I would leave and take the convoluted tube ride back to Bermondsey. Then I wouldn't answer her calls. Much as I tried to shut her out of my mind and concentrate on studying, I usually cracked within a few days. A long camphone conversation would ensue and we would be back to normal. I rarely lost my temper so crudely later in life with Diana or with Lizette, so, either I was provoked to greater extremes of anger by Gillian, or else I learned from her that such behaviour was counter-productive.

Whereas our first affair had lasted two months, this one survived for six. The morning after my post-finals celebration party, Gillian told me bluntly, as usual, that she had accepted a public relations position in Dublin. Dublin! She had decided weeks earlier but thought it best not to tell me for fear the news might affect my concentration in the run-up to the exams.

'And what about us?' was my inadequate response. I can remember the gist of the conversation, which did not last very long. We were sitting at the fold-down table in her narrow kitchen with toast and marmalade, and an over-sized plum-coloured teapot covered in blotchy scarlet elephants chasing each other round the curve.

'You'll get a job in Dublin, a good job. It'll only be for a couple of years. It's a great place. We'll buy a car and drive over to the west coast. I've got relations in Galway. We can rent a flat, and have friends come to visit. It'll be fun, exciting.'

'And my second interview?' I said calmly. Gillian had ignored this hurdle in her plans. I had been invited back for a second interview at Yorkshire House, where the government's Department of Communications was based. Having passed an exam, and been for a day interview conference, I was up for a junior grade post. Ironically, Gillian had encouraged me every step of the way, especially when I had expressed an instinctive reluctance to become a civil servant; I doubt whether I would have applied for the job without her encouragement.

'You never wanted the job in the first place. It's beneath you. Why jump at the first opportunity. You can't know what else might come along. A consultant will snap you up in Dublin for twice a civil servant's salary. Anyway, London's doing our heads in.' More often than not I treated these spontaneously-arrived assumptions – that my likes and dislikes, for example, matched her own – as amusing. A few times, though, they irritated me intensely.

'No. I'm not going anywhere.' I remained calm. I believed Gillian was joking or testing me in some way.

'You must, Kippy, you must come, or we'll have to end it.' That hit me in the face. She got up from her chair and started clearing away the table.

'I haven't finished.'

'You have.'

'I haven't. And I'm not going to Dublin. I want this job. You know I do. Why can't you try and get a similar job here?' I was trying to be reasonable.

'I'm going Kippy, and that's an end to it.' There was a firmness, and a finality about the way she spoke, that implied argument or further discussion would be redundant. Anger fired up inside me, and I wanted to shout, but words would not come. This was suddenly too serious. Instead I spoke with quiet bitterness.

'An end – to us, I agree. I am grateful that you had the decency to tell me to my face this time. Good-bye.'

I did a boisterous turn around the flat, collecting various possessions, mostly clothes, a few books, banging everywhere I went. I half hoped she would call me back into the kitchen and say 'let's talk about it', or 'we can work something out'. But she didn't. This time round, although I was personally stronger (and older), I was more severely wounded than before, suffering as I did from both the emptiness of losing her, and the bitterness of having been rejected.

To conclude this chapter of my life on a more positive note, I gained a good degree, three-five marks short of the best grade. I was offered, and accepted, a civil service post in the Department of Communications. I spent three sunny weeks in the Balearics, taking part in two beach volleyball tournaments, one with Alfred during his last European holiday before he returned to Lagos, and one with Peter de Roo. If Gillian visited my thoughts at night, during those weeks, they didn't disturb my sleep, nor my wild dreams in which the semi-fictional Gabriella was often the heroine.

EXTRACTS FROM CORRESPONDENCE

<u>Melissa to Kip Fenn</u>
May 2017

Mum and Rob away all w/e.

Tonight's Programme: Bill+Ben's 7pm; Rock 9pm; My Striptease Palace midnight or soon after!

Loving.

June 2017

Me/Gemma organising picnic after match. Stuck with Rob and friend, though, so they'll have to come. Bore.

Don't worry, we'll ditch them later. xxx

<u>Alan Hapgood to Kip Fenn</u>
August 2018

Thanks so much for your kind note. It was our pleasure, truly. You may have 'felt' awkward but you 'handled' the food as if a born Arab. Tamara was quite taken with you – as I am with her. After you'd left us at the hotel, she wanted to know why I couldn't find you a job at WWF. She thinks the oilserfs might get you for good!

Despite my fears, the meetings turned out to be more positive than I expected. Decision-makers will listen if you argue firmly and consistently, and back up your case with facts. After a stop in Copenhagen, we're back in Kiev now. There is so much work to be done, not only to convince the government to agree to our project, but to find and train technicians.

Keep in touch.

November 2018

Thanks so much for your note. I'm glad I was able to help. So, Ingrid [Kallström] gave a good show. I don't doubt it. Was any student bold enough to ask if being female and pretty helped open doors in the corridors of power? She has a stock answer: 'Doors open in different ways but it's what you do and say when you get in the room that matters.' Believe it or not she works so hard she doesn't have time for a private life. I took her out for dinner once – we're talking 12 years ago now when we were both working in Budapest and the flood problems were so severe – but she told me over the soup she didn't have time for boys. From all I hear, nothing has changed since. What a waste. And how's your love life these days?

Keep in touch.

September 2020
Remarkable document. Thanks. I'm not sure I should approve. For goodness sake don't get into any trouble.

Keep in touch.

December 2020
Many many happy returns for your 21st. I'm sorry I can't be there to celebrate with you, but we have composed, well Tamara mostly, and acted (!) a modest ditty for you, as you'll see on the camclip. That's Zaborovsky Gate in the background in case you were wondering. Tamara says you must come to visit us. And – it goes without saying – I agree with everything she says.

And all the best for the new year. It sounds interesting and fun working with Wilcox – tell me more when you have time.

Keep in touch.

PS: Good news about your mother getting the headship, it's no more than she deserves.

January 2022
Thanks so much for your note. I do know Triti Madan. She has quite a reputation among the NGOs, it's only a shame Western governments don't take her ideas more seriously.

Have you read any books by the political scientist Chaminda Dharmasena. He's a professor at Colombo University, and is most famous for his studies on government responses to terrorism. Although he works in a very different arena from Madan, their general conclusions often echo each other. For example, Dharmasena argues, using costs and benefits calculated with his own much-lauded methodologies, that the largely military/security response by the US and its allies to 11 September was an international catastrophe, politically and economically, and that they only paid to store up trouble.

Keep in touch.

Gillian Tilson to Kip Fenn

May 2020, End of the affair

Kippy Darling, delete this as soon as you've read it, won't you. I don't want to hurt you, I love you so. But I have to stop seeing you. Exams in a few weeks. I need to be without distraction, focused twenty four seven. I've been keeping you from your work too. There are so many things we don't have in common (and some we do). It's all for the best. (Your mother never liked the sound of me anyway – or so you said.) The very best. Maybe we can have lunch soon. Be good.

December 2020, Birthday

Kip Darling, where are you for your birthday? Are you in town? Shall I see you for martinis or zinis? You must celebrate 21, you must. You looked so well in Bruxelles mon cher. Call me, next time. OK. No excuses. Happy Birthday. Have a great day. Bye for now.

October 2021, re: End of the affair

Kippy Darling, shall we meet for lunch, my treat. Usual place 12:30. Don't be late.

Tom Fenn to Kip Fenn

December 2020

Son, it's a pity we can't get together this holiday/your birthday. It's been a difficult year for you and me in different ways. But, hey, things are on the up and up. At least you're not grounded with a mushy ankle like last year, and, you sound full of beans at work, with this Firey character. Sterling's a prat, I agree. And no, I never did get any feedback about your leaving/dismissal – why should I have?.

I've a month in Indonesia during the spring, politics willing, coincidentally finishing at the same time as the Bali Grand Prix, and a new girlfriend, Griselda – horrible name, lovely girl, tell you about her next time.

Lots of love, and love to your mother.

Horace Merriweather to Kip Fenn
December 2020

Sorry young chap, got there before you. I can report, confidently, there's no difference this side of 21 – all that key to the door stuff, reckon we get it when we're 14 these days. I'm madly jealous to hear you're working in the European Parliament – some of us are still slogging our guts out at uni. One more year to go. Cambridge has a lot to answer for – it's very 20th century. Desperate to be out there, making waves. I've promised myself to get elected an MP by 25. Tindle's said he might take me on as a researcher in the Commons. And a while ago, I met Spoon, one of the most promising young Conservative Members of Parliament. We hit it off straightaway. He was a Witley Academic boy too, but left the year before we started. It wouldn't surprise me to see him brought into the government when Owen Perry shuffles in early spring. Must dash, Mother has recklessly promised me 100 euros if I can beat her at golf – weather permitting.

So, many happy returns Kip for the day.

Peter de Roo to Kip Fenn
December 2020

Kip. What no party? Pete says you're becoming too serious. All tangled up in the net. Ha Ha. He should be taking you clubbing. Have a beer for me, have five. And get laid, you wanker. Happy Birthday.

PART THREE

Gillian, Caxton and the Net

'Integrity, loyalty and fairness, these are the qualities I have tried to bring to my personal and public life.'

'Unhindered access to information is essential to freedom, equality, and justice for all. Unhindered access to information for all is the key to a peaceful, democratic and progressive world.'

'Those who wish to control the flow of information, are those who wish to control our lives.'

A Man of the People by William Caxton (2029)

CHAPTER 23
ABOUT JAY, FLORA AND CHINTZ

In general, I see visitors here at Willow Calm Lodge between 6 and 7pm in the evening or on Saturday afternoons, and, I prefer to see one person at a time. I set the pattern soon after settling into this sunset hospice, this halfway house – halfway between life and death. Jay comes most often, partly because I encourage his visits since talking with him tires me less than with anyone else, and, I hope, because he likes my company. Also, in the last few months, since his partner Vince Wells ran off with a holiday tour manager, he has been lonely.

Most days I talk for a few minutes to Flora Pattison. She is roomed along the corridor, but, unlike me, can manage short spells in an Easy. I never bothered much with Easys, having moved straight from my last accident in a Swifty to this bed. Flora hums in, natters about the nurses and/or her pill menu and symptoms, and then hums out. She's so high-spirited, though, and so undemanding I don't wish to ask her to leave me out of her daily carrousel. She's scheduled her death on the same day as me, 31 January 2100, so I feel bonded to her in an odd kind of way.

And then there's Chintz. Ever since she asked about the Ferrez photo, she's taken to visiting me at the end of her shift. She stays until I say 'I'm tired now', and then kisses me on the forehead and leaves in an instant. I can talk to her, as I talk to Jay, about this book. They both help me put my thoughts in order; also, I can tell by their attention to my anecdotes how interesting they might be to someone other than me. Jay appreciates the family stories, the personal stuff; Chintz wants to know about famous people and exotic places. She's learned a thing or two about William Caxton, 'The man of the people', in the last few days.

I seem to have been prevaricating, picking out the best bits with which to impress her, rather than making the effort to reflect on seriously, and write about faithfully, this bleak period of my life. Unfortunately, in order to make best sense of events I need to flit backwards and forwards a little bit in time. Indeed, I might as well start at the end, as it were, on a day I experienced the most exquisite sense of *schadenfreude*.

CHAPTER 24
IN WHICH I EXPLAIN ABOUT CAXTON AND ME

Because they made an effort to do so, many remember where they were or what they were doing when they heard about Caxton's assassination. It was the kind of fashionable fluff talk you could hear at young people's fiestas throughout the 100 year golden era of oil and chips.

Tom, my father, who was 18 months old at the time, claimed he could remember his mother Evvie shouting 'Oh my god' when seeing John F Kennedy shot on television. Under cross-examination, he would eventually admit he might have been told this later. About John Lennon's assassination, my uncle Alan always remembered his English teacher at primary school insisting on a minute's silence, and giving a lesson about the Beatles' lyrics. Peter de Roo, who had a teenage crush on Vi Hoop, was painting the family barge when the pop music on his personal player was interrupted with news of the singer's murder.

I remember where I was when Caxton was assassinated – although I'm jumping a decade or so ahead here in my chronology – for two reasons: because of the sinful pleasure I experienced as I watched the giantscreen replay the moment over and over again; and because Diana demanded I tell her the full story. It was the first time I had told anyone other than Gillian. Part of it was in the public domain, but not my story, not my version. Perhaps his death had suddenly released me, or, perhaps I wished to impress Diana with uncharacteristic openness.

Diana and I had met only two weeks previously at one of Peter's festive gatherings, but this particular evening we were at Keizerskroon, a tulip palace restaurant, in the Dutch town of Zaandam. Diana looked radiant. She wore a long purple cotton dress, giving her a dash of added height, and a dark red velvet bonnet slanted across her forehead half hiding a round, cherub-like face. I have a kitsch photo of us. Here it is now, exactly as it was then, on a large wallscreen. A roving photographer had ushered us over to a banked display of tulips in flower, a veritable rainbow of colours, and snapped us a few times looking self-conscious and stiff. He said something I didn't understand fully, but Diana translated, over-emphasising the last but one word: 'Put your arm around the lovely lady.' So I did. Diana bent her fleshy body sideways into mine. I remember the sensation vividly, for it was the moment I realised she – to use an old-fashioned word – fancied me. The photographer said 'bravo'. Minutes later, the picture appeared on the wallscreen. There was a ripple of applause, one of many that night (and every other night), and I paid a small fortune for two large prints and for a copy to be sent me by email. But that night, as I say, was still far in the future.

William Caxton, or WC as the British satirical magazine *Private Eye* dubbed him for many years, died instantly on Saturday 14 May 2033 at 5:13pm in Moscow. It was 9:30pm our time when I caught a giant picture of Caxton's face on the restaurant wallscreen. I walked over to stand closer to a speaker so I could hear the commentary. One sequence showed the moment a bullet went through Caxton's forehead. Another showed a bearded youth, only five metres away in a crowd at the side of the street, holding a revolver with two hands out in front of his body, frozen for a few seconds, then rugby-tackled from behind.

Ten days later the assassin, Valentin Spichenko, bled to death in a Moscow jail. His wrists had been slit. In the weeks and years that followed, conspiracy theories abounded. One investigative reporter wrote a book, for example, claiming the Russian mafia had arranged the killing because a Caxton peep-hole or spycam had exposed, live on the net, one of their very best protectors, Georgia's home affairs minister. The man disappeared within hours and was never seen again. The author claimed Spichenko had told a guard he would never serve a prison term because he had very powerful friends. Another, frankly preposterous, theory claimed the UK's Special Armed Services were responsible. But I believed a simple explanation: an ordinary man had a mental break down and attacked the person he felt was to blame for his situation. Spichenko was a newly-qualified accountant with a young wife and a two month old child. His father had died six months previously and left him a substantial inheritance, but he had lost every last penny of it, and much more, by playing and betting on backgammon through one of Caxton's gaming sites.

I had met Caxton, he who was to become my bête noire, for the first time at school, when I had organised his giving a talk; and then I had met him again, a second time, while I was working for Firey in Brussels. Caxton came to us, in autumn 2020, to lobby on the Euronet revision bill. I remember how Bronwen ushered him and several assistants into Lionel Wilcox's office, and how he shook hands with Firey himself, then with Brian Vetch, then with me. Although I was 10-12 centimetres taller than him, I felt distinctly inferior.

'Ah, the tall young Fenn,' he said with alarming directness. 'I'm so glad we meet again.' He turned to talk to Wilcox for a second. 'We have both progressed since when you were a schoolboy and I was a junior minister.' We laughed with him for politeness. 'I'm glad you've opted for the Parliament. The European Commission might have been the more powerful institution in Delors' day, but no longer.'

There is no doubt I felt seriously flattered that he had remembered our conversation from several years earlier at Witley Academic. Nevertheless, I am gratified to recall that I allowed Firey's and Brian's opinion of the man to influence me fully. During the meeting they cut through his anti-regulation arguments with ease and disdain; and, once his entourage had left, they mocked him for being so profoundly full of himself.

This, my second encounter with Caxton was not wholly a matter of chance, and, because I do not wish to be accused of avoiding facts that give succour to those who believe we make our own luck and our own misfortune, I should set the record straight. If I had not been so intent on name-dropping, my life might have taken a very different course. The truth is that I mentioned, somewhat youthfully and boastfully, to Brian that I had met Caxton before. Without this petty brag, he may not have suggested I sit in on the meeting; and, if I had not been there, it's possible Caxton would not have picked on me later to be one of his squealers. But I was, and he did. And I learned, from first-hand experience, that William Caxton was not a man who played by the rules, nor was he a man who bluffed.

Apart from countless biographies, not to mention his own early auto-hagiography, information about Caxton can be found in every printed and net encyclopaedia, so there is no need for me to cull more than a few cursory background details from *Encyclopaedia Universal*. Ronald Shuttleworth was brought up in a large, non-religious, Catholic family by a succession of nannies, his mother being too committed to the Girl Guides, and his father being far too busy managing the packaging firm inherited from his father. He won the equivalent of 15 million euros on the lottery when he was only 18; and, after spending a quarter of his winnings in two years, he had a sudden and dramatic, possibly drug-fuelled, conversion to maturity. He then bought and grafted his way through Harvard Business School. On returning to the UK, Shuttleworth settled himself in an estate near Tenterden, Kent, bought several local newspapers on the cheap, and joined the Liberal Democrat Party. In the media business, he developed a commercially-successful way of sprucing up the town-based newspapers in conjunction with information-loaded local websites. In politics, a readiness to use his money and his media for the cause soon won him friends and influence.

Why did Shuttleworth choose the Liberal Democrats? The historical consensus is that he adapted his apparent politics to the party which he thought would give him the easiest ride. He did not win a seat during the 2010 election but, having done well in a tough constituency, he was eased into a safer seat which he won in 2015. In this, the first Labour-Liberal Democrat coalition, he was given a junior posting. He willingly withdrew from the day-to-day running of his burgeoning media empire and, otherwise, demonstrated a commitment to politics over and above business. In 2016, he was promoted to a ministerial position in the Department for Communications. But, having bluffed and bribed his way so far, he was unable, or unwilling, to hold his tongue. Barely a week went by without Shuttleworth himself making the news for trying to edge policy, particularly on net issues, away from the government line. His resignation in 2017 was a spectacular affair, filling far more column centimetres than news about any other junior minister might have done.

Thereafter, he courted more media attention by changing his name legally to William Caxton. He shrugged off criticism from his family and politicians by dismissing it as nothing more than a 'stage name'. He let it be known that he had always admired the original Caxton for being a man of the people, and that he felt an affiliation with his fellow publisher not only because of Tenterden, where he was born, but because of their shared background in the textile industry (great, great grandfather Shuttleworth had been a wealthy mill owner). Within four years, the 21st century's very own Caxton had launched the *Daily Truth* newspaper and the People's Channel. As is well known, they became phenomenally successful, although the former before the latter.

Our paths crossed a third time on 15 October 2024 (the day after Hurricane Emma caused so much devastation in the Caribbean and the east coast of the US) and when they did, the European Union's Euronet legislation was the reason once again.

On joining the Department of Communications, at Yorkshire House, in the autumn of 2022, I had been assigned to Alexander Duck, a lawyer by training, who acted as the British government's chief expert on European internet issues. The draft Euronet bill, the very same one I had worked on with Firey and Brian, had not made it onto the European Union's statute books: it had been stalled by an alliance of Central and Eastern European countries, the newest and poorest Member States. During the years in which it was stalled, though, there had been and continued to be a regular stream of proposals – from all quarters, the States themselves, the European Parliament, the Commission etc – as to how to overcome each impasse. Every one of these required examination and analysis. It was my job to do this, and to make recommendations to Duck, who would then consult his masters before forwarding them to the UK's negotiating team in Brussels.

At the June 2024 gathering of EU leaders in Warsaw, the Polish president, Walenty Czyzewski, skillfully negotiated a deal among the 30 odd European leaders on a range of high profile issues, one of which was agreement to make a final effort to resolve the Euronet proposals. This was a signal for the lobbyists to start up in earnest again. No doubt Caxton's team was busy in Brussels, pressing for the new laws to be as open and liberal as possible, but it was equally active in London, trying to persuade the British government to the same effect. During my two years in the Department of Communications up to then I had been involved in several meetings involving Caxton's companies, but the man himself had never been present. However, that October, he did turn up for a discussion with our minister. On this our third meeting he paid me no attention whatsoever.

Two nights later Gillian and I were arguing about arrangements for the weekend when my phone rang. I went to the office room to answer it. William Caxton. The line was unusually crackly, and the speaker didn't identify himself by name; but I knew who it was. As best I can remember this is what he said.

'Fenn. That was a pleasure to see you the other day. I have a modest proposition for you. A simple exchange. Information for money. I need inside information on the detail, every last detail, about what happens on the Euronet proposals after the ministers agree on the broad outlines next month. What a shame Wilcox is no longer on the case.' This was sarcasm since Caxton had been quoted in the press as saying he thought Firey's retirement in 2022 could be nothing but good news for the Euronet. I said nothing.

'As you know, negotiations on the Euronet proposals are hotting up – I understand the Council and the Parliament are aiming to reach final agreement some time next year.' There was a pause. 'I want reports, Fenn, regular reports.' Another pause. 'What?' he said. I continued to remain mute, my heart was beating fast, and my head was all scrambled. 'I hear you asking about your reward.' I still said nothing. 'Fifty thousand euros.'

Although I had heard rumours about Caxton's unconventional methods, I could not believe this was happening. He stopped talking, and I needed to fill the silence.

'Thank you Mr Caxton, but no, I couldn't do it.'

As I spoke, I knew there must be more to come. He tried again to convince me to take the money. He assured me that extraordinary efforts would be made to ensure that the information could not be traced to me, and that my job and future would be secure. When I refused and threatened to put the phone down and to report the conversation, he turned nasty. He mentioned some debts we had accumulated at the time, and then, when that did not persuade me, he referred to Lola, my net madam of three years.

I don't believe my relationship with Lola was, in any way, illegal at the time; and yet I did feel so ashamed of this secret that I was putty in Caxton's hands. He went on to explain in detail how he could expose the conflict of interest between my work on Euronet and my personal use of the net. Thus, under threat of public exposure in the *Daily Truth*, I did, shamefully, give in to his demands.

For the next year or so, I told myself I was only passing on information that would be in the public domain within hours. Besides, I firmly believed that Caxton's influence over a major international legal text – one which required agreement by the democratic European Parliament and a large number of European nations – would be less than negligible.

CHAPTER 25

IN WHICH I MARRY GILLIAN AND EMPLOY LOLA

I realise, though, that I have raced too far ahead and not explained enough about my personal life.

Gillian did go to Dublin. Having lost my calm when she told me about her decision, I relented and proposed we see each other at weekends. She declined, and it was on her insistence that we broke up yet again. She resented the fact that I would not follow her to Dublin; plus, I am convinced, she never lost the feeling, deep down, that I wasn't good enough for her. After all, I was not handsome and I lacked character (how often did she tell me that over the years). Poor Gillian, she had been spoilt by her theatrical mother, Constance, and could never cope with being ordinary; and, although in some ways she was brighter than I, she lacked any ability to see herself truthfully or to think intelligently about who she was, and how she fitted into the world around her. It took me a long time to recognise and fully acknowledge this, blinded as I was by her social competence and extroversion.

For the best part of a year, autumn 2022 to summer 2023, we did not see each other, apart from one memorable lunch in Lewis's a few days before Christmas. I remember it because there were vast crowds in Oxford Street and long queues at the self-service restaurant. We argued the whole time about the immigrant hunger strikes which had just begun across the Union. They were to dominate the continent's political agenda for months, and lead to 50 or more deaths. Gillian, taking an extremist view, said they should be allowed to die. I wanted her to understand about the long-term advantages to Europe of significant immigration and integration of cultures, and, therefore, the need for softer, more subtle controls. She insisted on the rights of democracy and of giving way to the cry of citizens for protection from the ills of immigration and the crimes of immigrants. But what a pleasure it was to debate with her. She could argue, unlike so many of her friends, without losing a sense of logic. When our intense debate came to a natural conclusion over some Chinese tea brew (to counteract the duck fat in our meal, I was told) Gillian suddenly recanted.

'I think you're right, on the whole. I was only teasing. I don't want them to die. Of course I don't.' I said nothing. I was thinking how much I had missed being with her. And then, as if she had not already done enough to recharge my feelings towards her, she added in a typical off-hand way, 'You know, Kippy, you're one of the most intelligent men I've ever met. I do miss you.' A few seconds later she was gone.

During the spring, we exchanged a few short meaningless messages, while I allowed myself to be dated by a girl called Popsicle who, aptly, died her hair bright colours and wore jeans with neon flashes. We met at The Photography Place where I'd gone after work to see an exhibition of Irish stereo photographs from the 1860s. Some of the photographs had been mounted as large black and white prints, very slightly out of focus and in denial of the stereoscopic effect. However, the exhibition also included a dozen or so stereoscopes placed strategically on shelves allowing one to bend over and experience the full glory of the three-dimensional effect created by the near-twin prints (made from left-eye-view and right-eye-view negatives). I had my eyes glued to a scene called *Picnic by the Dargle*, possibly by Frederick Holland Mares.

I did see the same photograph through a stereoscope again, decades later, which might explain why I can recall the 3D image so well. Despite 250 years of technological development, I cannot reproduce the same effect on my wallscreen, and I must make do with this slightly out-of-focus reproduction to remind me of the detail. In the foreground, a group of ladies and gentlemen, wearing formal dress, are seated at a picnic table, looking at the camera, or drinking, or talking. They are all framed by a bower of trees. In the background, to one side, a river flows towards and past the picnickers.

What I remember most is how the picture carried my eye: first to the front of the long picnic table, past an upturned top hat, and from side to side examining each face, bearded or bonneted, to the far end; from there across the luxuriant foliage behind the picnickers to a cascade in the river set far back; down with the river widening into the foreground towards a darkish pool at the side; and, from there, finally to a second upturned top hat on an empty stretch of bench in front of the table, thus providing the visual clue to return to the other top hat. My eye was then free to examine the people again, this time more leisurely, and to wonder who they were, why they were there, and what I might say to them if I were sitting at the same table.

'Can someone else have a peep?' Having dallied in black and white on the soft and pleasant banks of the Dargle, I was rudely thrust back into the acute present, by a shrill voice and then, on turning round, by multicoloured clothes. I stepped aside in mild shock.

'Wow.' She stood up after a few seconds and, finding me still there, opened a conversation. 'Isn't it amazing that they could do this stuff so long ago. It makes you wonder what we've achieved in the last centuries doesn't it?' It wasn't a rhetorical question, and I couldn't agree with her, so we ended up in the tearoom talking for an hour or more, before moving on to her pad nearby.

Popsicle, who made a living by photographing furniture for advertisements, proved a fun companion for a couple of months. More importantly she was instrumental in nurturing my interest in old photographs. But photography was the only thing she could take seriously; otherwise, she divided her time between watching soap operas on television and 'going out'. It didn't matter where, a club, a gallery, a cinema, anywhere. We were so unsuited, it was bizarre: I would no more introduce her to my work friends, than she would admit to her shallow arty/clubby friends that she was fucking (or rather not fucking) a civil servant. We only survived as a couple through to the spring because she saw my impotence as a real challenge. I gave way to her vain and utterly ineffective attempts to deal with it because I was lonely, and because I was becoming increasingly concerned about my growing reliance on Lola.

One day in late June – this is still 2023 – Gillian messaged me: 'Kippy darling, You must come to Dublin. Come for a week. Come in August, I'll take holiday and show you round. You'll love this town and the country. Not the last week, though. Let me know soonest.' The sub-text was clear – she wanted to try again. And so did I.

Apart from seeing Gillian, and a visit to the splendid Liffy Theatre to see a dense play about the 20th century troubles, the highlight of my week in Ireland was a trip to the Wicklow mountains. I'm not convinced we found the right picnic place by the Dargle river, but it was very similar to the one in the photo. We walked along the shingle in Bray, took an Irish cream tea in Enniskerry, and at Powerscourt Falls grumbled together about the inadequacy of waterfalls in the British Isles, Gillian having experienced Niagara and I having been to Iguaçu. There was one day when Gillian had to work, so I took myself to the National Library and, in the photographic print department, chatted amiably for more than an hour to an elderly expert on albumen prints.

Towards the end of the week, we were sitting in one of Bewley's coffee shacks talking about the delights of Ireland, when Gillian suddenly announced she was fed up with Dublin and her job and would be returning to London in the autumn. I responded with genuine delight. Although I tried to elicit a reason for the change of heart, she would not explain it. Instead, she suggested, as casually as if she were asking the waiter for another menthol tea, that we should marry and live together. It took a few seconds for the marriage proposal to sink in, and then another few to compose a response. Gillian stared at my eyes, as if daring me to be flippant, or to say 'hold on', or to argue. So I did none of those things. Instead I spoke meekly.

'That's a good idea.'

Later on, I tried to quiz her several times about why things hadn't worked out in Dublin, but she would never say. Whether there was a man involved, or she didn't take to the work, or she had failed to establish a social life, I never discovered. Dublin's loss was my gain, or so I thought at the time.

Thus it was that, by November, we (as in Gillian) had decided on a duplex apartment in a terraced house on Torbay Road, not half a mile from her previous flat (which she had rented out while in Dublin and then sold for a reasonable profit). Tom gifted me 50,000 euros, which allowed my share of the deposit to equal that of Gillian's. Mostly, I let her organise the decor, and the fixtures and fittings, offering only token resistance here and there to expensive items. Over and above a sizeable kitchen, a lounge and our bedroom, there were two further rooms. I took the one downstairs as my office, but not before a major row with Gillian who insisted that if I was to have an office than she needed one too, which meant we would have no spare bedroom. In addition, there was a walled yard at the back which carried a patch of lawn and a few neglected shrubs.

In January 2024, Gillian began work as a public relations 'junior executive' for Mandrill Publications. It is worth noting that the company was sold to H.O.N. in the early 30s and subsequently submerged into the Caxton empire, but not before the megalomaniac himself had departed the world.

In March, we married. It was a simple affair at the Marylebone Registry Office. I'll list a few of the people who were there, if I can find a photograph. Here's one. There's my mother Julie looking perturbed and flushed with Alan's arm around her shoulder. She looked old on that day, I remember, much older than six months earlier when I'd joined her and some friends for a dinner to celebrate her 50th birthday. It was Gillian that noticed my mother's distressed looks, she thought they were directed against herself. I thought they might have more to do with Tom's presence. He was there with an ugly girl in high heels. Horace Merriweather took the role of best man, although, to be honest, I would have preferred Alfred, who sent a very touching camclip from Lagos. At the reception in a nearby brasserie, Horace embarrassed me with several anecdotes from our time at Witley Academic.

On Gillian's side, her wayward mother Constance was there with a husband who Gillian flatly refused to talk to let alone consider as a step-father. Her mother's father, John Tilson was in a wheelchair aided by a distant relation of hers that Gillian had never met before. Gillian, and I for that matter, had a lot of time for her grandfather John. We visited him in his Hertford retirement home once a month, and often took him out to visit show gardens or to sit and watch the anglers by the River Lee. He was born on the eve of the Second World War. After spells in the army and the hotel trade, he spent most of his life trying to run bars of various types. He was good at it, or so he said, but could never settle in one place. He told excellent tales about London in the 1960s, which is where and when he played happy families with Constance's mother, Sydney in the 1970s and 1980s, and Spain in the early 2000s, after all of which he returned to the UK for free health care. In addition to family, Gillian invited a variety of friends, but Yvonne – she in this photo with a thorny look in her eyes – is the only one I remember.

Of my friends, there was Pete Sampson, Peter de Roo with Livia, by then his wife, and Phil Rumble, a work colleague who played in the civil service volleyball team, with his girlfriend Melanie Koper.

Two weeks later Julie told me about the tumour in her left breast, diagnosed only days before the wedding. With a combination of pills, surgery and radiotherapy, she recovered by the end of the year. Oddly, the illness helped Julie and Gillian bond; without it, they might never have softened towards each other.

I have not forgotten that I am backtracking, trying to give some shape to my life in the 20s, and to the part played by Caxton and his dirty tricks. I had been a client of Lola, off and on, since the year I'd spent in Brussels. Initially, I had balked at paying a premium for personal service, but I soon tired of trawling the net for photos or clips to arouse and satisfy my needs. For a modest fee, Lola, whoever she was and wherever she was, looked after me. To begin with, she provided a regular supply of high quality striptease clips. Then, inspired by Popsicle's passion for art photography, I became keen on black and white photos of innocent-looking girls caught in various states of undress by an apparently hidden camera. Lola had no difficulty in providing me with an endless supply. Surprisingly, she also had access to an excellent library of classic erotica, much of which I stored on Neil. Subsequently, I began to delve into the delights of voyeuristic camclips, despite worrying about how they might have been obtained. Lola reassured me they were all fake, and that I should 'just enjoy them'.

Lola was good at her, or his, job. I assumed she was a woman, but she may have been a man for all I really knew. She was well educated and almost certainly British by the evidence of her writing. Apart from the obvious difference that we never met, our relationship was similar to one I might have had with a physical fitness trainer or therapist. I always felt she was interested in me, and would give thought to what I wanted and would appreciate, surely the mark of a successful professional. But, with Gillian's return to London and our marriage, I made a determined effort to forego Lola's excellent services.

Soon after settling into our Kilburn home, Gillian and I sank into a habitual pattern of sex once a week on Saturday night. Most of the time, I was able to function adequately, there being no pressure to seduce or perform, but there was very little pleasure in the act, neither for her or for me. And there was no question of any discussion or experiment. This was all the more disappointing because I could never put out of my mind the night Gillian had waltzed naked around the bed and shown off a lacy bra; I never stopped hoping I might witness that persona again. Within months (this is embarrassing to confess), I was back, secretly, furtively, at the computer screen. My relationship with Lola, who remained attentive to my changing needs for over ten years until the day she net-vanished, was to outlast that with my wife. This is surely a comment on the 21st century or on me or on both.

Sex was not the only problem. Gillian had a habit of sulking for the most trivial of reasons. I viewed her behaviour as a remnant from childhood, and my behaviour as diplomatic coping. But, in fact, I was no more in control than one of Pavlov's dogs and would do my utmost to try and please her back into a good mood, at least in the early years.

On a few issues, I did take a stance, and then, when it became apparent that the sulking had not worked, a big row would ensue. The very fact that I had allowed things to get that far, usually meant I was not prepared to give way at all. Since both of us hated losing our temper, we suffered afterwards to different degrees. I suspect Gillian deemed such arguments as a flaw in the marriage, and evidence that she had made a wrong decision in marrying me. This caused the kind of conflict in her psyche that she was poorly equipped to deal with. I do not know if inwardly she thought about these things at all, but outwardly her sulkiness took on a nasty tone. Whenever, after one of these arguments, I attempted to appease her, she would snap out some vicious comment, thereby subjecting me to a week or two of what can only be called punishment. Although such problems in our relationship became more complex later, especially with children in the frame, the basic pattern did not change.

CHAPTER 26

IN WHICH I SNOOP FOR WILLIAM CAXTON

After the dreadful call from Caxton and my weakling submission to his bullying, it did not take long to discover that my net service provider (NSP), a company called Velocity, was part-owned by Caxton's empire. In my files at Yorkshire House, I searched out a study of the European NSP market and discovered that the London-based Caxton Enterprises, directly or indirectly (through 27 different companies including Velocity), controlled 22% of the mainstream Union-based market for NSPs. I can only guess at the rest: Caxton must have used an army of personally-appointed technicians whose job it was to collect and interpret information about key people whom he wished to manipulate. How many others were there? I had no idea. Most of Caxton's biographers steered clear of making any detailed accusations of illegal activity. One sensational book, published after his death, did quote extensively from an anonymous inside source who went so far as to call him an 'habitual blackmailer'.

The revised Euronet Regulation was finally agreed in April 2025 – more than six years after I had worked on the original proposals with Firey Wilcox in the European Parliament. And even with that agreement in place, there was a furious row about the location of the new Euronet Agency which wasn't settled for another few months, not until the Stockholm meeting of EU leaders, in June 2025.

Since its inception, the Euronet had been run by an off-shoot of the European Commission in Brussels, but the new Regulation legislated for a much grander Agency, independent of the Commission. Dozens of documents relating to this, and the siting of several other agencies, had crossed my desk. It was a multi-layered, multi-faceted auction between the EU's Member States that had gone on for over a year. Every conceivable permutation had been touted by every interested party. Cardiff, Milan, Bonn and Warsaw were all on the short list. The Stockholm meeting was the EU's self-imposed deadline for a decision. A week prior to that meeting, Reuters claimed a scoop to the effect that Bonn would get the Agency. Chancellor Magdalene Kessler, she who had come to public attention more than ten years earlier with vigorous criticism of government policy on immigration, denied the story immediately. So did the rest of the EU's leaders. But the Polish premier, Walenty Czyzewski, was not satisfied with these denials. He broke ranks and told *The Wall Street Journal* that, at the Warsaw conclave the previous June, he had been promised the Agency in exchange for his support for the overall Euronet legislative package. Fuelled by this evidence that such furtive arrangements really did take place in secret, the media went white hot, even though everyone with half a live brain knows that such deals are at the heart of politics. It was fun to watch from the inside and the outside. Warsaw won in the end.

Incidentally, it gave me enormous satisfaction to see the text of the final legislation crystallise with Firey Wilcox's three tier system firmly in place, substantial funds, paid directly by EU taxation, and sufficient legislative controls and remedies to give it a real chance.

Between October 2024 and April 2025, during the final period of negotiations, I spoke to Caxton's go-between, who called himself Carter, an average of twice a month. Having been advised not to change my NSP, Carter gave me access codes so we could talk in a way he assured me was secure. Fortunately or not, Gillian, who had fallen pregnant in early autumn, became too self-absorbed to enquire into why I had office calls at night. I did not like lying to her, and, at times, I wished she had quizzed me more intrusively, for I might have been tempted to explain all. I gave Carter the nitty-gritty of each Euronet meeting I attended, both important and unimportant, as well as any extra information I had gleaned from paperwork coming in from Brussels. At his insistence, I also outlined the forthcoming schedule of meetings so he would know when to contact me.

I did have the presence of mind to call Pete Sampson for help in setting up a discreet way of recording Carter's calls. He chided me lightly for only getting in touch when I needed something, and then for not bothering to confide in him about the purpose of my shenanigans. But, truth be told, he had become increasingly involved in academic life and had gravitated socially towards other potential profs, while my own free time was largely under Gillian's control. Pete's effort was wasted. I was never able to manoeuvre Carter into mentioning Caxton's name, nor get him to provide a hint of why he, Carter, was interested in my information. If I said, for example, 'Are you sure, Caxton really wants to know all this detail?', Carter would answer me, ingenuously, 'Who?'. All the wrongdoing in these taped conversations was mine.

On Easter Monday, days after the Euronet legislation – the Agency's location apart – was finally agreed, a hand-delivered envelope, addressed to me, lay on the mat at the foot of the stairs inside our front door. It contained a bundle of 100 euro notes – 500 of them. The money itself gave me a slight buzz of guilty satisfaction, but it was far more pleasing to think that this distasteful episode in my life was over. Gillian was asleep, so I hid the envelope in my office. Thereafter, I withdrew only two or three notes each week.

Caxton had clearly put much effort into lobbying on the Euronet Regulation, yet, at the final count, I could not detect any specific way he had affected the outcome, nor could any of my colleagues with whom I discussed the subject generally. Having lost the main battle for a free and easy regime to continue, his people focused on ensuring that the complex technical aspects of the telecoms world suited, or did not conflict with, the way his companies were developing their network systems and customer relations, about which I knew nothing.

CHAPTER 27
IN WHICH I BLAME CAXTON FOR THE SPYCAM SCANDAL

That said, I do believe it was Caxton who orchestrated the great spycam scandal. Although it was never proved, and again no biographer was ever willing to point the finger directly, it had all the hallmarks of Caxton showmanship. If I am correct and it was him, then it was a rare error of judgement. He must have calculated that exposés of public figures would lead to general outrage, and consequently make it awkward for EU politicians who wished to support a tightening of the regulations, which might outlaw or hinder such important exposés. Caxton was right about the level of public interest, as magnified by the media, but he was wrong about the political response.

In brief, this is what I recall. During that winter, 2024-25, the one in which the final and intense negotiations on the Euronet Regulation were taking place, there was a series of extraordinary live relays on the internet from secret cameras inside offices and homes of important/famous people. The spycams, it later transpired, were installed on some pretence such as a gas leak or a telecom problem by tradesmen who subsequently could never be traced. It was not only advances in microcam capabilities that made this scurrilous activity possible, but in battery technology, meaning that such cams could be tiny and transmit data for a reasonable amount of time without requiring an external power supply. For each episode, a producer, sitting in Albania or Georgia or wherever, monitored the feeds from a set of cameras and, at the moment one of them contained something newsworthy, broadcast it live on the internet through a specially designed website. Instant messages sent to key media around the world ensured widespread coverage.

The first episode led to the resignation, and subsequent suicide, of Jonathan Underwood, a High Court judge, who the world saw beat his wife in their bedroom. Only a few witnessed the two minute clip live, but it was repeated endlessly on news and net broadcasts for days and weeks with the netsite address visibly stamped into the clip. The second episode came three days later, by which time millions had signed up for an email alert from the site. For seven minutes, we watched in amazement as three members of the Irish government sitting in cosy armchairs discussed the possible assassination of Sian Linton. Linton was a fierce campaigner in Northern Ireland against the pace of movement towards a unified Ireland, and had, by then, become a hero to many old people in the province who did not want to become Irish. It emerged later that the Irish MPs, all suspected of being Irish Republican Army (IRA) sympathisers 30 years earlier, had been secretly asked, by active remnants of the IRA, for their private opinions on the killing of Linton. The clip ended with a phone call, and one man, fear pulsating across his face, ushering the other two out of the room. The Irish government fell the next day.

This second episode resulted in all mainstream net service providers being persuaded to block access to the exposé site and to any sites set up to replace it. But such efforts were useless. Many, simply signed up, almost overnight, to renegade net providers, beyond the Union's frontiers, and the several more spycam exposés were circulated as wildly and widely as the first two.

Ted Ullswater, a hugely popular family comedian and actor, was caught at his computer terminal sifting through a collection of paedophile pornography. He ended up in jail, as did several company chairman who were shown to have hatched a stock market fraud. Some of these spycamclips did have a clear public interest element, but the purpose of others was less clear. There was one which exposed the illegitimate child of the BBC's chairman, another in which we saw an attractive young Labour MP begin canoodling with a man other than her husband, and a third in which we watched the daughter of the most senior European Union official involved with telecoms regulation mouthing off to a friend about her father and his racist views.

Although only a dozen episodes were seen on the net in this orchestrated campaign, a further 100 or so individuals or organisations owned up to having found illegal spycams. But surely millions of us must have checked and double-checked every nook and cranny of our homes and offices.

The public loved these scandals. The media loved them too, especially since the owners of the site and the spycams were anonymous and were in no position to enforce copyrights. Despite various legal and political actions to censor repetition of the episodes here and there, the media found ways to get round whatever restrictions were imposed, and rejoiced in doing so. Caxton, I feel sure, hoped these episodes would, one way or another, provide convincing proof that regulation should not be so tight that it would end up sheltering people from the truth. He miscalculated. The EU's Member States and the European Parliament made no further liberal concessions at all: the agreed Euronet Regulation effectively legislated for three controlled nets – Solar (a largely open net which proved in time to be an effective alternative to the internet), Doré (business) and Sage (academic) – and tight regulation of net service providers. It also made provisions to ensure that telecom access to non-EU providers was either very expensive or illegal.

Recorded and edited spycamclips became a media staple, especially those legally obtained, or illegally obtained but with such powerful public interest they could not be ignored, yet it was only in the more liberal developing countries, especially Brazil and Russia, that live spycam broadcasts were witnessed on a regular basis for a further decade or so. The most famous of these, of course, was the one that exposed the Georgian home affairs minister as being in the pay of the Russian mafia, and which may or may not, as I said earlier, have led to Caxton's murder.

CHAPTER 28

IN WHICH WE SEEK THERAPY AND CRYSTAL IS BORN

To return to more domestic matters, Gillian informed me of her pregnancy one evening in September 2024. I arrived home from work and found her peeling potatoes in the kitchen. She spoke without even turning around to acknowledge my presence. I said something inane. Under Gillian's direction and in her social world, we transformed seamlessly into a couple who were expecting their first child.

Apart from the constant shadow of Carter's calls and my feelings of guilt, this was a happy time for Gillian and me. She was rarely unwell, and she liked her work. We both enjoyed sharing our daily experiences in the evening. But, whereas I would simply listen to her accounts, she would become involved in mine, deftly exaggerating my own criticism of colleagues' work or behaviour and reinforcing the importance of what I was doing and how I was dealing with policy issues or departmental manoeuvring. Gillian was especially adept at advising me on how to deal with over-ambitious colleagues and on how to make sure my own position was properly valued by those above me. It is Gillian I must thank for my civil service grade promotion since she persuaded me when and how to argue for it, and – later – for saving my civil servant's status after the awful *Daily Truth* business.

Crystal arrived on 25 May, within two days of the predicted date, and only a few weeks after I had received my payoff from Caxton. Gillian was not keen on ante-natal (or post-natal) advice, and we never discussed the consequences of her being pregnant nor did we make any plans together. Whenever the subject came up at a dinner party or with friends in a bar, it always surprised me how much she had already thought about, and planned for our child. After one scan, she told me, in an offhand way, that our baby was a girl. About three weeks before the nine month period was up, she finally took maternity leave, and used the time to convert her office into a baby room. She opted for Miss Princess wallpaper and matching cot, but I was not involved in the choice of decor or baby paraphernalia. Nor was I involved – and this did rankle – in the choice of name. A few weeks later, we purchased a fashionable and expensive sofa-bed for the lounge which we could use when Gillian's mother, Constance, or occasionally my mother, came to stay for a night or two.

Tom was abroad the day Crystal was born, but he sent a message of congratulation. He approved of the numerical date 25/5/25. 'Must be magical,' he wrote, making a slight quip against Gillian's mother. But he also noted, with dismay, that Martian Four was due to be launched only three days hence. Julie came to London to give Gillian a touch of motherly comfort since Constance was unavailable.

It was 18 years later that I learned, from Crystal herself, about her name, about how, as a teenager, Gillian had been enamoured of an author, very famous at one time, called Lucretia Quant. She had written several post-fantasy books with an anti-heroine called Crystal.

On that same occasion – I am skipping far forward here – it was late summer in 2043, I was delighted that my daughter wanted to see me, and optimistic that she might have good news, about a job perhaps, or a permanent boyfriend. However, I was perturbed that she had decided to spend our time together walking in the poorer areas around Paddington. To begin with, we talked backwards about things we had never discussed, her mother, our separation, and about Crystal's early schooling; only then did we talk about her current friends and her ex-boyfriend, Vidrio. I asked about her situation and plans, and she began telling me about the notorious Pearl Worthington. I could and should have been wiser and seen her talk not as a wilful teenage stunt, a poke in the eye to society, but as an agonising personal cry of pain. If I had, she might not have taken the Pearly Way only a few weeks later. No, that's fanciful self-recrimination, I am not convinced there was anything I could have done at that late stage.

Why do the worst memories, the bad and the sad, always flick into one's thoughts far more often, far more easily, than the best? And why are they easier to write about, to define and to reflect on?

Gillian and I had a difficult six months, more or less until she stopped breast-feeding. Crystal then slept through the night, and we took on a local childminder for five or more hours a day, so Gillian could return to work part-time and so we could socialise some evenings and weekends.

I aimed to be a father by the equality book as they used to say, but Gillian did not want, nor could she suffer, my input or involvement in Crystal's caring. If I had concerns about her needs or wants, it was simplest to keep my own counsel. What I found most disturbing, though, was Gillian's mechanical responses to Crystal's bawling. She would try, in turn, a combination of the possible causes for the distress – the need for drink/food, winding, or a change of nappy – and if none of them worked, she would let her bawl until she fell asleep. I was not allowed to comfort her, unless Gillian deemed it the right thing to do. But, as I say, after that initial period of six months or so we settled down, and for a year lived in relative harmony.

Every two or three weeks we were on the move with Crystal, whether to see Julie, and Alan if around, in Godalming, Constance (so long as her husband was out) in Canterbury, Gillian's grandfather John in Hertford, or friends wherever. We got on particularly well, I remember, with Phil and Melanie Rumble. They lived in a large apartment, bought by Melanie's parents, in Greenwich, and had a baby boy a few months younger than Crystal. They both, though, found it impossible to remain friendly after the *Daily Truth* article – a matter which I must soon get to.

It is possible that the fresh breakdown in my relationship with Gillian, which became apparent in January 2027, was indirectly caused by the effect on me of new demands from Carter/Caxton. However, I do not believe my behaviour changed in any noticeable way. If I was partly responsible, it was Gillian that announced we had a problem; it was Gillian that proceeded to prove it by finding reasons for endless bouts of sulking and snapping criticisms; and it was Gillian that insisted, because I was causing the friction, that I see a therapist. I do not wish to over-use therapy language, but this was a denial of reality, a relapse too many, a power trip too far. I flatly refused to do any such thing. The truth was too obvious: having become diverted for a while by owning a child, Gillian had, once again, grown tired of me.

I proposed we both see a partnership therapist. Gillian was horrified at first, but when I continued to challenge her plan that I alone seek therapy, she reluctantly agreed. She chose Rosemary Acklow, on the recommendation of one of her friends. It was an uncomfortable experience. Gillian confessed, on leaving Acklow's Hampstead premises once, that she found the whole thing 'dirty'. She employed the word 'filthy' another time to describe a session in which Acklow had tried to broach the subject of our sex life, Gillian having earlier exclaimed definitively that our problems had 'nothing to do with sex'. Most often, we simply sat in the consulting room answering questions and saying as little as possible. While I would spend long periods, journeying to or from work on the crowded metro or during some banal meeting, going over these discussions in my mind, I doubt Gillian gave them a moment's consideration beyond our own brief post-session comments.

With several months of inadequate progress behind us, Rosemary suggested we should install, in one or two rooms at home, cams and the necessary recording equipment so that we could 'review together', with 'the facts before us', what was happening in our relationship. Since the early 20s, cam-therapy had been fashionable: examples of couples willing to expose themselves filled the inside pages of life-style magazines; and minor film and sports celebrities found financial comfort in selling edited therapy camclips and camstills to the media. Some obsessed and very rich clients would set up a direct live link to their therapist so they could be honestly monitored at any time. I had learned about this in *GlobeOne*, the biggest selling Western political weekly. I had also read, I should confess, Julia Derwent's pop-science classic from the 2010s, *Why Humans are Trees or the Hardships of Adulthood*, which took a massive swipe at the whole psychotherapy industry. In summary, Derwent argued that it was as impracticable for an individual to change his or her major behaviour traits as it would be for a mature tree to reconstruct its branches, or, I suppose, for a leopard to change its spots.

Neither of us would make up our mind about Rosemary's proposal. On the plus side, Gillian favoured the idea because it carried a degree of social kudos, while I secretly expected the recordings would show me in a reasonable light. Conversely, I loathed the thought of the extra expense we couldn't afford, in addition to the 1,000 euros a month we were paying for the therapy, and Gillian bridled at the possibility of sordid revelations. I think the reason we finally agreed to rent the equipment stemmed from our mutual trust of Rosemary Acklow, for she had somehow managed to keep a straight bat despite our various off-cutters, leg-spinners and googlies.

Predictably, the money we paid to Acklow was wasted. To begin with, Gillian and I were too conscious of the cameras, which constrained our behaviour in the lounge and eating area where the cameras were located. She and I would spend an hour or so prior to the sessions with Rosemary, speeding through the recordings in search of something suitable to show her, but for six weeks there was nothing remotely useful.

Then, out of the blue, Gillian announced she was with child again. It was Crystal's second birthday, a Tuesday in late May, at breakfast, when she casually informed Crystal and me that she was pregnant. Crystal, whose broad uncomprehending smile was covered over by banana mush at the time, was more interested in the pile of presents waiting for her.

'I hope you don't mind,' Gillian said. 'It'll be a boy this time, I know it will. I did the test this morning. It must have been the weekend Mummy was here, which makes it five and half weeks. I was shocked when I saw the test result, but now I'm thrilled. Thrilled.'

'A lounge baby then,' I said light-heartedly to cover over my lack of emotion at the news. Odd but true, we had better, i.e. less inadequate, sex on the sofa-bed than upstairs in our own bedroom, where Constance and Julie both slept when visiting. Maybe I should have tried to focus Acklow's learning onto that enigma.

'It's perfect timing. If we'd left it any later they'd be too far apart to play together when they got older. Crystal, you'll adore him. We'll have to move of course. Get somewhere bigger. How about Finchley, or Barnet.'

'Not yet. Can we finish breakfast.' Having been sidelined by Gillian over Crystal's nurturing, I was short on enthusiasm second time round.

'I don't want to tell anyone yet, not even Mummy.' She carried her bowl through to the sink, and on her way back stopped to wipe Crystal's face. She plonked a kiss on her fair head, and moved sideways to plonk one on me too, on the dark uncombed mess that was my hair. 'I'm sorry. Let's dump Acklow. Let's move on. It's a waste of money. And, anyway I think you're winning. The weather's looking reasonable. It's Southampton on Friday isn't it. Merriweather had better make it, or I'll kick his ass.'

Thus, almost instantly, she became better natured, more interested in me and my work; and she actively re-engaged us socially. The cam equipment contract was cancelled and we said goodbye, with feigned reluctance, to Rosemary Acklow.

Gillian. Gillian. Gillian. She could make me feel so bad, so un-able; and then, in an instant, she could turn me round.

***

I mentioned leg-breaks and googlies earlier, which I knew at the time were inappropriate metaphors, but as I write I have one eye on a corner of the wallscreen where England are doing well in the second of the triangular two day internationals against Australia and India being played at Lord-it Lords. Lord-it at Lords! What a crass advert the cricket establishment employed during the years when England slipped out of the five year Test League. I was diverted from writing earlier this morning as Flora revealed that her famous son, Barnaby Pattison, now dead, had bowled for England on no less than 53 occasions. She proudly rattled off his various impressive statistics before charging out mid-sentence to stop herself from boring me.

CHAPTER 29

IN WHICH HORACE IS ELECTED TO PARLIAMENT

After a full five year term in which the Lib-Dems had worked effectively with minority support from the Green Party, there was a long-awaited general election that very Thursday, after Crystal's birthday, and Horace Merriweather, who was contesting a seat for the first time in the Southampton Test constituency, had insisted we come to a celebration/commiseration party on Friday.

Before being selected by the local Progressive Party group, thanks in part to his friendship with the Member for Southampton Itchen, up-and-coming Terrance Spoon, one local paper had strongly objected to Horace on the grounds that he had no connection with the area. He responded immediately by buying, and moving to, a house in Totton, which was the venue for the Friday gathering. Nevertheless, he retained the Kensington pad (for me, conveniently near The Photography Place) as a useful London base, not only for scooting to Westminster, but for too many short-term love affairs with fickle lads.

Initially, Gillian had dismissed the idea of us making a weekend of it, and ordered that I should go alone; but, having announced her pregnancy at breakfast, by nightfall she had organised a weekend holiday, starting with Horace's party. It also included a day-trip to Cowes, a visit, at my request, to my grandmother's memorial in the scented remembrance garden at Parsonville, and Sunday lunch with my mother on the way back.

Horace's commitment and hard work paid off. He was elected with a slim majority, lower than his predecessor who had retired, but better than the local polls had been predicting. He joined a larger group of opposition right-wing MPs than there had been in the previous parliament. The Liberal Democrats were again the largest party, but their leader, Adam Jones, found himself forming a government not only with the Greens but also – incredibly – the Republican Party. The Green Party, which had only been able to tinker with government policy during the previous administration, was to wield far more power in the coming years.

As for coalition with the Republicans, it was widely known that Jones was not in favour of abandoning a monarchy, but that, during his previous five years as prime minister, there had been reports of tetchy meetings with King William. The Liberal Democrats and the Greens had a majority of 12 in the new parliament and some argued that Jones could have made do without the seven Republican MPs. He foresaw, though, that he could use the Republicans to make life easier for himself in Parliament, while, at the same time, sending a political signal to the King that it was time to win a few friends and influence people. Jones did not concede to the main Republican demand – for a referendum on the monarchy – until the spring of 2030. Even though there was a huge majority for keeping the King and all his trappings, and the poll effectively ruined the Republican Party, Jones was harshly criticised from several sides both for having gotten into bed with the Republicans, and then for allowing the referendum so soon. Some historians, however, believe Jones saved the monarchy for the next half century. Without Jones's forthright approach, and without the early referendum, the Republican Party might have continued to expand.

Jones resigned a few weeks after the vote, insisting there had been no link between his decision to call a referendum and to resign. In *Jonesy – The Autobiography*, he claimed that, from the moment he made the deal with the Republican Party in 2027, he had a good idea of how he would handle the issue, since he knew the referendum would have to come in the second half of the parliament, and he wanted to resign before the next election campaign. Moreover, he claimed it was for the sake of the Party that he planned to deflect onto himself some of the negative public opinion stemming from the decision to call the referendum. His selfless act did not make much difference: by the time of the next election, in 2031, the public were very tired of the Lib-Dems, and alarmed by the rise of the First Tuesday Movement. Moreover, they were greedily interested in a revived Conservative Alliance (as dominated by the Progressive Party), and excited by the formation of Caxton's People's Party.

Returning to 2027 and Horace's party, my old school-friend was on outstanding form. Having spent the day dashing from one interview to another and touring the constituency thanking various groups and helpers, he was ready to have a drink, and let his hair down with a few friends. Crystal conveniently fell asleep in a spare bedroom (from whence you could see the famous Eling tide-mill) so Gillian and I could join the other 30 or so guests. Timothy, Horace's younger brother who was training to be an accountant, kept everyone's glasses full. Horace's agent, whose name I forget, left early, but not before having a large group of us in stitches with a stream of electioneering jokes.

Not all of Horace's nearest and dearest were there. His parents, who had been staying in a plush hotel, flew back to their villa in Nice that afternoon. Nor was Horace's then partner present, having not been invited. None of us knew about him, not that is until a couple of years when he sold his story to one of Caxton's rags. He'd done so in a fit of jealousy having found out about yet another of Horace's rent boys in London. The story effectively scuppered Horace's chances of being given a junior minister position during the short Conservative Alliance-People's Party coalition in the early 30s.

Terrance Spoon – he who was to be a minister in the 30s and prime minister for three short years in the 40s – dropped in to the party for a few minutes, no longer than he could remain the centre of attention. We all stopped our conversations to gather round him and Horace. Spoon asked us to drink to one of 'the youngest and certainly the brightest' of the new intake; and Horace asked us to raise a glass 'to a gifted politician who will go far, very far'. There was loud applause. I slipped out of the room to check on Crystal. I gently tried to pull a thumb out of her mouth, but when she threatened to wake, I desisted. I wonder to this day if Horace had not pinned his banner so firmly to Spoon's rickety flagpole, whether he might not have achieved more than he did, despite the early setback caused by Caxton's scandalmongering.

CHAPTER 30
IN WHICH I EXPLAIN ABOUT UNACCEPTABLE CONTENT

More than 18 months after the first pay-off, and the winter before Gillian became pregnant again, Carter returned into my life. The phone call came in early January 2027. He said it would be to our 'mutual advantage' if we started talking again on a regular basis.

The Euronet Agency in Warsaw was due to launch the three tier Euronet system a year hence, on 1 January 2028. By this time, I had been given more responsibility to guide the policy and legislative interface between London, Brussels and Warsaw. Duck remained my chief, but his own portfolio of jobs had widened, which meant I often dealt directly with junior government ministers, or, by cam-conference, with high-ranking officials in the European Commission and the Agency. In late 2026, the Commission put forward new draft laws affecting the launch and operation of the Agency and its regulated system. It was necessary, the proposal said, to close various loopholes that had come to light, and improve the efficacy of the already approved legislation in ways that had not been imagined earlier. In addition, the Commission put forward draft guidelines on Unacceptable Content.

Before concluding with the lurid details of my own particular involvement in the matter, I need to explain about Unacceptable Content. Within ten years of the internet being widely available and used in the home, there was already general concern that it could lead to unfortunate and unacceptable consequences for society. In some parts of the less-democratic world, governments were able to exercise a high degree of control over their citizens' access from the beginning; but in the free western world, where unfettered access had been championed from day one by those who had developed the concept of the internet, and where data privacy was of public concern, it was more challenging to prove the need for control, and consequently to set up effective regulation. The early Euronet had failed to expand, but damning evidence against the unregulated net continued to accumulate. This evidence took two main forms: the exposure of sites linked to illegal activities, such as terrorism, paedophilia, racism or human-trafficking; and sociological and psycho-sociological research showing how certain net activities (particularly pornography, gambling and netgaming) were undermining elements of society's social fabric.

Although there were, of course, several sides to every argument, by the late 2010s, the weight of opinion was beginning to coalesce around the view that, for example, the widespread, cheap and easy availability of hardcore pornography to young people, especially teenagers, was contributing to a worringly high proportion of single and socially inadequate men, an acceleration in the breakdown of marriages and long-term relationships, and a continuing decline in the birth rate. The EVE movement, which expanded rapidly and became a very effective lobby during the debate on Unacceptable Content, emerged rather belatedly in response to the pornography explosion during the early part of the century.

In some ways, the gambling issue was similar, since, as with pornography, the internet made it possible and very easy, for a large number of youngsters, impressionable and still developing their characters, to indulge in, and become addicted to, a habit which for many people, as the research shows, led them into life-ruining situations. And, with regard to netgaming, there were serious concerns about permanent psychological damage to some individuals, focused on a concept called 'general alienation' and, more specifically, on bursts of 'random violence'.

There had been no attempt to define Unacceptable Content in the original proposals that Firey, Brian and I had worked on in Brussels. The European Commission's aim had been to win agreement on the general idea of having a harmonised censorship regime, rather than to get bogged down in the details too early. The long delays in agreement on the Euronet Regulation were partly caused by a few countries awkwardly insisting on an early and clear definition of Unacceptable Content. And, ultimately, the European Union had only been able to adopt the new Euronet legislation in 2025 because a decision on the details of what material the Agency would prohibit was deferred.

Very simply, the legislation stated that the operational and content guidelines for the business-oriented Euronet (Doré) and the academic Euronet (Sage) would be decided by the Agency's management board which included many different types of experts and officials. But, for the basic Euronet (Solar), which was to be an open net, guidelines for Unacceptable Content would be drafted by the Commission and then agreed at European Union level. This would be no easy matter, with many and opposing political interests having strong voices throughout the many Member States.

Working documents from Brussels and policy positions from lobby groups had been crossing my desk on a regular basis, though it was not until the draft guidelines were presented in December 2026, that real negotiations started in earnest. It was tough going, but the guidelines were adopted as EU law during 2028, leading, finally, to the actual launch of the three tier Euronet the following July, 18 months later than planned. Although, the guidelines were not as rigid as many, such as those in the EVE movement, wanted, they were much tighter than the FreeNet movement, in unholy alliance with privacy campaigners, had demanded. Furthermore, the fact that they existed at all meant it would become much easier thereafter to adjust them, tightening or loosening strands of the policy according to the winds of political and social change.

CHAPTER 31

IN WHICH I APPEAR IN THE *DAILY TRUTH*

And so, back to Carter's phone call in January 2027. I refused
to talk to him. But, when I had cut him off a second time and
he took such a bullying tone on the third attempt, I feared he
might turn up at our front door. So, foolishly, I listened to
what he had to say. Either his voice had deepened over time,
or else it was a different person. I didn't care. He asked for
more of the same, straightforward information on the negotiations about, and progress with, the proposals on Unacceptable
Content. He offered the same stick and carrot: exposure of my
relationship with Lola if I refused to play ball, and, this time,
100,000 euros if I agreed.

A more practical, sensible sort of person would have closed
down his Velocity subscription and chosen a non Caxton-
owned net service provider. But, on receiving the first pay-off
some years earlier, it had seemed too much trouble, and, I
suppose, I never considered I would be of any further interest
to Caxton. Yet, of course, he was still lobbying and pressing
and cajoling and, clearly, blackmailing his best to ensure the
Euronet ended up as open, free and liberal as possible, utterly
uncaring of the negative social consequences.

If I am honest, and I continue to write these Reflections
trying not to compromise the truth in any respect, I do not
believe the money swayed my decision, it was more the fear of
my private habits being exposed to Gillian, my mother, my
colleagues and all – however harmless they were in compari-
son to much else around. Nevertheless, I did think the money
would come in handy.

By this time, Gillian had run up substantial debts, and was
paying excessive interest rates on bank and credit card loans.
She had never mentioned the debts, nor had I hinted that I
knew about them. When she asked that the monthly sum I
paid into her account for housekeeping be increased, I agreed
without question. I also helped by paying whenever we went
out or bought anything together, which had not been the case
previously. As far as I could tell from her paperwork, the debts

began not long after Crystal was born: her credit card statements, for example, revealed bills from companies called The Gold Rush and For Your Eyes Only.

When Gillian returned to work at the end of her maternity leave, and during the 12 months that followed, she came close to clearing her debts. Then, not long before we started therapy, when she had become dissatisfied with me and her life, the debts began escalating again. I puzzled a lot about when and how she was finding the time or privacy to lose so heavily. Her computer was situated in a corner of the lounge, and it was rarely switched on when I was in the house. On most days, though, in the period I am talking about – after she had returned to quasi full-time work and when Crystal's day care was shared between a nanny and a local kindergarten – Gillian was at home for an hour in the morning after me, and for an hour or more in the evening before I got back. Yet, whenever I returned from work unexpectedly early, she invariably appeared busy enough with Crystal. Given Gillian's general reluctance to discuss anything personal and her surly and uncooperative behaviour at the time, it was my thought that I might catch her in the act, and this would spur a confession. I never did. Nor, I should add for balance, did Gillian ever surprise me with my pants down, as it were, in the study.

I did not seriously consider how I would explain to Gillian the gain of 100,000 euros, nor how I would manage to give a large part of it to her without admitting I knew about the gambling debts. But the thought of the money did, as I say, comfort me, for a while.

I gave Carter what he wanted for nine months. His calls came less often than before, but they still came. That summer, Gillian, all happy and light-headed with her new pregnancy, confessed having temporary money problems. So, rashly, I asked Carter for a goodwill payment of 30,000 euros. The 20,000 he actually gave me up front went a long way to resolving Gillian's debt, though she never once asked where the money came from.

Months later, on Saturday 16 October, the day after Gillian's birthday, a stocky man with dark glasses and claiming to be Carter sidled up to me in Grange Park where I was watching Crystal in the playground bopping around on a funny spring chair with ears. He did not look at me, but stood by my side.

'We've had new instructions.'

'We?'

'You and me. I've been given them to pass on to you. The chief is very pleased with the way things are going.'

'The chief? You mean Caxton?' On the phone, he had never referred to any other person or to having received any instructions.

'I've 30,000 euros to give you right now, and the other 50,000 will be yours by the end of November, at the latest.' He paused. 'If.'

'If?'

'If we can ... how shall I put this? ... do a bit of nudging.'

A bit of nudging! Having reeled me in with relatively innocent (I had to believe that) information-gathering activities, Caxton now wanted me to try and influence the direction of UK policy, not on anything too obvious, too political, but on some techno-legal issues. I protested that I had no influence at all, but Carter knew well enough from our many conversations that my position allowed me to argue points of view and to draft possible responses to external suggestions. I tried to appeal to Carter's reason that it would be considered uncharacteristic of me if I were to start pressing too firmly on any particular issue. He said he was confident of my ability to ensure this would not happen. We stood there in silence for a short while.

When Crystal stumbled on her way from the bouncy mouse to the climbing frame, I darted forward to help her get up and to flick off some wood chips that had stuck to the side of her coat. She tried to pull away; for a second, I wouldn't let her. I half twisted her body round so she would be looking at me, and so I could kiss her cheek.

'Daddy loves you,' I whispered.

'Very touching,' Carter said, with conviction, on my return to his side. 'I like kids.' And then he started to explain how this new stage in our relationship would work, and how it would involve me receiving, now and then, a few papers. I stopped him talking.

'Carter, I'm not doing this. I'm not going any further. You can tell Caxton, he's not getting another thing from me. I'm finished with this deceit. You can keep your money, and please don't call again.' I moved round to take the pushchair and wheel it over to reclaim Crystal from the climbing frame.

'You're making a mistake Fenn, I've seen what the chief does to others.'

'I don't care. I don't care.' I did care, but Caxton had misjudged how far he could lead this particular animal before his slaughter.

Carter tried to persuade me to change my mind by phone twice, although he was clearly constrained in what he could say without incriminating himself, and once more in person, again in Grange Park. Implicit in these conversations was the threat of exposure in the *Daily Truth*, not only of my relationship with Lola, but also my 'spying' activities, and Gillian's gambling problem – thankfully, Gillian was never to discover that anyone but me knew about this. I remained resolute to have no further dealings with him or Caxton. I would like to think that Caxton's demands had finally awoken my moral sensibility, and that I stopped being a spy because I wanted to do the right thing, behave in the right way. I suspect, though, that my decision was sparked by a catalytic conjunction of common sense with self-preservation. Had I gone any further, I would have been Caxton's forever.

For about one month, over Christmas, my birthday and into the new year, I lived in a state of near-happy delirium. Carter's calls stopped, and there was no media intrusion into my life whatsoever. As each day passed, I felt more sure that I had called Caxton's bluff and won. Gillian had taken maternity leave already in the middle of December. She was the size of a sumo wrestler. As when she was pregnant with Crystal, she was full of good humour and generosity. She positively enjoyed playing mother and housewife during this time. Our second child was due in the third week of January.

The call came on 4 January, a Tuesday morning before I had left for work. A high-pitched male voice introduced himself as a journalist from the *Daily Truth*. He said he needed an interview that very morning so I could put my side to a story which was of great concern to the General Public. I stood there, in my office room, stunned, petrified. I could sense my life crumbling instantly all around me in many different directions. My initial thought was to put the phone down immediately, then I decided I should find out what the hack was planning to write. I considered calling Tom's solicitor who I had met once, but, in that moment, the issue was still a personal, private one and it seemed unnecessary to discuss it with a lawyer. So, I agreed to meet the journalist mid-morning in a guzzleshop more than a kilometre from Yorkshire House.

He was stocky, middle-aged, and had a face with rat-like features. I may have imagined the last bit. The interview lasted less than five minutes. He would not tell me where the story came from, and what was in it. I would not tell him when I last had sex with Gillian or other intimate details he badgered me for. Nor was I prepared to comment on the suitability of an internet porn addict being involved with government policy on internet policy regulation. I returned to work, informed my secretary that I was not feeling well, and made my way back to Torbay Road. Gillian was asleep on the sofa, and the screen was showing her favourite soother of slow-motion shots of seabirds in flight with Satie piano music on low. Crystal was at the kindergarten for the first time since Christmas. I sat down so I could watch Gillian sleeping for a while. She looked uncomfortable, half propped up against the sofa's arm-rest, cushions pushed in to support her back, and her legs bent up and slightly apart. I understood so little about what made this woman tick that I had no idea how she would react. Nevertheless, I felt I had to make some attempt to talk to her about it before the story appeared the next day. I put on the kettle, made a pot of her favourite menthol tea, and brought a tray into the lounge. I switched off the media console, and gently woke her.

In an uncharacteristic emotional gush of words, I apologised for everything: for waking her, for deceiving her, for allowing this to happen so close to the new birth, for letting us both down, for bringing shame on our family. I begged her not to interrupt while I explained myself in full. With some effort she did keep quiet, but then she soon began looking away and shutting her ears, I expect. In conclusion, I pleaded, like a weasel, that I wasn't so bad because I had, after all, put an end to the matter with Carter before deserting my principles altogether; and, lamely, I suggested that getting my rocks off through pornography was hardly a capital crime. For some reason, I omitted the sordid details of my relationship with Lola even though I fully expected these to be listed in graphic detail by the *Daily Truth*. Gillian grimaced. It was a horrible grimace. I sat there sheepishly, helpless.

The next day the article with three photos – one of a Marilyn Monroe-type blonde bombshell – appeared on page five of the *Daily Truth* with a flash on page one. In addition, the story took a head position on the company's netsites, and was distributed to 25 million subscribers around the world, via a free advertising-packed email.

I read the story first on the internet in the middle of the night. Then, before dawn, I went out and bought a copy of the newspaper. This was the only time I ever paid money for that rag. Although bursting with shame, especially at the thought of my family and friends finding out about this private behaviour of mine, I was very relieved that there was no hint of the information-gathering activities. I guessed, at the time, it would have been too difficult for Caxton/Carter to make accusations in my direction without implicating themselves either immediately or later were an official enquiry to ensue. At 6am, the phones started ringing so I put them on automatic. In those days, the privacy laws were as ineffective at prohibiting unsolicited pestering calls on personal phones as they were at protecting net data abuse. I rang my mother to give her the gist, and said I would speak to her later. I emailed Tom too, and suggested we meet at the end of the week. Gillian had dressed Crystal and given her breakfast. We ignored the doorbell rings, and, when I took Crystal to the kindergarten, I politely refused to talk to reporters waiting in the street. By the time I returned, my wife had read the paper. She was in fighting mode. This was not a personal predicament I had to face alone, but a practical problem she and I would overcome together.

Over breakfast, we agreed there was no question of legal action, or any initiative on our part that might propagate the story. This meant the immediate cancellation of any telecom services owned, or partially-owned, by Caxton, and their replacement, which was a pain to organise. It also meant no interviews of any kind; and Gillian had kindly called her mother and forced a promise out of her to keep mute, which was very much against her nature. Otherwise, our main objective was for me to keep my job. I took Gillian's advice on this. In a crisis, she was the perfect commander, my very own Churchill. She told me, for example, that humility was absolutely out of the question, as was any appeasement of my superiors. I was to take a firm line and stick to it, whether in conversation with my colleagues, or in any written memos to my seniors: the *Daily Truth* accusation concerned a personal matter and had no connection at all with my work or the way I carried out my duties.

CHAPTER 32

IN WHICH MY NOTORIETY HAS FEW CONSEQUENCES

A few follow-up articles appeared in different media, mostly in those owned by Caxton; but, within ten days, the journalistic intrusions had died out. Thus, by the time Bronze was born, on 25 January, our life had quietened down. Again Gillian decided on the name without any input from me. Gold was common for boys and girls by then. I thought it far too ostentatious and/or ambitious. Silver had a touch of class. The name Bronze was unusual, although it did become more common later. To my mind, it suffered from being the metal used for third place medals, and, as such, indicated lesser quality. At that time, Gillian had taken to the colour bronze and was buying knick-knacks made of the alloy. Most of all, she liked the sound of Crystal and Bronze together. Oddly, after our divorce, she declined to insist on the children taking her family name, Tilson (although Bronze chose to later). She had always disliked it, partly because her mother's full name, Constance Tilson, was slightly awkward to pronounce. Unfortunately, Bronze was anything other than bronze, as a Mediterranean baby might have been. He was pale and thin. I couldn't help thinking 'poor little bugger' for arriving in the midst of all our troubles.

The media interest may have flattened out quickly, but I still had to deal with the fall-out at work, and among my friends.

At work, Gillian's strategy worked admirably. I ignored/ resisted any suggestion that I should take the simple way out by seeking a job in the private sector. I declined paternity leave for fear that, in my absence, rumours would proliferate. Within a month of the article, I was offered a sideways move to the Department of Industry and Technology. I decided to take it. Duck, who acknowledged my contribution to the section, was 'very sorry' to let me go.

The same cannot be said of my colleague Phil Rumble. He cold-shouldered me in the Yorkshire House canteen; and, in advance of a long-planned inter-departmental volleyball match, he sent me an email, copied to the team members, asking me to step down 'to save the team's embarrassment'. On Gillian's cue, I resisted, continued to keep my head high and made no concessions to ignominy. When no one else in the team backed him, Phil found an excuse not to play. At around the same time, Gillian had tried calling Melanie, Phil's partner, to tell her about Bronze, but Melanie would not speak to her. That was the end of our three year friendship.

More than a decade later, I ran into Phil at the retirement cocktail party of some high-level civil servant. He apologised for having been such a prig all those years earlier. He told me that Melanie, by then his ex-wife, had been a committed member of the EVE movement at the time, and had, he said, 'infected' him with her views. When I asked why we had never seen this side of either of them at dinner or during pushchair walks on Hampstead Heath and in Greenwich Park, Phil explained that because of my work he had always insisted Melanie steer clear of any related subjects. He went on to embellish his apology – needlessly and cringingly – by telling me that, when Melanie had walked out on him, he too had found plenty of comfort in the virtual world.

The *Daily Truth* article had no lasting impact on my other relationships. With few exceptions, if the subject was mentioned in conversation with friends, the discussion focused on the role of the media and the privacy laws. I never did talk to my mother about it any further. During one of the two weekends between the article's publication and the birth of Bronze, I met up with Tom, for the first time in ages, at a cinema bar. He found my troubles amusing and could not resist making the odd joke about Bangkok, and his own, non-virtual, sexual demeanours. I found him irritating, and was quite relieved when we were called in to the film. I think it was a new print of *Bus Stop*. If not then, we saw it a few months later. I remember because Tom leaned over at the appearance of Marilyn Monroe.

'There's Lola.' He laughed like a hyena, drawing hisses from others in the audience, and couldn't resist adding in a quieter voice, though his unwelcome reference needed no further explanation, 'You know, the girl in the photo. Ha. Ha.'

I should acknowledge that, unlike Tom, Gillian never once made a snide remark or any comment about Lola, nor did she refer to my behaviour as debasing me or her or us. Some three months or so after Bronze was born, she restarted our regular bouts of passion-less sex on Saturday night as though nothing untoward had occurred to affect that side of our relationship.

Horace Merriweather, as it happens, was too busy being a good Member of Parliament to see me much around the time of these events. He came to Torbay Road, self-consciously incognito with a scarf wrapped round the lower half of his face, to inspect Bronze. I went once to Kensington where we spent the evening talking politics. It was more than a year before we met in public again. I suppose he was right to be cautious, but I didn't feel as sorry for him as I should have done when it was his turn to be laid bare before the public: 'My MP lover hid me away', read the *Daily Truth* article. I made a point of inviting him to lunch at a very public restaurant soon after the article appeared and while he was still being hounded. He did not take the opportunity, as Phil would do much later, to apologise for having ostracised me. I doubt he realised he had done so. He was great company, and a good friend in other ways, especially as I never expected too much, so I did not take offence.

I tried to write an email to my uncle Alan encompassing both the news of Bronze's arrival and the *Daily Truth* business. But to someone as close as Alan, I couldn't make any sense of the latter without revealing the blackmail aspects, and I was not prepared to do so. It would be another five years before I told anyone other than Gillian, and that would be on the night of Caxton's murder, as I've already described.

Thinking back on the whole degrading episode, as I have done from time to time during my life, it struck me as bizarre that our society, which had become so inured to sex in general, maintained such a sensitivity about masturbation. Needless to say my relationship with Lola did not end. Soon after changing my net service provider, I was back online and thanking her for being discreet: I doubted not that the *Daily Truth* had sought her/him out and that the picture of her was a fiction. She sent me back a message confirming the absolute confidentiality of her client relationships, but thanking me in return, with a double exclamation mark, for the publicity.

I thought carefully before deciding to dredge up this matter here in these Reflections. I even discussed it with Jay. He could see no reason to mention that side of my life at all. I think, to be fair, he was simply embarrassed. I am sure the *Daily Truth* article was not much noticed in the wider world – after all it was only published because Caxton wished for revenge. As scandals go, it was distinctly minor, and it may have sunk into the mire of my unwanted and unremembered memories but for one thing. Years later, when I was important enough to be the subject of a few media profiles, the topic was often dragged into the interview, as a piece of unpleasantness that had to be dealt with, like a dirty nappy in the car, or a rotting mouse in the closet. And thus Caxton's intrusion became a blight on my life, one that I would have to explain to my partners and children in turn, and, occasionally, to powerful people who were trying to decide if I was a fit person to take on a particular task. My use of Gillian's strategy might not have persuaded journalists to omit that part of my life from their profiles, but it was sufficient to protect me against further prejudice in professional and practical ways.

Ironically, by the time I had moved to Holland and become involved with the beginnings of the International Fund for Sustainable Development, I was already grateful to Caxton (about-to-be-deceased) for having inadvertently diverted my career.

CHAPTER 33

IN WHICH ROB REAPPEARS AND SO DOES CAXTON

There is one more consequence of the *Daily Truth* article I wish to mention. A few days before Bronze was born, I received a call in my office at Yorkshire House from the reception desk on the ground floor. A man, who would not give his name, wished to see me on a personal matter. When I asked if he was a journalist, the receptionist's voice descended to a confidential whisper and told me that my visitor looked very unkempt and distracted.

It was Rob, brother of Melissa, my school girlfriend. The receptionist had not exaggerated. His unshaven face, wild hair, and torn, stained overcoat suggested he might have been living rough. He did not say so, but I assumed media coverage had triggered his memory and signalled how to find me. I took him to a nearby cafe and bought him a late lunch. At first he remained surly, and made no attempt to tell me why he had sought me out. I asked questions about where he had been, what he was doing and whether his mother was well, which elicited scant information. I thought he might have wanted to talk about Melissa, but I was being too generous. It was money he wanted, money for drugs.

Neither Gillian nor I were given to helping those less fortunate than ourselves. We did not take in stray cats, for example, or worry about the homeless; nor, as we were regularly being urged to, did we help out at the old peoples' home round the corner from Torbay Road. But I couldn't turn Rob away. I called Gillian to explain the situation. Since she was in a happy pregnant state, overloaded with natural stimulants, she agreed to invite him to the house. We insisted he shower, we lent him clean clothes, and gave him wine and food. He talked with a stutter and with his head bowed; and he often contradicted himself.

Much affected by his sister's coma, he had left school and home at 16, and moved to London. Under the liberal drug regime introduced by the Lib-Dems/Labour coalition in the late 2010s, Rob had been drawn into the use of cannabis and other decriminalised substances. With a group of Scavengers, he learned how to get by without a regular job and to use harder drugs. Then he followed a heroin addict to Hamburg, where a crusading doctor put him on high doses of Solama. This stabilised him for a while. He held down a job for some months. Unfortunately the income helped him feed a growing, and illegal, chemical habit. He came back to England in 2026 when his mother died. After selling the house she had part-owned and paying various debts, he had less than 30,000 euros. He moved back to London, found a pad with druggy friends, and squandered the money. Since then, he had been living on the streets, in turns angry, desperate, ill, and suicidal. He had enrolled on various rehabilitation programmes but never lasted the course. The police stopped and searched him regularly but never arrested him. All he wanted from me was money for more chemicals, to relieve for a few hours the unrelenting hopelessness of his life.

Rob made my problems appear negligible. He stayed the night on the sofa. Neither Gillian nor I had any idea how to help. We knew from the media, and from what we saw in the streets occasionally, that Rob was by no means an isolated case. In the morning, before he woke, I made calls to my mother and a couple of friends who I thought might know more than we did. I was given a few addresses and telephone numbers of rehab centres and recovery houses, and advised not to get involved. I didn't. We gave Rob breakfast, the contact details I had gathered, and 200 euros. And we said goodbye.

Only when he had gone and Gillian and I had reassured ourselves that there was nothing else we could do, did I allow myself a few still-strong nostalgic, pleasurable and sorrowful, memories of Melissa.

And what of Caxton? He was, without doubt, one of the most extraordinary public figures of this or any other century. Others have likened him to a youthful cross between Beaverbrook and Berlusconi, two larger-than-life characters in recent European history, from whom he said he learned a great deal.

A key characteristic of all three men was that their ambitions could not be contained within commerce but needed a political arena. If Caxton had lived, who knows what his special combination of brilliance, populism and thuggery might have achieved. Not content with a media and telecoms empire that had become nigh on as large as possible under the EU's competition laws, and had coiled its tentacles around many enterprises in third countries such as Russia and China, Caxton set up his own political party.

By no coincidence, he launched the People's Party, with great fanfare and a huge party at Wembley arena, on 1 July 28, the very day the new three tier Euronet went live. I received two invites to the party, one at work, signed by the campaign manager, and one at home signed by Caxton himself. It said, and I quote exactly: 'Bygones? – The People's Party could use a man like you.' How he had the time and the memory to keep me, a very minor pawn, so firmly in his sights, I have no idea. I took pleasure in tearing up both invitations, but regretted my actions when I saw the spectacular show broadcast onscreen. After his death, I also lamented not having kept the personal invitation as a keepsake.

The history books show well enough that the People's Party, and its supporting media, campaigned heartily with most other political parties, excluding the Republicans and Greens, for keeping the monarchy in 2030. It then went on to win 50 or so seats in the 2031 elections and to form a government in coalition with the Conservative Alliance, with John Lyndquist as prime minister. Caxton, after supposedly distancing himself from his commercial empire, was made minister for an expanded Department of Industry, Technology and Enterprise. Thank goodness I had already moved on to the Department of the Environment.

Following Caxton's murder, the People's Party, which had been constructed on the foundations of his money and ambition, imploded in slow-motion. The coalition government collapsed within months, though Lyndquist then formed a new coalition, this time, to everyone's astonishment, with the

Green Party, which had already spent much of the 20s in government allied to the Liberal Democrats. Gregory, the controversial pop-historian, has a lot of time for Caxton who, he believes, brought a welcome tornado of change into the European media industry, and provided an important brake on the ambitions of the regulators. Despite his great insight, I am not convinced Gregory knows as much about the man as I do.

As a final homage to Caxton, I am taking my last look on the screen at a reproduction I have stored on Neil of a collage created by the genius Tamson Bunting. At the centre is a camstill, as I first saw it in the tulip palace with Diana, of Caxton the moment after the bullet went through his head. Skillfully blended around the central picture are news and publicity camclips, merging in and out of each other, alternating in tones and tints, giving the impression, to me at least, of a complex powerful man with dark and grimy secrets. Zoom in on one eye in any representation of him, and you come out of another. Zoom in on the writing and the words transmute as you try and read them. For me, Bunting says more about Caxton in this piece than Gregory does with all his words.

CHAPTER 34

IN WHICH WE MOVE HOUSE AND TAKE A HOLIDAY

Chintz caught me this evening indulging in an old Movie
Martyr flick – *Time and Sight*. The artist's name was familiar
but she had never seen one of her films. Chintz drew up a
lounge chair and sat down by the side of the bed and watched
the screen with me in silence. At the sad bit, where Movie
Martyr's mother goes blind – her editing is over-sentimental
on occasions, but this in no way diminishes the acuity of her
observations – I saw Chintz cry and somehow she reminded
me of Crystal as a vulnerable infant, crying often.

***

Gillian was not a good mother. Have I said this before? She
tried in fits and starts, but she never knew instinctively what
to do; and, as often as not, she chose the wrong approach.
When things were not going well, she distanced herself from
the problem without letting anyone else (me, for example)
deal with it. The problems with Crystal stemmed partially
from Bronze's ill-health. As a child, as a teenager and as an
adult, I can barely remember a time when Bronze was not
complaining of some disorder or other. It is true that he was
cursed with a body that did not function very well, but he
never grew to compensate for that, instead his mental and
physical life acted to exaggerate his misfortunes.

I do blame Gillian partly. Unlike with Crystal, she pan-
dered to his every whinge, scratch, cough which only encouraged more whingeing, more scratching, more coughing. It
started not long after he was born and went on, as far as I
know, for most of his childhood and beyond. This was not
only bad for Bronze, to my mind, but unfortunate for Crystal
too. Gillian had never bonded with Crystal in the way mothers
are supposed to bond with their children, especially their
daughters, as happens in story books and breakfast cereal
advertisements. Crystal was a job, a chore for Gillian, rather
than a pleasure or a passion. The job was containable while

Crystal was a baby, but became seriously troublesome when Crystal moved into toddlerhood. By the time Bronze came along, Gillian was ready to divert her attention to the new baby. Crystal became irritable and demanding which only alienated Gillian further.

During the summer after Bronze was born, we bought a 20 year old four-bedroom semi-detached house in Lacey's Lane, Willesden. That was the summer when the worst floods in modern history, driven by a cyclone and a tidal wave in Bengal Bay, killed nearly half million people in eastern India and Bangladesh. The world watched horrified as the death toll mounted day by day.

When Alan first visited us in Lacey's Lane, he had recently returned from the area. He told horrific stories about how whole towns in the Ganges delta had simply disappeared without trace, how millions of people were lost and homeless, and how large areas of Calcutta looked like a war-zone. Alan blamed the United States for failing to back the Kyoto Protocol on climate change 30 years previously, and for refusing to support actively further measures beyond it. To his mind, because of that failure, subsequent international efforts came too late, and delivered too little. The floods that year all over the world, not only in the Indian subcontinent were, though, to rekindle efforts on greenhouse gas control, and focus new efforts on climate damage response.

The Lacey's Lane house we (by which I again mean Gillian) chose was in reasonable decorative condition. Gillian was already back at work and did not want to live in a building site. I took the rear upstairs room for my office. From there I could glimpse a speck of green in Gladstone Park, which sported a more adventurous playground than Grange Park. Gillian and I talked at length about the advantages of a live-in nanny, but, thankfully, for I had no wish to live with a stranger, Gillian decided to manage without. However, I suspect that the succession of temporary nannies, childminders and childminding arrangements we employed did nothing to diminish our children's later problems. I blame myself as

much as Gillian. With Bronze in her lap, she was less proprie-
torial over Crystal, and, if I had persevered, I might have been
able to give our daughter more self-assurance. Unfortunately,
she never showed much interest in me, and only ever wanted
Gillian's attention. When tantrums didn't work, she became
withdrawn, sullen and silent, sucking her thumb excessively
and watching the virtually realistic cartoons for hours.

I realise that I have, inevitably, left out much of the detail
from my life, our lives. For example, Gillian and I did a fair
amount of travelling in the latter half of the 20s, although not
often together. While I was at the Department of Communications and working on internet regulation, I made day trips to
Brussels and two-day trips to Warsaw every few weeks. Three
or four times a year, Gillian spent several nights in a major
European city helping to promote Mandrill publications at a
conference or a publicity event. I looked forward to her absences as they allowed me to pay more attention to Crystal
and Bronze, not that they noticed.

Once or twice a year, we managed to get away for a holiday. On the whole, these weeks were among the happiest of
our times together. Gillian took a traditional view of how a
holiday should be and therefore made a special effort. While
on maternity leave, in the autumn of 2025, we pushed Crystal's buggy awkwardly around Florence and Rome, cramming
both cities into one week. A year later, she decided we should
go on an expensive club holiday to Morocco – not that we saw
much of the country. The facilities for toddlers were excellent,
as were the beaches. Gillian found some pleasure in taking up
tennis, while I hustled my volleyball skills.

And there was one holiday, to the Algarve, which has
become my favourite memory of the four of us as a family. I
recall none of the detail, but the character and sense of it
became fixed in my memory by one photo. This one. We are
on a sandy beach, and behind us in the sea are arches made of
sandstone with coloured layers. I can see the water's edge,
milky-yellow and then turquoise. All four of us are grouped
together in the centre: Gillian, in a white t-shirt and white

shorts, is cradling Bronze in her left arm; he has a khaki sun-hat protecting his tiny head. I am kneeling; Crystal is on my shoulders, also dressed in white with a pastel blue baseball cap. My hands clasp her ankles. Gillian has her right arm around Crystal's shoulder, and Crystal is holding, somewhat awkwardly, one of Bronze's hands. We have all been caught in a moment, unselfconscious, smiling and happy. Even Bronze looks as though life is treating him well.

CHAPTER 35

IN WHICH I AM DISMISSED ONE LAST TIME

By the winter of 2028-29, Gillian had sunk into a depressed, sulky state that was impervious to my attentions and efforts to help. During the last year of that decade our life deteriorated bit by bit. She began to find Bronze as difficult as Crystal. We passed through periods of seemingly endless dinner parties and banal weekend visits, and others in which Gillian preferred working to being with us, her family. I was a buffer. When she was tired or busy, I organised the practical arrangements with childminders and transport to and from the kindergarten, and, when she wanted to take over again, I stepped back. We tried therapy together a second time, but without resorting to cams in the home this time round, on the pretence that the problem might be mine; and Gillian employed a different therapist alone on the pretence of improving her already successful life.

There was a respite in 2030 when Gillian managed to persuade her doctor to prescribe a course of the 'miracle' drug Solama. She had gone to the surgery for one of Bronze's problems, but had mentioned in passing 'a very mild depression'. Solama was only prescribed in this country for a maximum of six months with a lead-in and tail-off period at either end. (A few of the many who bypassed the law by changing doctors fuelled the suicide statistics that were to start accelerating in the 40s.) Solama worked for Gillian. She began an affair with a colleague at work which lasted as long as the drug did. She never tried to hide her actions, in the sense that she stayed away some nights, and never explained why. I accepted her behaviour because it seemed to be linked to a lighter and more carefree mood, which I felt was beneficial for our children. But when the Solama ran out, her affair must have burnt itself through, and once again she became impossible to please and chronically moody.

Towards the end of the year 30, I became seriously worried about Gillian's gambling bills. With so little to lose, since she was scarcely communicating and as gloomy and unap-

proachable as I had ever seen her, I took a decision to confront her about the debts. I chose a Saturday night, when the
children were asleep. I pretended that I had discovered the
bank statements when looking for something of mine in her
drawers. I spoke to her in a stern righteous tone, as Julie
spoke to me when I was five, or in the way I spoke to the
bullies in the playground when I was nine. I must surely have
tried the tactic, one of few I possessed, on Gillian in our early
days together, but no doubt she had quickly learned to disarm
it. On this occasion, she made no attempt to counter-attack or
to defend herself. I employed dramatic soap opera statements
such as 'we have children now' and 'our very home is at stake'.
I told her that, under no circumstances, could I allow this to
go on. It was an all-or-nothing effort. She looked directly at
me with horror or shock or both – in silence. When I ran out
of sternness and righteousness, she sat there, deflated and
quiet, her head bowed towards her hands in her knees. After a
minute or two, she rose from the chair, left the room and went
to bed.

I stayed up late into the night watching *Heart and Cold*,
the second of the Sensations series which brought Movie
Martyr worldwide acclaim. What she did, which no one had
done before in the mainstream film market, was to show, by
filming her own life in excruciating detail, how awareness of
self and acute consciousness could help one cope with life's
excesses while, at the same time, enriching life's experience,
whether good or bad. Somehow, she managed to provide each
film with a personal story about herself, a member of her
family or a friend, sequences of comic action to rival the great
Charlie Chaplin, and bags of unexpected insight into the way
we lived and who we were. Some critics hated her films. They
argued that because she lived her life in such a way as to
create the drama and comedy, her insights were not valid.
Personally, I could see no difference between Movie Martyr's
approach and that of the great travel writers of the 20th
century who actively sought out situations which would
provide material for good prose. I do not think it is a coinci-

dence that I mention Movie Martyr here. For me, personally, the late 20s was a nightmare, and she provided some good honest commentary on what it was like to be human.

The next morning, Sunday, Gillian went out without saying where or when she would be back. I drove Crystal and Bronze to Godalming to see Julie. Gillian returned two days later but would not communicate. Christmas came and went in a sour domestic fog. In January, she announced she was going to live with her mother, by then single again, in Canterbury, and commute to work. I protested vehemently, not for myself but for the children. She ignored me, as she usually did, and for a month I was left to juggle the children's care arrangements and work – I had transferred to the Department of the Environment in Shropshire House the previous autumn but I'll have to return to this.

Then she came back and, in effect, threw me out.

By Crystal's sixth birthday, in May 31, we were divorced. I tried not to think about the fact that most friends and acquaintances would find a link between the failure of our marriage and what they had read or heard about in connection to the *Daily Truth* article. I settled down in a second floor pad with high ceilings in a Victorian house along Randolph Avenue, Maida Vale, while Gillian installed a nanny into my old office room in Lacey's Lane.

I was surprised at how great a relief it was to be in charge of my own life. The downside was my separation from Crystal and Bronze. I had never been very close to them but, while we had lived in the same house, I hadn't recognised the reality of the emotional distance between us. This lack of a closeness mattered much more when we lived in separate homes. I saw them every weekend to begin with, then, as they grew older and more able to express their boredom with me, the schedule slipped and I saw them only once a fortnight. As time went by I thought about them often; and, even more often, I tried not to think about them.

As far as I know, from the day I forced Gillian to face the truth of her addiction, she never gambled again. My intervention did her no good. She did not seem to recover from that period in our life: I never saw her as happy again as when she was pregnant those two times. Nor, I came to understand later, did Crystal and Bronze recover from our inadequate parenting.

EXTRACTS FROM CORRESPONDENCE

Kip Fenn to Alan Hapgood

June 2027

Thanks for your letter, and I'm sorry I haven't written for ages. Mum is well. She had her check-up recently, and everything was clear. When we saw her on Sunday (we lunched at the Barley Mow) she was very upbeat about her plans at Boxgrove for 'extending the definition of education'. She's been working on a pilot programme for years (I didn't know much about it), and now she's been given a bigger grant to expand on it.

I have news too. Gillian is pregnant AGAIN – only six weeks or so. She insists we keep this a secret, but as you are in foreign parts, you don't count, though don't tell Mum. I should have been overjoyed at the news, but I wasn't. I feel a bit guilty about that, but Gillian didn't notice, and, to tell the truth, we had been having some difficulties. We saw a therapist. I won't go into details. Gillian's pregnancy, though, has brought us closer again, and I've started to become excited at the thought of a second child. Crystal's two now. In case you don't believe time is marching so fast, I've attached a photo Julie took. Doesn't she look a picture. She sucks her thumbs all the time, and has a tendency to talk gibberish for long periods. I imagine that's normal.

As I'm sure you've read, Adam Jones has agreed to form a government with the Greens (good news – your friend, Jill Asquith, may be our environment minister in a few days) and with the Republicans. I don't think many expected that. The Greens say the UK will now have to press the EU to accelerate the climate programme. I doubt Jones will have much choice.

Do you remember Horace Merriweather, one of my buds at Witley Academic. He and I (and, later, Jeff Zimmerman) were the top debating team for a couple of years. We've stayed friends since then. I'm not exactly sure why. He's a protégé of Terrance Spoon and has just been elected MP for Southampton Test. Gillian, Crystal and I went down there last Friday for a celebration party. On Saturday, we took the jetfoil to Cowes for a few hours. Gillian sailed a bit when younger, and was thinking we might take it up as a family. But her notions come and go as quickly as the wind changes direction.

And what's new with you, uncle of mine?

PS: While I remember them here's a couple of election jokes told me by Jekyll (Horace's agent when sober) and Hyde (a stand-up comedian when drunk).

1) 'Mummy, mummy, mummy, do all fairy tales begin with "Once upon a time"?'

'No, dear. Nowadays, lots of them start with "If I am elected ...".'

2) Finally it's the day of the UK general election. An innovative portable-type electronic voting machine, much improved on the previous version, is being used across the country. Then, in one local village hall a machine breaks down. The returning officer arranges for a support technician to be called in. One hour later he arrives and, after tinkering around for a few minutes, manages to repair it. As he comes out of the polling station, a poll volunteer asks, 'Well, is the machine fixed?' The technician thinks for a second, then before hurrying on to his next assignment, replies, 'Now, now, we don't like to use the f-word on election day.'

3) Have you heard the one about a man who walks down the street and is suddenly struck by a falling brick? 'What an outrage. You can't walk anywhere without a brick falling on your head,' cry the people who gather around. Then one of them notices the victim is a candidate in the forthcoming general election. 'What an outrage,' the crowd says, 'there are so many of these candidates, there's no room for bricks to fall!'

Oh dear, why did I bother, they were funny at the time, honest.

Alan Hapgood to Kip Fenn

June 2027

Thanks so much for your letter. I haven't heard from Julie for a while, so I was glad of your news. I shall write her next.

Congratulations are in order. Do give my love and best wishes to Gillian. I know from my own experience all relationships go through ups and downs, so don't be disheartened. By having children, you've already taken a much more difficult route than I ever did. Crystal looks so pretty. I forgot her birthday. I was travelling until yesterday, but I'll send her a surprise soon. What about a Russian doll?

Horace, yes, I remember him. I came to watch you debate once. He was very confident and impressive in his speaking, while you were rather diffident and appeared to be in awe of him. I took you out for a meal afterwards. And what happened to Alfred, your volleyball bud? There was something very noble about him, he even towered over you.

Good for the UK Greens. Jill and I may have had our differences but that doesn't mean she won't make a good environment minister. Did I really tell you about our college flirtation, that was very indiscreet of me. It's not only in the UK that environment parties are making gains, I see it across Eastern Europe, in South America, and in some parts of southeast Asia. It's not surprising really, when you quantify, as we do at WWF, the rise in climate-related disasters of one type or another. I'm sure I've told you, I've been working now for three years on a major report concerning the incidence of floods and related damage to homes, agriculture, etc.: when you take ten year rolling averages, the figures show a progression that is more geometric than arithmetic. The figures for actual loss of life are not so clear, but I fear the clarity will come.

I'm back in Kiev now for a while. Keep in touch.

PS: Not to be outdone on the joke front, here's two golden oldies sent me by an American colleague.

1) In the beginning god decided to make the earth, but first he was under orders from CEPA (the angelically-staffed Cosmos Environment Protection Agency) to implement an environmental impact assessment. When he was ready, god appeared before the CEPA council. After some consideration, the council said it could see no practical use for earth since it

was 'void and empty' and 'darkness was on the face of the deep'. So god suggested, 'Let there be light.'

This caused a further problem. One member of the CEPA council wanted to know how the light was to be made, and whether there would be strip mining, air pollution, nuclear contamination and/or defilement of the landscape with oilrig/windmill monstrosities. God explained that the light would come from a huge ball of fire. Nobody on the council really understood this, but, nevertheless, it was provisionally accepted, on certain conditions: no smog or smoke to result from the burning; a separate burning permit (to be awarded by a CEPA sub-committee); and, since continuous light would be a waste of energy, a halving of the burning time.

When asked by CEPA how the earth would be covered, god said, 'Let there be land made amidst the waters; and let it divide the waters from the waters.' No one understood this either, nevertheless the Council decided that, before proceeding, god would be required to seek a further permit from IPBWM (the Inter-Planetary Bureau of Water Management).

The council then asked if there would only be water and land, which is when god said, 'Let the earth bring forth the green herb, and such as may seed, and the fruit tree yielding after its own kind.' The council agreed with this so long as all seeds were approved by UGA (the Universal Gene Authority). As to future development, god added, 'Let the waters bring forth the creature having life, and the fowl that may fly over the earth.' Here again, the council took no formal action since this would require a further approval by UGA.

The council was about to give its conditional approval when god explained that he needed to complete the project in six days. The council said his timing was completely out of the question since IPBWM and UGA between them would need 12-18 millennia, and thereafter CEPA itself would need a further few centuries.

On storming out, god yelled, 'To hell with it!'

2) President McFeather and his secretary of state are sitting in a zini lounge. A lady walks in and asks the barman,

'Hey, isn't that McFeather and Nielson?' The barman says, 'Yep, that's them.' So, the lady walks over and asks, 'Hi, what are you guys up to?' McFeather says, 'We're planning to invade Mexico.' The lady says, 'Really? Wow. What's going to happen?' McFeather answers, 'Well, we're going to imprison all Mexican immigrants, bomb Mexico from the east coast to the west coast, and close down the three taco guzzleshops on Broadway.' The lady exclaims, 'Hey, why are you gonna close down the taco guzzleshops?' McFeather turns to Nielson and says, 'See, I told you no one would worry about the fate of immigrants or what happens to Mexico.'

NEWSPAPER CLIPPING

Daily Truth (5 January 2028, page 5)
Civil Servant in Internet Porn Shocker
Communications official caught in compromising position
The Truth about our policy-makers
Kip Fenn, a senior official in the Department of Communications, employs a personal net madam. Her name is Lola, and there is no type of porn she will not commandeer for him.

We do not wish to go into detail since the *Daily Truth* is a family paper.

What is wrong with this, we ask ourselves. On the surface, nothing. Long may Lola serve her clients, so long as she does so within the law. (And we have no evidence that Lola has ever done anything illegal.)

But Mr Fenn is no ordinary civil servant.

Mr Fenn is part of one of several teams of public servants involved directly with assisting government in setting policy concerning the net, and its regulation.

Important negotiations are currently under way in the capitals of Europe on net regulation. Would you trust Mr Fenn to be involved in deciding Unacceptable Content?

We at the *Daily Truth* are strongly in favour of a free regime. We argue for a strictly enforced worldwide ban on pornography with violence, children or animals. Lock up anyone who makes or uses such filth forever. Otherwise, leave us grown-ups free to decide for ourselves.

For all we know, Mr Fenn, with his perversions, might take this same view and help in our campaign. But we cannot keep the Truth to ourselves. And no more do we wish to rely on perverted officials. We want the government to make the right policy because it is right. We do not want to rely on individuals who might pervert the course of action, whether in the right direction or not.

Can Mr Fenn go on working at the Department of Communications? We don't think so.'

Three photos and captions that accompanied the article
A photo of Gillian, looking very pregnant, taken in Torbay Road.
Caption: 'We feel sorry for Gillian – the loving wife. Mr and Mrs Fenn have one child, with another on the way.'

A fake photo of Lola looking like Marilyn Monroe.
Caption: 'As a client for many years, Mr Fenn has been good business for Lola. Some estimates suggest there could be as many as 250,000 net madams.'

A photo of Kip Fenn exiting Yorkshire House (with the building name clearly visible above the entrance).
Caption: 'Would you trust Mr Fenn to be fair about how to censor the net?'

List of characters

This is a full list of characters appearing in one or more of the trilogy volumes (excluding those referred to only once) by surname (where mentioned in the text) or, otherwise, by first name. For national leaders, dates for their period or periods of office have been noted (as listed in *Encyclopaedia Universal*, 2098 edition).

A

Abd al-Jabbaar, David (son of Sami and Iona) – VOL 3

Abd al-Jabbaar, Iona (wife of Sami Abd al-Jabbaar's) – VOL 3

Abd al-Jabbaar, Sami (Kip's neighbour) – VOL 3

Acklow, Rosemary (therapist) – VOL 1

Ajose, Alfred (Kip's friend) – VOL 1, 2, 3

Ajose, Fayola (Alfred's wife) – VOL 2, 3

Ajose, Fela (son of Alfred and Fayola) – VOL 2, 3

Akilina (Anna Mastepanov's cousin) – VOL 3

Almond (half-brother of Yewla) – VOL 3

Al Zahir (Muslim leader) – VOL 2, 3

Amado, Jorge (Brazilian author) – VOL 1, 2, 3

Anders (stillborn child of Diana and Kip) – VOL 2

Andrasta (Mercurio Sanderson's friend) – VOL 3

Angela (daughter of Alicia Gonçalves) – VOL 3

Antonia de Malancas, Pedro (aka Pam, Mexican director) – VOL 1, 2, 3

Arklington, Betty (US president: 2047-51) – VOL 2, 3

Armstrong, Neil (US astronaut) – VOL 1, 2, 3

Asquith, Jill (Alan Hapgood's friend) – VOL 1

Asser, Eduard Isaad (Dutch photographer) – VOL 1, 2

B

Bayard, Hippolyte (French photographer) – VOL 2, 3

Beale, Martin (teacher) – VOL 1

Beato, Felice (British photographer) – VOL 2

Belinda (administrator) – VOL 2, 3

Bergmann, Zoe (German historian and author) – VOL 3

Brin (Jay Sanderson's friend) – VOL 3

Bronwen (Lionel Wilcox's secretary) – VOL 1

Buffer, John (volleyball coach) – VOL 1, 2
Bunting, Tamson (British artist) – VOL 1, 2

C
Carter (Caxton's go-between) – VOL 1
Caxton, William (née Shuttleworth, Ronald, politician/entrepreneur) – VOL 1, 2, 3
Chambi, Martin (Peruvian photographer) – VOL 2, 3
Chaplin, Charlie (US film actor/director) – VOL 1, 2
Chintz (nurse) – VOL 1, 2, 3
Choolee (prostitute) – VOL 1
Chowdhury, Tommy (IFSD official) – VOL 2
Corazon, Neco (Brazilian president: 2030-40) – VOL 1, 2, 3
Costa, Luigi (Italian prime minister:2043-47, 2049-52, 2055-59) – VOL 3
Courret brothers (Peruvian photographers) – VOL 2, 3
Cowerbridge, Arnold (museum director) – VOL 3
Czyzewski, Walenty (Polish prime minister: 2020-28) – VOL 1

D
Davidson, Augusta (Diana Oostlander's friend) – VOL 2
Davidson, Ike (journalist) – VOL 2
Delors, Jacques (European Commission president: 1985-1995) – VOL 1, 3
Delvreux, Kolin (Anglo-Dutch poet) – VOL 3
de Roo, Arnout (son of Rudy) – VOL 1, 3
de Roo, Livia (Peter's wife) – VOL 1, 2, 3
de Roo, Peter (Kip's friend) – VOL 1, 2, 3
de Roo, Rudy (son of Peter and Livia) – VOL 1, 2, 3
de Roo, Ulla (daughter of Livia and Peter) – VOL 2, 3
Derwent, Julia (US author) – VOL 1
Donna (Crystal Fenn's friend) – VOL 2
Duck, Alexander (British civil servant) – VOL 1
Dufkova, Giselle (museum director) – VOL 3
Dumas, Alexander (French author) – VOL 3
Durring, Lindsay (school pupil) – VOL 3

E
Elly (childminder) – VOL 2
Engelhard, Karl (Diana Oostlander's friend) – VOL 2, 3

F
Fenn, Barry (Tom's father) – VOL 2, 3
Fenn, Crystal (daughter of Gillian and Kip) – VOL 1, 2, 3

Fenn, Evvie (Tom's mother) – VOL 1, 2
Fenn, Gillian (née Tilson, Kip's wife) – VOL 1, 2, 3
Fenn, Julie (née Hapgood, Kip's mother) – VOL 1, 2, 3
Fenn, Tom (Kip's father) – VOL 1, 2, 3
Ferrer i Germa, Joaquima (Catalan film maker) – VOL 2
Ferrera Magalhães, Conceição (Kip's friend) – VOL 1, 2, 3
Ferrez, Marc (Brazilian photographer) – VOL 1, 2, 3
Fortune, Matt (British politician) – VOL 2, 3
Fragrance (Tom Fenn's second wife) – VOL 2, 3
Fuller, Garth (British prime minister: 2037-45) – VOL 1, 2

G
Gabriella (bus passenger) – VOL 1, 3
Gagarin, Yuri (Russian astronaut) – VOL 1, 2
Garibaldi, Giuseppi (Italian military leader) – VOL 3
Gemma (Alfred Ajose's girlfriend) – VOL 1, 2
Gonçalves, Alicia (née Magalhães, daughter of Arturo) – VOL 2, 3
Gonçalves, João (Alicia's husband) – VOL 3
Gregory, Crispin (British historian) – VOL 1, 2, 3

H
Hapgood, Alan (Kip's uncle) – VOL 1, 2, 3
Hapgood, Eileen (Julie Fenn's mother) – VOL 1, 3
Hapgood, Oswald (Julie Fenn's father) – VOL 1
Harris, Chuck (US author) – VOL 3
Hilde (Wood Junior's secretary) – VOL 1
Hitler (German dictator: 1933-45) – VOL 1, 3
Hoop, Vi (Canadian singer) – VOL 1, 2
Horeva, Ninel (IFSD official) – VOL 2, 3

I
Imogen (Rob's friend) – VOL 2
Inti (son of Guido Oostlander-Fenn and Mireille) – VOL 3

J
Jackmann-Ives, Rhoda (Lizette Sanderson's friend) – VOL 3
Jensen, Sydney (British materials science professor) – VOL 3
Jespersen, Bobby (journalist) – VOL 2, 3
Jessop, William (doctor) – VOL 1, 2
Johns, Unwin (British poet) – VOL 1, 3

Johnson, Wilma (British history professor) – VOL 1, 2
Jones, Adam (UK prime minister: 2022-32) – VOL 1, 2

K

Kallström, Ingrid (Swedish environmental campaigner) – VOL 1
Karel (son of Tamara) – VOL 3
Kingston (Crystal Fenn's friend) – VOL 3
Kiselev, Boris (IFSD official) – VOL 2
Koper, Melanie (Phil Rumble's wife) – VOL 1
Krishnamurty, Pravit (IFSD official) – VOL 2, 3

L

Lambert, Aaron (British film director) – VOL 2
Le Gray, Gustave (French photographer) – VOL 2, 3
Liphook, Philip (aka Flip, teacher) – VOL 1, 2, 3
Lipman, Rupert (doctor) – VOL 1, 3
Lobo, Se (Brazilian journalist) – VOL 3
Lock, Josephine (née Shuttleworth, daughter of William Caxton) – VOL 2, 3
Lola (net madam) – VOL 1, 2
Lomax, Lorraine (technical director) – VOL 3
Luz (Arturo Magalhães's friend) – VOL 3
Lyndquist, John (UK prime minister: 2032-37) – VOL 1, 2

M

Madan, Triti (Indian international politics professor) – VOL 1, 2, 3
Magalhães, Arturo Fenn (son of Kip and Conceição) – VOL 1, 2, 3
Magalhães, Edna (Arturo's first wife) – VOL 2, 3
Magalhães, Eliane (née Silva, Juliano's wife) – VOL 2
Magalhães, Fatima (Arturo's second wife) – VOL 2, 3
Magalhães, Ignacio (son of Arturo and Fatima) – VOL 2, 3
Magalhães, Juliano (son of Arturo and Fatima) – VOL 2, 3
Magalhães, Tina (daughter of Fatima and Arturo) – VOL 2, 3
Magalhães Silva, Maria (daughter of Eliane and Juliano) – VOL 2, 3
Mallow, Vincent (aka Mush, British actor) – VOL 1, 3
Marcella (Olive Norrington's partner) – VOL 3
Maria (Pope: 2052-74) – VOL 3
MarySue (secretary) – VOL 2, 3
Mastepanov, Anna (Alan Hapgood's partner) – VOL 2, 3
May (Mercurio Sanderson's friend) – VOL 3
McFeather, Andrew (US president: 2017-21) – VOL 1
Meijer, Dominique (née Oostlander, Diana's sister) – VOL 2, 3

Meijer, Jurian (son of Waltar and Dominique) – VOL 2, 3
Meijer, Lukas (son of Waltar and Dominique) – VOL 2, 3
Meijer, Waltar (Dominique's husband) – VOL 2, 3
Melissa (Kip's girlfriend) – VOL 1, 2, 3
Merriweather, Horace (Kip's friend) – VOL 1, 2, 3
Merriweather Tim (Horace's brother) – VOL 1, 2, 3
Mistral, Amy (British film/theatre director) – VOL 2, 3
Monique (Alan Hapgood's girlfriend) – VOL 1, 2, 3
Monroe, Marilyn (US film actress) – VOL 1
Montechristo, Felix Rico (Ecuadorian entrepreneur) – VOL 3
Movie Martyr (US film director) – VOL 1, 2

N
Naiambana, Chidi (IFSD official) – VOL 2, 3
Nash, Liam (Diana Oostlander's cousin) – VOL 2, 3
Nolan brothers (US astronauts) – VOL 1, 2
Norrington, Olive (Lizette Sanderson's colleague) – VOL 3

O
Oakley, Finbar (British playwright) – VOL 1, 2, 3
Ojoru (Nigerian president: 2027-35, 2037-47) – VOL 1, 2, 3
Olivier, Jean-Michele (REACH official) – VOL 3
Oosterhuis, Pieter (Dutch photographer) – VOL 1
Oostlander, Anders (Diana's brother) – VOL 2
Oostlander, Dana (Diana's sister) – VOL 2
Oostlander, Demeter (aka Dimi, Diana's sister) – VOL 2, 3
Oostlander, Diana (Kip's partner) – VOL 1, 2, 3
Oostlander, Neeltje (née van der Klein, Diana's mother) – VOL 2
Oostlander, Powles (Diana's father) – VOL 2
Oostlander-Fenn, Guido Tom (son of Kip and Diana) – VOL 1, 2, 3

P
Pacciotti (Italian film director) – VOL 1, 3
Paride Bernabo, Hector Julio (aka Caybe, Brazilian artist) – VOL 1, 3
Pattison, Flora (Kip's friend) – VOL 1, 2, 3
Pedrosa, Maria (Brazilian actress) – VOL 3
Popsicle (Kip's girlfriend) – VOL 1, 3
Pouille, Henri (photograph curator) – VOL 3

Q
Quant, Lucretia (British author) – VOL 1, 3

Quasim (Angela's partner) – VOL 3

R
Rachel (Julie Fenn's friend) – VOL 1, 2
Raisa (Clarity Sampson's friend) – VOL 3
Renato (son of Angela) – VOL 3
Rob (Melissa's brother) – VOL 1, 2
Robinson, Henry Peach (British photographer) – VOL 1
Rocard, Didier (Diana Oostlander's friend) – VOL 2, 3
Rocard, Helene (née Chastrain, Didier's wife) – VOL 2, 3
Rocard, Mireille (daughter of Helene and Didier) – VOL 2, 3
Rocard, Veronique (daughter of Helene and Didier) – VOL 2, 3
Rumble, Phil (British civil servant) – VOL 1

S
Sampson, Clarity (Pete's wife) – VOL 2, 3
Sampson, Joan (daughter of Clarity and Pete) – VOL 2, 3
Sampson, Pete (Kip's friend) – VOL 1, 2, 3
Sanderson, Esos (son of Mercurio and Andrasta) – VOL 3
Sanderson, Irene (daughter of Lynn and Samuel) – VOL 2, 3
Sanderson, Jay (son of Lizette, and Kip) – VOL 1, 2, 3
Sanderson, Lizette (Kip's partner) – VOL 1, 2, 3
Sanderson, Lynn (Samuel's wife) – VOL 3
Sanderson, Mahonia (daughter of Lynn and Samuel) – VOL 3
Sanderson, Mercurio (aka Rio, Lizette's brother) – VOL 3
Sanderson, Mervyn (Lizette's father) – VOL 3
Sanderson, Samuel (Lizette's brother) – VOL 3
Sanderson, Saul (son of Samuel and Lynn) – VOL 3
Sanderson, Wendy (Lizette's mother) – VOL 3
Sanfrancissisi (aka Sanfry, Nigerian volleyball player) – VOL 2, 3
Shakespeare (English playwright) – VOL 1, 2
Singleton, Jude (British civil servant) – VOL 1, 2, 3
Spoon, Terrance (British prime minister: 2045-48) – VOL 1, 2, 3
Stalin (Russian dictator: 1929-53) – VOL 1, 3
Stockmann, Angelika (German playwright) – VOL 2, 3
Subramani (teacher) – VOL 1
Sumani, Leona (public relations specialist) – VOL 3

T
Tamara (Alan Hapgood's girlfriend) – VOL 1, 3
Tarbuck, Steve (US president: 2051-59) – VOL 2, 3

Thomas, Rike (British civil servant) – VOL 2

Tilson, Bronze (son of Kip and Gillian) – VOL 1, 2, 3

Tilson, Constance (Gillian's mother) – VOL 1

Tilson, John (Gillian's grandfather) – VOL 1

Tindle (British politician) – VOL 1, 3

Tuohy, Clint (Lizette Sanderson's husband) – VOL 3

Turnbull, Doug (Kip's friend) – VOL 2, 3

Turnbull, Lucy (daughter of Miriam and Doug) – VOL 2, 3

Turnbull, Miriam (Doug's wife) – VOL 2, 3

Turnbull, Susannah (daughter of Miriam and Doug) – VOL 2, 3

V

van der Klein, Anders (Diana's grandfather) – VOL 2

van der Klein, Betje (Diana's aunt) – VOL 2

van der Klein, Kaatje (Diana's aunt) – VOL 2

Vaughn, Leo (photograph curator) – VOL 3

Vetch, Brian (British political adviser) – VOL 1, 2

Vidrio (Crystal Fenn's boyfriend) – VOL 2, 3

Villalonga, Eduardo (IFSD official) – VOL 3

Voll, Max (Argentinian billionaire) – VOL 3

W

Wells, Vince (Jay Sanderson's partner) – VOL 1, 2, 3

Wilcox, Lionel (aka Firey, British politician) – VOL 1, 2

Williams, Cos (media producer) – VOL 3

Wood Junior, Sterling (oil executive) – VOL 1

Worcester, Paulina (British prime minister: 2056-59) – VOL 2

Worthington, Pearl (teenager) – VOL 1, 2

Worthington, Xanthe (Pearl's mother) – VOL 2

X

Xiangjun, Liu (IFSD official) – VOL 3

Y

Yewla (daughter of May and Mercurio) – VOL 2, 3

Yvonne (Gillian Fenn's friend) – VOL 1

Z

Zanichelli (Italian composer) – VOL 2, 3

Zimmerman, Jeff (Kip's friend) – VOL 1, 2, 3

FAMILY RELATIONSHIPS

BACKGROUND

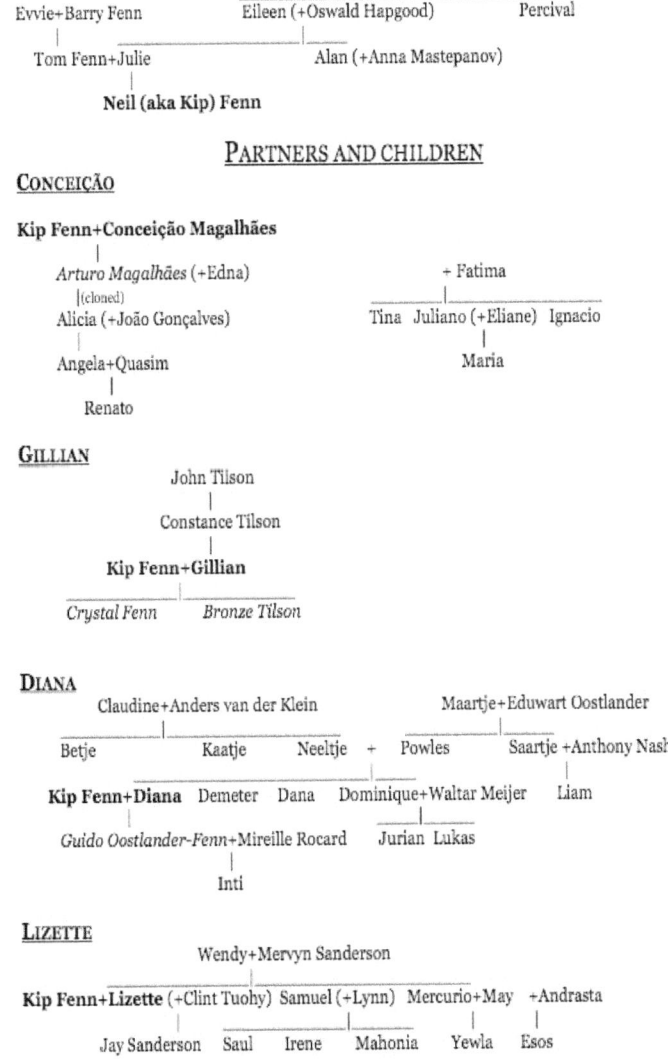

Evvie+Barry Fenn   Eileen (+Oswald Hapgood)   Percival
|
Tom Fenn+Julie   Alan (+Anna Mastepanov)
|
Neil (aka Kip) Fenn

PARTNERS AND CHILDREN

CONCEIÇÃO

Kip Fenn+Conceição Magalhães
|
Arturo Magalhães (+Edna)   + Fatima
|(cloned)
Alicia (+João Gonçalves)   Tina Juliano (+Eliane) Ignacio
| |
Angela+Quasim   Maria
|
Renato

GILLIAN

John Tilson
|
Constance Tilson
|
Kip Fenn+Gillian

Crystal Fenn   *Bronze Tilson*

DIANA

Claudine+Anders van der Klein   Maartje+Eduwart Oostlander

Betje   Kaatje   Neeltje + Powles   Saartje +Anthony Nash
|
Kip Fenn+Diana Demeter Dana Dominique+Waltar Meijer Liam
| |
Guido Oostlander-Fenn+Mireille Rocard   Jurian Lukas
|
Inti

LIZETTE

Wendy+Mervyn Sanderson

Kip Fenn+Lizette (+Clint Tuohy) Samuel (+Lynn) Mercurio+May +Andrasta
| | | |
Jay Sanderson   Saul Irene   Mahonia   Yewla   Esos

www.ingramcontent.com/pod-product-compliance
Lightning Source LLC
Chambersburg PA
CBHW061323200626
46813CB00017B/2832